FOREVER ENGLAND

Forever England

By

David Luddington

Dedication

I would like to dedicate this book to my wife and best friend, Sarah. The person who gave me fuel for my dreams and the wings to fly. I would also like to thank the people of Spain, especially the Alpujarran region who have made us so welcome in their country.

Author's Note

This book is the result of much research and personal sacrifice. Unfortunately much of that research had to take place in sunny locations in and around the Alpujarras where the people are friendly and the beer is chilled. This book is a work of pure fiction but many of the incidents and characters are drawn from people and places I've encountered.

P.S. The School Bus moped is real.

Chapter One

I twisted the little yellow switch on the remote detonator and the crisp night air ripped apart in a magnificent display of colour and sound. I felt the usual involuntary smile relax the tension in my face.

As explosions go this certainly wasn't my biggest, that honour belonged to the Eiffel Tower and an out of control Apache helicopter with Bruce at the controls. Or was it Arnold? I can't remember now, I've worked with most of them over the years. It wasn't even my smallest explosion, the safe deposit box in the vaults of the Monaco Casino wins that one. But by a long way, this was my most personally satisfying. Little bits of yellow metal clattered across the A38, still smoking as they settled onto the deserted tarmac. I removed the earplugs and dropped them into my shirt pocket then kicked the remains of the speed camera into the ditch at the side of the road. The grey metal post that just five minutes ago proudly held the camera high above the road now cast a stark and twisted image against the night sky. Perfect, though maybe not quite up to my usual pyrotechnical displays but still not bad for a spur of the moment bang.

I slipped back into the seat of my Triumph Stag and the engine started on the fourth attempt. Driving a classic car is a great honour but one does have to make allowances for the old lady's age. As the car swung onto the road and we resumed our journey, I wondered if that had been one of the new digital cameras. If it was, then the images of my number plate were already on their way through cyberspace to the local police headquarters. But what the hell. By this time tomorrow I'd be gone.

***

Empty houses often have a sad feel about them, almost as if they are mourning the fun and laughter the walls once contained. My house simply gave an air of being slightly relieved. The last couple of years had brought the joys of economic disaster, endless rain and the arrival of Karen's mother. I sat on the floor with my back to the wall and stared at the fireplace which I had built myself from scavenged Victorian bricks. I really should have got round to finishing off the edges properly. Watson nudged at my leg. Nothing quite compares with the unconditional love and total loyalty offered by a hungry cat. I took the hint and headed for the kitchen. By the time I'd reached the box of cat food the other three had heard the sounds of imminent food and threaded through my legs as I struggled to open the packet with a penknife. I had been left with the barest of essentials with which to survive the last twenty four hours in the house along with four cats. A borrowed camp bed on which to sleep, basic cutlery for my fish and chips and five varieties of cat food. And of course a list of instructions that extended across two pages and most of which consisted of 'Cat Instructions'. I duly played Cat Waiter, ensuring each cat had the correct bowl according to Section Two on page one then locked up the house and headed for the Camelot Hotel.

"Evening, Terry," greeted Mike from behind the bar. "Pint of Hedge Monkey to remember the old town by?"

"Just the one to start with." I settled on the bar stool and watched him pour the frothing pint with the care of master craftsman.

"Your room's the first on the left at the top of the stairs. It's the bridal suite. Thought we'd make it a bit special for you for your last night in England." He set the pint on a Glastonbury Ales beer mat in front of me. "Besides, it's not been used as a Bridal Suite for three years, they all go to Ayia Napa these days."

I pulled hard on the beer and half the glass disappeared. I was going to miss this. "Thanks for the room, Mike. I really appreciate that."

"No problem. Can't have you kipping on the floor round there, that's not right. What time are you off?"

"Ferry leaves Plymouth at four, need to be there a couple of hours before, so I suppose I need to leave around midday."

"I'll have a Full English ready for you in the morning."

My phone rang and in my surprise I fumbled to pull it from my pocket and it dropped to the floor. By the time I'd retrieved it the ringing had stopped. I studied the screen. '1 Missed Call - Karen'.

I put the phone on the bar.

"Problem?" Mike asked.

"Karen. No doubt she'll ring back if it's –" The phone burst into life again and vibrated on the bar. I picked it up. "Karen? Everything alright?"

"They've blown up Mum's suitcase." Karen's voice exploded across fifteen hundred miles of airwaves.

"What?" I can't have heard that right. "Slow down and tell me what's happened. Where are you?"

"We're still at Malaga Airport. Been here all day. And Mum's had one of her turns."

Mike pointed at my empty glass and I nodded.

"But you should have been at the hotel four hours ago?"

"Tell these idiots here that," she yelled, causing my phone to distort. "It's got all her underwear in it."

"I'm sure they have underwear shops in Spain, I clearly remember seeing one," I said. "They blew it up?"

"Oh, they called it a controlled detonation but then you'd know all about controlled detonations, wouldn't you? You lot with your –"

"Karen," I interrupted, "what actually happened?"

I managed to drink my pint whilst listening to her tirade against the incompetent security staff at Heathrow who had decided their x-rays showed suspicious items inside Dot's suitcase and exploded it in a security shed behind Baggage Handling.

"What on earth was it?" I replaced the empty glass on the bar.

"Curling tongs. She'd bought some gas powered curling tongs and half a dozen spare cylinders."

"I should imagine that made quite a satisfying bang," I suggested, my professional interest piqued. "Why gas powered?"

"She thought there'd be no electricity here. They say she's

3

due twenty pounds compensation." She started sobbing into the telephone. "This is a dreadful place. I don't know why I let you talk me into this."

"It will be alright. Get to the hotel, we'll sort it all out when I get there."

"Have you fed the cats?" The master of the unexpected trick question but I'd prepared for that one.

"Yes, they're fine. They're curled up here with me now," I lied.

Karen gradually calmed down and I said I needed to preserve phone charge as I had a big day tomorrow then ended the call.

"Cats?" asked Mike.

"She thinks I'm at the house keeping them company for the night."

"Of course."

"They'll be fine. It's not as if they can go anywhere."

***

Of course I hadn't reckoned on the escapology skills of Miss Marple, the feline equivalent of Steve McQueen. The following morning's headcount of furry little heads had come up one short. I scoured the house and even checked the loft. Nothing. In three hours I was supposed to be driving down the M5 with a full set of cats in the back of the car and I was one down. Karen would be sure to notice. I checked my watch and thought about postponing the crossing but the furniture was probably meandering its way across the Pyrenees about now and I would need to be at the house when it arrived. A second search of the house revealed a small gap in the top section of a bedroom window. A gap with which an anorexic spider would have struggled but clearly offered little resistance to a determined Miss Marple. I slid through the front door, taking great care not to let any of the others out then set about searching the garden for the missing cat.

I gave up after half an hour of rummaging, calling and much rattling of cat food. She was probably mousing in the next village by now and I would just have to deal with the fallout when I got to Spain. That wouldn't be pretty. As I slipped in through the front door I managed to lose a second cat, Sherlock. Two hours to go and I was down now to fifty percent of my cat quota. Karen had prepared this section of The Grand Move with a degree of precision that would have left Sun Tzu in awe. The cat baskets had been labelled, the back of the Stag resembled a cat prison camp with wire mesh blocking of all possible routes of escape. We had driven the feline contingent around the lanes of Somerset in a series of test runs and I had rehearsed under her watchful eye the ingress and exit procedures I was to follow on The Big Day. And now I had lost two of the little buggers before I'd even started.

I herded the two surviving cats, Watson and Columbo, into their respective baskets and double locked the doors with cable ties. I checked the time, ninety minutes to the off and I hadn't loaded the car yet. A tapping at the kitchen window startled me. I turned and at first couldn't see anything then the tapping came again, courtesy of a cat paw reaching up to it. Sherlock slid into view and padded to and fro along the narrow window ledge. I opened the window and he sat just outside on the ledge. I crept as slowly as I could, arms outstretched.

"Come on, boy, there's a good boy." My fingers reached towards him. My phone rang loudly. I jumped, the cat jumped. I grabbed the phone as I watched Sherlock disappear into the bushes at the bottom of the garden.

"Terry?" Karen's voice. "How's things going? All set for the off? You have put the cat biscuits in their baskets with them?"

"Oh, yes. All good. Biscuits." I stared out of the window and watched Sherlock darting from bush to bush. "How's your mother?"

"She's feeling better. We had a call from the airline. It's seems they didn't blow up the suitcase."

"Oh, that's nice." I poked cat biscuits through the bars on the cat baskets.

"Yes, apparently it was only the gas cylinders they

exploded. Probably because they can't speak English properly here."

"Well, there you go then. Must go now, dear. Got to finish loading the car." I put the phone down and rushed into the garden. Sherlock sat by the bushes staring at me.

"Come on, boy. Cat biscuits." I held my hand out to show him the cat biscuits.

He stood and stretched languidly then slowly strolled over to me to sniff at the biscuits. As soon as he was within reach I snatched at the scruff of his neck and hung on tightly. He thrashed and snarled, claws tearing chunks out of my skin. I carried him at arm's length back into the house and stuffed him in his cage.

"And you're not getting any biscuits either," I told him as I snapped the cable ties through the bars. "Get out of that!"

I had to wipe a smear of blood from my watch before I could check the time. Fifty minutes to go. The house was still littered with bits and pieces that were by now supposed to be tightly packed in the back of the car. I grabbed my overnight bag and the box labelled 'Cat Essentials' and dropped them on the passenger seat of the Stag. On my way back into the house I scanned the garden for signs of Miss Marple. Nothing. The three captives moaned loudly as I crossed their line of sight in the kitchen and returned with my case of vintage Scotch whiskey. I'd been told by Mike that it was almost impossible to buy good Scotch in Spain so I'd spent months assembling a collection of Scotland's finest offerings only to be told by Grumpy George, the removal van driver, that he wouldn't take it.

"Can't take alcohol into Spain," he'd said. "They'll impound my van. And that's my living, that is."

I'd tried explaining that one of the few advantages of the European Free Market was the ability to transport copious amounts of alcohol across its borders but he'd stubbornly refused to take it and left the case in the middle of the lounge floor. Along with my antique civil war sabre, "Dangerous weapon," my Sky satellite box, "Illegal in Spain," my box of books on explosives and weaponry that I needed for my film work, "Material likely to be of use to a terrorist," and my bronze statuette of lovers entwined, "Pornography."

The boot on the Stag was never really designed for anything more substantial than a wicker picnic basket and a pair of folding chairs and it struggled to accommodate the rejected removal items. I had to rearrange everything several times to get it all to fit. I just prayed that Spanish customs wouldn't open the car or they were likely to lock me up for being an alcoholic terrorist with a penchant for pornography. The back seat of the Stag had been turned into a cat sanctuary complete with cushions and litter tray tucked down behind the seats. The whole lot had been enclosed with a makeshift plastic wire mesh fence which should keep them all safely in place. I lined up the cat baskets, three occupied and one vacant, on the back seat and locked the fence.

A quick tour of the house turned up a lampshade and a stepladder. How does one overlook a step ladder? The boot just about took the added strain of the lampshade but refused the stepladder. I found a piece of rope and tied it to the top of the boot.

Back to the house and with list in hand I checked off doors, windows, gas, electricity and water. All secure. Ten past twelve and I was already eating into my traffic jam contingency time. I slipped the front door key under the mat for the new owners then dived in the car and headed down the lane to a chorus of meows from the back seat. This was going to be a fun fifteen hundred miles. Halfway down the lane I noticed a cat sat by the side of the road watching me rush past. That looked like...? I hit the brakes and reversed until I was level with Miss Marple. She didn't flinch as I approached and just sat on the verge staring at me. I leaned across and opened the passenger door. She sniffed at the door for a moment then climbed onto the passenger seat alongside my overnight bag, curled up and went to sleep. I closed the door and continued my journey. Fifteen minutes late but at least I had my whiskey and a full complement of cats.

Chapter Two

Brittany Ferries proved to be ruthlessly efficient. A helpful female security guard even climbed into the car with me to scan the cats' microchips. The embarkation went smoothly and I was directed to my parking place and within fifteen minutes I was in my cabin. I had a room the size of a child's wardrobe but still managed to contain a pair of bunk beds and a small bathroom. I freshened up and headed for the bar which was already overflowing with English football supporters and Spanish truck drivers. I took a pint of some generic beer and headed out to the rear deck.

Plymouth faded into the background, the details becoming lost in the afternoon mizzle that seemed to have become the norm for a spring day in England. I tried hard to feel something. Fear? Sadness? Excitement? But there was nothing, just another job to be done. The same sense of resignation I used to experience when I had set up some complicated series of special effects for a film shoot and then when the button is pressed you just have to watch. At that point the outcome can't be affected, not by feelings or by any action I could take at that point. I felt the same here. The button had been pressed and the plan was in motion. The furniture had gone, the house had been sold and the cats were safely stowed below. The cats? Oh hell, feeding time! I checked my watch. I was fifteen minutes late. Brittany Ferries offered cat owners the opportunity at set times to go to the car deck to feed and water their pets and I was late.

The French attendant at the information desk was condescending but courteous. A unique skill the French have cultivated over centuries of dealing with the English, condescending courtesy. He assured me it was no problem when clearly it was because he had to pull somebody off their break to escort me down. The cats knew I was late. They have finely tuned internal clocks that make the atomic clock in Geneva look like a hooky Chinese Rolex. The plaintive wailing as I approached the car seemed to fill the car deck and was clearly audible even over the deep rumble of the engines. The deck hand stood by as I poked food through the small opening in the mesh. The cats ate hungrily and I locked up again and returned to the bar.

The football fans were singing songs and the Spanish truck drivers chatting loudly behind their growing piles of empty glasses. I returned to the outside deck but by this time there was nothing to see. Just gently rolling waves and the phosphorescent wake we left behind. I sat for a while and pondered over how I had come to be here. It had never been my life plan. That had been a detached cottage somewhere in remote Cornwall with a vegetable patch and a pair of Alsatians. But the universe had had other plans. After thirty years being the Go-To Guy when Broccoli or Cameron wanted something exploding the computer nerds had arrived. Now they can blow up the White House on a laptop for a fraction of the cost of a sound stage model. They also get to have several goes to get it right, whereas I only ever got one. Of course it's never the same. Computer graphic imaging will never replace a well laid pack of C4 but the accountants and the Health and Safety brigade were much happier. My periods between jobs became longer and one day the telephone just stopped ringing. Then on an extended break to Spain I became intoxicated with the vibrancy of the country, and not a little of their gin, and I was the proud owner of a nearly finished villa in Bahía Blanca on the Costa Tropical.

I collected a bottle of Bell's from the Duty Free shop and headed for my cupboard.

The following morning the cafeteria was already thronging with families and Spanish truck drivers, although no sign of the football supporters. Considering my Full English breakfast had been prepared by a Yugoslavian on a French ship it looked surprisingly good. A trio of Spanish truck drivers vacated a table by a window and I nabbed it quickly. I had to push a collection of wine bottles to one side to make room for my tray and made a mental note to keep a good distance between my car and Spanish trucks on disembarkation. I ate as much of my breakfast as my hangover would allow then pushed the plate to one side and watched the sea roll gently by as I drank my coffee.

"You going south?" a voice asked.

I turned to see an attractive looking woman standing next to my table. She wore faded jeans and a multi-coloured silk shirt that clung gently to her slim frame. I guessed her to be in her late thirties or mid-forties, although her weather-hardened face indicated she may be older.

"Sorry?" I said.

"South, I'm looking for a car-share south." She slid into the seat opposite me. "I'm good company."

"No. I mean yes. I am going south but I'm full. Cats. A car-share? How does that work?"

"It's the environmental imperative. We all have to be green and share cars, Tony Blair said so. Are you going to eat that sausage?"

I glanced at my plate containing the remains of my breakfast. "No, help yourself."

She picked up my fork and speared the sausage then twisted in her seat to grab an abandoned bread roll from the table behind her. "So, I thought I'd be a responsible partner with the planet and car-share. You haven't got any ketchup I suppose?"

"No, sorry." Why was I apologising for not having ketchup?

"I'm a good co-pilot. You'll never find your way out of Santander without a co-pilot."

"I've got satnav and I'm sorry but I've got four cats in the car."

She gave me a slightly puzzled expression. "You do know they have cats in Spain already? You don't really need to take your own."

"They're the wife's cats. She's there already. We're emigrating."

"You don't want to trust satnav in Spain. It'll turn you in circles then dump you outside the Guardia Civil where they'll be waiting to fine you for driving whilst lost. Really. It happened to a friend of mine." She dabbed a paper serviette at the corners of her mouth.

"I'd give you a lift if I could but really. It's only a small car and the removal driver threw a sulk and left a pile of stuff behind."

"No worries." She stood and cast her eyes around the cafeteria. "Take care of the cats now and good luck."

I watched as she approached a lone trucker at a nearby table. "You going south?" I heard.

***

I made my way back to the cabin, picked up my overnight bag and headed for the front deck to await the first view of my new adopted land. It was a clear day and soon the mountains broke above the horizon and for the first time I felt a slight thrill at the adventure ahead. I watched as more of the shoreline came into view then an announcement called owners to their cars and I hurried downstairs to the car deck. There was no sign of the cats as I slipped into the car, they were all probably in full sulk mode by now and hiding in dark places. The offer of cat biscuits through the mesh brought three out from their hiding places but there was no sign of Miss Marple. But then a black cat in a black hiding place was never going to be easy. I was about to have a better search when I noticed other drivers getting in their vehicles and starting their engines. She'd missed biscuit time now and it served her right. As I waited I noticed the passenger door of a large English truck swing open and the girl from the cafeteria jumped out. She was clearly upset and was shouting back up towards the cab although over the noise of the car engines and the ship's rumbling I couldn't hear anything. A rucksack flew out of the cab and landed at her feet and the door swung shut. She hefted it over her shoulder, gave the cab a middle finger salute then threaded her way forwards between the parked vehicles.

We sat there for another five minutes then the vehicles in front of me started to move. I eased the car forwards, keeping pace with the car in front of me. After about ten metres the car in front suddenly stopped and on went the hazard lights. The cars either side continued to nudge forwards and with seconds the noise of horns blaring filled the metal cavern. One of the cars in the lane to my left came to a sudden stop and he was immediately rear-ended by a German camper van. More horn blaring as the occupants of both vehicles emerged and started a heated argument. The car driver was gesticulating at something forward but the German wasn't interested and was busy writing notes and taking photographs. As we were clearly going nowhere for a while I switched off the engine, checked the cats' mesh was secure and slipped out of the car, closing the door securely behind me. Other people were wandering around, some seemed to be peering underneath various vehicles. I slipped between a truck and a minibus to try to see what was going on. Then to my horror I realised what the problem was. In front of the lead vehicle of the stalled group sat a black cat. A pure black cat with the brightest green eyes and a flickering pink tongue. Miss Marple. A young girl made a lunge for her and the cat darted underneath a blue Mercedes. My mind swam. How had she got out? I'd only left the tiniest gap in the window and I'd been ultra careful each time I'd opened the door. I began to wonder if there was a hole in the floor but that was ridiculous. I then realised all the chaos this little cat was busy creating and felt a strong desire to sneak back into my car and hide. I'd never catch her in here anyway. Far too many places to hide, especially when she was in full panic mode. Anyway, if I owned up they'd lynch me from the yardarm or something. She'd survive. Lots of fish in a sea port. I'd just have to put up with Karen's wrath. It wasn't my fault. I turned my back on the chaos and weaved my way back to the car. Then I weakened and returned to the front to join the search. I spotted her darting between the vehicles and called to her by name. That was probably a bad move as it immediately turned the group anger towards me. People shouted at me, at the cat and at each other. Horns blared and vehicles threaded their way through the chaos. I tried to ignore them all as I remained in pursuit of the scampering Loki-possessed Miss Marple. She suddenly emerged from underneath a caravan and headed across the clear part of the deck. Straight into the arms of the girl from the cafeteria. She scooped Miss Marple up and tucked her into her jacket, looking at me as she straightened up. I stood frozen for a moment until the sound of a truck horn behind me vibrated every bone in my body. I jumped at the noise then nodded at the girl to head aft towards my car. I quickly cleared room on the passenger seat and she slid in, still clutching the cat in her jacket. I took Miss Marple from her arms and poked her into the back of the car.

"Thank you," I said.

"Going south?" she replied.

Chapter Three

"Have you got your passport ready?" I asked as we approached the border control.

She fished a battered envelope from her hip pocket and extracted an equally battered passport. "All legal," she said.

I handed her mine as she would be closest to the border police window as we drew up. "I'm sorry, I don't even know your name?"

"Harley," she announced. "Mum and Dad flipped a coin to name me. Mum lost."

"I guess your dad wanted a boy?"

"No," she said as she handed the passports through the window to the waiting policeman. "He actually wanted a motorbike."

We waited while the policeman scanned our passports into his computer then returned them to Harley. "Gracias," she said.

"I'm Terry, my friends call me Tel."

"Pleased to meet you, Tel." She smiled and nodded coyly at me.

The Guardia Civil officer waved us through the border point with no concern for my smuggling paraphernalia in the boot and we were in Spain. The sun streamed in through the windscreen as I tried to see the screen on my satnav to programme it for Bahía Blanca. The screen blinked off momentarily then announced, 'System update in progress. Please wait.' One of those ubiquitous progress bars appeared at the bottom of the screen and stubbornly sat at 22%. I yanked it from the windscreen threw it into the back to the sound of an affronted meow.

"Can you read a map? There's some behind your seat."

She pulled a handful of maps out and leafed through them. "What do you want? Ordinance Survey map of Somerset? Short walks in the Cotswolds? Or a street atlas of Basingstoke?"

I pulled over onto a gravel patch just before the exit from the docks. "Give those to me."

Harley was right. My assortment of maps was going to do little to help us navigate through Santander on a busy Tuesday afternoon.

"I had one, I know I did. In fact I bought two just in case." I reached behind the seat and groped around, coming up only with a Classic Rock magazine and a three week old copy of the Telegraph. "Fat lot of help that'll be." I stuffed them both back behind the seat.

"I can navigate," she said.

"Do you know your way round Santander?"

"Well, not exactly. But how hard can it be? I mean, it's on the coast so fifty percent of your choices turn out to be water and if we see a sign for either France or Portugal we go the other way."

I stared at her for a moment. There was a certain logic to her argument and in the absence of alternatives we had little choice. There was a sudden flurry of activity in the back with lots of meows and much hissing. Clearly the cats were bored.

"Which way do you think?" I asked as we approached a T junction.

"Left... No, right. Hmm... Left, definitely left."

I waited for a break in the traffic and turned left.

"Where are you going?" Harley said.

"You said left?"

"I meant right. I'm not very good with lefts and rights."

We managed a U-turn in a petrol station and soon found ourselves locked behind an English caravan with a sticker on the back which read, 'Running Free.' I guessed he would be likely heading south so decided to stick behind him. Before long our momentum stalled as the traffic thickened and we inched forwards, painfully slowly. From the wrong side of the road it was difficult to see what was happening ahead.

"Can you see what's going on?" I asked Harley.

She poked her head through the window. "No, it's all... Oh wait, yes. There's something big ahead, people are pulling out around it."

We came to a standstill for a moment then the caravan pulled out to the left and the source of the trouble lay directly in front of me. For a moment it was impossible to see the exactly what it was as we were too close to see but as soon as Harley gave the all clear to pull out and follow the caravan the full enormity dawned. A massive wind turbine blade straddled two parts of an enormous heavy haulage vehicle. The blade itself must have been three metres high and it seemed to go on forever as we drove slowly past it, encouraged by a Guardia Civil officer with a red flag. I guessed the turbine blade to be around eighty metres long, at least the length of a dozen vehicles.

Once clear of the behemoth the traffic moved freely and eventually my plan to follow the caravan turned out to be a wise choice as he led us straight onto the A67, the main road south. Just as we cleared Santander and hit the autovia, a voice from the back seat announced, "You have reached your destination. Turn right."

"He probably got confused," Harley said.

"Who?"

"The satnav man. Waking up in Spain must be rather confusing."

"Hmm. See if you can re-programme it, will you?"

"Where are we going?"

"Bahía Blanca. It's on the Southern coast, down near Almuñécar."

"Oh good. I've never been there."

I glanced at her to see if she was being serious. Her deadpan face told me she probably was. "Did you not have anywhere special you were supposed to be?" I could see turning up in Bahía Blanca with Harley on board probably wouldn't go down too well with Karen.

"Not really. I've got friends in Órgiva so I might drop in there at some point. Do you want to avoid toll roads?" She poked at the screen of the satnav.

"What? Oh, no. Toll roads are okay. Where's Órgiva?"

"Just south of Granada, up in the Alpujarras. There you go." She clipped the satnav back in its holder.

"Never heard of it." I felt acclimatised to the wrong side

of the road now and let the Stag have her head. She roared as we overtook a convoy of trucks.

"It's where you go when the rest of the world begins to feel disjointed."

A full scale cat war suddenly broke out in the back. The meows and hisses had turned into snarls and a flurry of boiling cats threatened to explode through the mesh.

"Can you see what's going on?" I asked.

Harley twisted in her seat and made cat soothing noises until they calmed down. "Difficult to see," she said. "They all seem to be hiding again."

***

The Stag ate up the miles, or kilometres, with the hunger denied by years of captivity. The bright sunlight, warm through the windows, belied the snow still gathered on the higher hills. We made good time as far as Madrid so once to the south side of the city I pulled off the motorway and into a roadside restaurant.

I ordered a couple of beers which arrived with tapas of local ham and manchego cheese. We drank and ate, enjoying the peace and sunshine. Two more beers arrived without me seeming to do anything.

"You need to keep an eye out for the traffic cops," Harley said, nodding towards the beers. "They're on bonus points since the Germans asked for their money back."

"You're probably right, but these are only little ones."

"They have spy helicopters with cameras that can tell what you're thinking. At least that's what Indian Steve says."

"Indian Steve?"

"Well, he's not really an Indian." She paused thoughtfully and sipped long at her beer. "And his name's not actually Steve, that's just what everybody calls him on account of his spiritual affinity with eagles. And the fact that he always wears feathers in his hair."

"Oh, I see. But why Steve?"

"Because that was the name given to him by his Spirit Guide."

"Steve?"

"He's got a tepee in the valley with a herd of goats, half an acre of hash plants and three wives."

"Well, live and let live," I mused.

Harley thought for a moment then, "Unless they're zombies."

"Zombies?"

"You don't want zombies to live and let live. That's when the trouble starts."

"Zombies."

"What's your zombie apocalypse plan?"

I was rapidly losing the thread of this conversation and wondered if the beers had been stronger than I'd thought. "Never given it much thought," I admitted.

"Everybody should have a zombie apocalypse plan." She looked at me as though I were a child not understanding some fundamental truth of the universe.

"You don't really believe in zombies, do you?" Having worked on countless zombie movies I felt I had a privileged view of the subject and could attest to their fictional nature.

"Zombies, aliens, Taliban, European bankers. Doesn't matter what's coming, if you're ready for the zombies then anything else is easy."

There was a certain logic to that argument and although I didn't realise it at the time, a logic which was set to have a profound effect on future events.

As we went back to the car I noticed a lot of vehicles gathered around the exit to the car park and people were out of their cars wandering around. It looked like the access road to the motorway was blocked, although I couldn't see what was causing it from here.

"I'm just going to see what's happening," I said.

Harley followed me as I threaded my way through the jumble of cars and people. I caught the flashing lights of emergency vehicles and some people were holding camera phones above the heads of the crowd. With lots of British politeness I dispensed my 'excuse me's' and 'pardons' as I pushed my way forwards until I could see what was causing the commotion. It took a while to understand what I was seeing. There was another of those massive haulage vehicles and wind turbine blades at the front of the mess. It appeared to be partway up the on-ramp slip to the autovia. A closer look revealed part of the slip road had crumbled, presumably under the weight of the truck. The enormous vehicle had, it seemed, tried to reverse back down the slip road only to wedge the fin of the turbine blade firmly between the articulated sections of a following oil tanker.

"That's something you don't see every day," I heard Harley say from my left. "And sort of ironic really."

Guardia Civil officers waved animatedly at various drivers and vehicles giving conflicting directions in an attempt to untangle the mess. Each vehicle that moved only seemed to deepen the mess.

"Well, that'll be number two," I said.

"Huh?"

"These turbine blades, there's usually three of them. I wonder where the other one is?"

We headed back to the car and sat there for a while as I tried to work out what to do. I was half tempted to risk reversing back onto the motorway and might have attempted it but for a quick glance which showed the off-slip was starting to clog up.

"There'll be a service road," said Harley. "So the staff can get to the restaurant and such. Always is."

"How do you know that?"

"Used to work in one of these places outside Biarritz."

"That's France?"

"All the same, trust me. Apart from the croissants. I hate croissants. "

As the only other option seemed to be to wait here in the blazing heat with a car full of increasingly irate cats I reluctantly followed her suggestion. We pulled slowly behind the buildings but there was no sign of a road. Only what looked like a goat track.

"There you go!" Harley announced proudly. "Told you so." She grinned endearingly.

I bumped the Stag up the track, avoiding the largest of the boulders and the deepest of the troughs. She'd not been built for this. We weaved between some scrub vegetation and a collection of cactus plants, following the track as it meandered through the wilderness.

"Are you sure about this?" I asked. "It doesn't seem to be going anywhere."

"Have faith, I'm sure there'll be... Watch out!"

Her warning came too late. I swerved to avoid a hidden pothole, catching a glancing blow on a piece of jagged rock to my right. The tyre blew with a surprisingly loud bang and the front of the car sank slightly as we slid to a halt.

"Bugger!" I cursed. I climbed out of the car, the heat hitting me like opening the door of an oven mid-roast.

"You got breakdown cover?" Harley arrived next to me and stared at the torn tyre.

"I don't think the R.A.C. will come out this far. They struggle with Somerset."

"Got a spare then?"

"Of course, it's in there," I pointed at the stuffed boot. "Somewhere."

We unloaded the contents of the boot onto the track.

"What's all this?" Harley held up one of my bottles of Talisker.

"Whiskey. Be careful."

"You're not only importing cats into Spain but alcohol as well?" She sounded incredulous. "You do know Spain is famous for both its cats and cheap alcohol?"

"It's not cheap alcohol, it's a rare vintage single malt."

She continued to unload, passing occasional comments on my possessions as the pile grew. "That's nice." She held up the statuette of the entwined lovers to admire. "You're a bit of a dark horse."

Eventually I was able to drag the spare wheel free. Having been a lifelong member of various breakdown services I had never had the opportunity to change a wheel before. Harley on the other hand seemed remarkably adept.

"That bit fits in there... No, there... Where the groove is under the... Give it to me."

She took the jack from me and shuffled on her back under the wing of the car. The muscles in her legs flexed through

20

the tight denim and her shirt rode up, exposing a tight midriff. "Pass me the handle."

Once the jack had been assembled into place I took the man's role once more and pumped at the handle until the wheel cleared the ground. We worked together quickly and efficiently despite the searing heat and before long we were back in the vehicle sucking in the cool breeze from the air conditioning. Loud meows from the back complained.

"So," said Harley. "I think if we follow this down a bit more we should come out on the main road."

I stared out of the windscreen seeing nothing but scrubland but I was too hot and tired to argue.

As it happened Harley was right in her assessment. The track broke free onto tarmac and we followed it down until it linked to a service road that led to the next motorway junction. Before long we were eating up the miles south and keeping half an eye out for spy helicopters, we sped down the autovia. We caught up with the third turbine blade about fifty miles further on. It was struggling to climb a gentle slope between two mountains. Fortunately traffic slid past it without undue concern. We hit Granada at the peak of the evening rush hour. The clear, open roads suddenly gave way to traffic treacle and we slowed to a crawl. After several near misses with weaving vehicles I settled into the nearside lane and stayed there watching the mayhem. There seemed to be a collective belief that the closer one drove to the vehicle in front the faster it made the traffic move. When that didn't work then enthusiastic horn blowing was the eternal fail-safe.

We crawled along like this for thirty minutes then as suddenly as the traffic had appeared it vanished again and once more we seemed to have the road to ourselves.

"That was odd," I said.

"Granada is a mess of narrow streets and nobody drives through it," Harley said. "So everybody going home or out for the evening uses the motorway to get from one part of the city to the other."

Dusk collected ahead, bathing the mountains in dark shadows against an indigo sky.

"Turn off here," Harley suggested. "We'll go down the old coast road. More interesting than the motorway."

"Isn't that the long way?"

"Not this time of night. Besides, it'll keep you awake."

The evening sky scattered bright stars over our heads as we approached the coast road and headed west towards Bahía Blanca. I grew tired and Harley, recognising my failing concentration levels, kept up a continuous commentary on the area.

"Hannibal landed here. You know? The guy with the elephants? Must have scared the locals shitless. I mean, can you imagine? And just down there it's where the last sugar cane fields are in Europe."

She jabbered continuously until the lights of Bahía Blanca appeared in front of us. The change in driving conditions brought me into full attention again as I nosed the car along the brightly lit sea front.

"Well, here we are," I said. "Where do you want to be dropped?"

"Anywhere. Never been here before so here's as good as there."

I pulled over opposite an English All-Day-Breakfast bar.

"Here you are then," I said.

"Do you want a blow job?"

"What?"

"A blow job. You've been so good bringing me all the way down here. My way of saying thank you."

"No... No thanks. Although I appreciate the offer."

"Fair enough." She gave me a coy smile that nearly made me reconsider.

"Will you be alright?"

She dragged her rucksack out and stretched as she stood. "Of course! I'll probably stay here a few days and then move on." She cast her eyes up and down the road, taking in the neon. "Or maybe tomorrow."

"Well, you take care now," I said. I felt slightly guilty leaving her here after the companionship we'd shared for the last eight hours.

"Hasta luego." She hefted the rucksack over her shoulder

and disappeared up a narrow side street, leaving the car feeling suddenly empty.

I turned to the cats in the back. "Nearly there, guys. One more night in kennels then it's off to your new home."

I pulled up outside the Hotel Miramar and locked the car, carefully ensuring just enough window gap for air but insufficient escape opportunities for even the most determined Miss Marple. I rang Karen's mobile.

"I'm downstairs," I said.

Karen appeared a few moments later and headed straight to the car.

"How are they?" she asked. "Have they eaten lately?"

"I'm fine," I said. "Easy journey really. Just a bit tired now though."

"Poor little things." She eased her way into the car and peered through the mesh. "Were we cruel to you? Locking you up like this, oh poor dears."

I pulled my overnight bag from the car to give her more room. "The keys are in the ignition. I'm going to the bar for a quick one before we move the cats."

Karen appeared not to notice so I headed inside. I dropped my bag at reception and found the bar, a big and mostly empty room of shiny tiles and equally shiny wood and leather. A waiter appeared the moment I sat down and I ordered a large beer. We'd chosen the Miramar as our temporary residence as it was only a short walk from our villa and they had a small kennels in an annexe for guests' pets. Apart from that it was a soulless, generic hotel, one of thousands that littered this part of Spain. I picked at the olives and realised I was starving. The beer arrived, cool in a frosted glass.

"El menu?" I asked.

"Si, señor."

The menu arrived at the same time Karen returned. "Can't really see them in there," she said. "We need to move them. They're so unhappy, I know they'll never forgive us."

"Can I just get some food first?"

"Oh, for goodness sake, Terry. Let's settle them down first. They don't understand, poor little mites."

The waiter hovered. "Momento," I said, tapping the menu. "In una momento."

I drove the car round to the kennels and we were met by an efficient young woman in jeans and tee-shirt. My poor attempts at learning Spanish failed me when trying to explain we had four cats booked in so we continued the conversation in English, a language with which she seemed totally comfortable. I felt slightly guilty.

Karen and I put into action our well rehearsed plan for the decantation of cats from car to kennels. She stayed inside the car, grabbed a cat, stuffed it into a basket, sealed the mesh then handed the basket out to me. The plan worked perfectly four times. Four cats safely transferred from back of car to kennels in four very smooth operations. Until...

"Terry?" Karen said from the back of the car.

"What is it, dear?" I recognised the tone and tried to calculate what I'd done wrong. "They're all alright. All safe in the kennels."

"Terry?" she repeated. "How many cats did you start out with?"

This was a trick question. My mind raced. We'd transferred four cats. I'd handed them over to the girl myself. Miss Marple, Sherlock, Watson and Columbo. All there. "Err, four of course."

"Then who the hell is this?" She handed me another cat in the basket. A pure black cat. The exact double of Miss Marple.

I floundered. My tired and slightly beer tinged brain trying to make sense of this. "Um... Miss Marple's evil twin?"

Chapter Four

We sat in the bar while I devoured a cheeseburger and chips. The simplest thing on the menu I could find. Karen's mother, Dot, joined us complaining that Spanish lifts were far too bright inside and moved much too quickly.

"So, you stole the ship's cat?" accused Karen.

"Well, not exactly. I sort of accidentally saved her. She would have been run over by a lorry otherwise." I tried appealing to Karen's cat maternal instincts.

"Well, that was very caring of you but I still don't understand how you completely forgot you had an extra cat on board. I mean, didn't the others complain?"

I remembered the cat fight around Madrid and the dreadful cacophony emanating from the back of the car that sounded like a thousand cats being eaten by alive by a flock of pterodactyls.

"No," I said. "They were all as good as gold."

The waiter appeared and I ordered a gin and tonic. It was Spanish strength and hit the spot at first sip. I began to relax.

"The airline delivered mum's luggage in the end," said Karen.

"They still owe me a set of curling tongs. Where am I going to find curling tongs in this country?" Dot poked at her teabag-on-a-string as it stubbornly floated on the top of a glass of lukewarm water. "And why can't they make a cup of tea in this country?"

"You just need to give it time to brew, Mother."

"I'm seventy five, I haven't got that much time left."

"I'll find you some curling tongs, Dot," I said then to Karen, "Have you checked with Stuart we're still all set to pick up the keys tomorrow?" I asked.

"Yes, he said to go to his office at eleven and he'll have them," Karen said. "He's got a viewing before that. Showing a couple from Birmingham a Sports Bar on the front."

"And he's sure all the paperwork's in order?"

"Oh yes. He says it's all perfect and ready to go."

***

"Slight problem." Stuart, our estate agent and the person to whom we'd entrusted power of attorney, shuffled a pile of papers on his desk.

"Go on," I said.

"You appear to have bought next door's house by mistake," Stuart said.

"Next door's house?"

"Yes, it's quite funny when you think about it. You see –"

"I'm sorry, how is this in the remotest bit funny? I didn't want next door's house. If I'd wanted that one, that's the one I'd have chosen!"

"Hmm, yes, I can see how you might not find it so funny from your end." Stuart slid his chair back from the desk, as if trying to put distance between us. "Mind you, Mr and Mrs Frazer are not overly excited either."

"And who are the Frazers?"

"Oh, they're the couple whose house you've just bought. They're none too happy with you. Mind you," he paused as if trying to sum up the Frazers. "They never seem to be very happy about anything."

"How did this happen? I mean... Surely somebody checked the Land Registry or whatever the equivalent is here?"

"Ah, that's where the problem started. You see, the builder called your house Plot twenty three, Calle del Mar and next door was twenty nine."

"Twenty nine?"

"It was the order he built the houses in. The trouble was twenty nine was built on the land of a previous house that was number twenty three because at that time there were only fourteen houses in the road."

"Fourteen?"

"So when the Ayuntamiento registered the deeds they called your house twenty nine because twenty three already existed on previous records but in the meantime the

Correos, the Post Office, designated your house nineteen because they started counting all over again from the end of the road."

"Nineteen? So I have three addresses?"

"Nothing to worry about. Happens all the time, this is Spain. And actually you have four addresses because the local Town Hall forgot to re-designate the area with the regional Junta de Andulucia who still think that the road is Avenida de Malaga."

"So what number am I supposed to be in Avenida de Malaga?"

"I haven't the faintest idea."

"But this is a nightmare." I stood and paced the office. "Our furniture's arriving later today. Which house do they put it in?"

"Calm down, Terry," said Karen. "I'm sure Stuart didn't do it on purpose." She turned to Stuart. "You didn't do it on purpose, did you, dear?"

"No, of course not," Stuart said. "These officials round here are a sodding nightmare and none of them speak English properly."

"Well, what do we do?" I felt my voice rising and tried hard to remain calm even though the temptation to blow something up was becoming overwhelming. "How long's it going to take to sort this mess out?"

"Shouldn't take too long. The good thing about Spain is that buying or selling a house is actually quite simple. As long as you get all the right people in the right place at the right time, of course."

"Well can we at least have the keys so we can let the furniture in?"

"To which house?"

"My house!" I slammed my hand on the desk. "I want the keys to my house. Number twenty three."

"Twenty three is where the Frazers live, you want nineteen." He smiled. "Easy mistake."

On the promise that Stuart would sort the mess out by the end of the day we took the keys to number nineteen, which he assured me was the house we'd viewed.

The cats seemed pleased to see Karen, or maybe it was just her special cat treats of tuna, chicken and chocolate flavour cat shaped biscuits courtesy of Marks & Spencer's.

"What are we going to call the new one?" she asked as she reached into their run and tickled various ears as they passed by.

"That sort of presupposes we're keeping it?" I said. "I thought we'd agreed four was enough?"

"Well you brought him home, what do you suggest? Take him back to Brittany Ferries?"

"Maybe we'll find a new home for him, probably plenty of people in Spain would like a cat. Come on, we've got to get to the house and air it before the furniture arrives."

***

The first thing we noticed as we drove into Calle del Mar was what seemed to be a radio telescope observatory sat on top of our villa. A huge satellite dished scraped the sky in what appeared to be an earnest search for signs of life on Sirius Four. We pulled up behind a van marked 'Costa Gardening, Drain Clearance and Satellite TV'.

"What the hell...?" I stood in front of our villa watching the massive dish swing lazily from side to side.

A head peeped around the side of the dish. "Oh, hello, didn't know you were back." Darren, the satellite dish man, came round to the edge of the roof and looked down at us. "Have it sorted for you by the end of the day."

"Isn't that a bit on the large side? I only wanted the BBC, not the local news from Alpha Centauri."

Karen stared up at the roof in disbelief. "Won't it upset the neighbours?" she said.

"They've already had a moan but it's just jealousy," Darren said, pointing to the house opposite.

"I'm not surprised. It's just blotted out their view of the mountains," I said.

"They'll come round. When you've got the latest Premiership football and all they've got is Cooking with Pedro," Darren said cheerfully.

"I can't stand football," I said.

"Will it get Strictly?" Karen asked.

"You'll see the join on Brucie's syrup with this beauty!"

"Oh."

"Take it down," I said. "You'll have to put up something smaller."

Darren looked crestfallen. "I thought you'd be pleased, I got a special deal on this." He patted the edge of the dish and it wobbled alarmingly.

"From where? NASA?" I noticed we'd collected an audience as residents of the peaceful calle ventured out of their front doors, blinking in the bright morning sunlight like startled moles. "Good morning," I said, smiling at them. "We're moving in."

"It's usually very quiet here," said an elderly man in a dressing gown and slippers. His fellow neighbours shuffled and mumbled like lethargic zombies in search of prey.

A gentle breeze fluttered up the calle and I heard a clattering from the roof. I looked up to see Darren clinging to the edge of the dish as it dragged him in an arc around the roof. "Might need to tighten it up a bit," he said.

"Take it down," I yelled, slightly alarmed. "A half decent wind and that'll have my roof off!"

"It's the Spot Beam, you see," he said as he tried to hold the dish steady under another whispery gust. "You need something this size these days since they've pointed the Astra satellite at Woking instead of Benidorm. Never get the Beeb on anything smaller now."

"What about Strictly?" Karen asked, a slight note of panic in her voice.

"We'll sort something out," I said then turned to Darren, "Please take it down before it picks up my house and takes it off to Kansas."

We let ourselves into the house just as the dish landed in the garden.

"No worries," I heard Darren shout. "I've got it."

The villa smelled faintly of fresh paint as we moved from room to room opening windows and checking lights. It was a spacious single storey affair with a large open lounge, a huge marble and chrome kitchen and three bedrooms, each with an en-suite bathroom. We had bought it during a holiday in the town when sunshine and optimism had blinded us to the estate agent's wishy-washy promises that the building work would be finished within the month. It hadn't, of course. The builder had gone bust before the ink was dry on the Compraventa, leaving us to finish the work. Stuart had been full of apologies and offered to oversee a local British builder as the villa was finally brought to habitable status. But of course the bills had accumulated as quotations were redefined as estimates then approximations and finally wild guesses.

"It looks lovely!" Karen said as she tested drawers and cupboards in the kitchen. "They've done so well. I love the worktops." She ran her fingers across the shiny black marble.

"So it should." A knock on the door snagged my attention. "Come in. It's open." I headed to the hallway expecting to see Darren. Instead it was an elderly man in faded khaki shorts and a well-worn T-shirt emblazoned with the Saltire, the Scottish national flag. He held a large brown envelope in his hand and waved it towards me.

"It's no right, ye know." The thick Highland accent was almost impenetrable.

"Ah, Mr. Frazer?" I held my hand out.

"You'll no get away wi' it," he said, ignoring my offer of a handshake. "Ye cannae just turn up and buy a body's house an' hope they'll no notice. Ye ken?"

"Yes, sorry. Mix up at the estate agents."

"The gangsters in the town hall tried that. Tried to snatch all the houses here." He waved the envelope in a wide arc. "Said they were illegal. Tah! They'll no mess wi' us again. Ye ken?"

"Yes. But we –"

"We had a petition. Collected a hundred and thirty eight signatures and took a full page in the Bahía Blanca News."

"I can see how that would –"

"So, what are ye going to do wi' this?" He shook the brown envelope towards me.

"Stuart said he'll sort it. He's –"

"Stuart!" Frazer waved both arms in the air. "Stuart? Yer nae talking about that idiot down at Costa Casas are ye? Tah! He could nae sort out a tea party in a doll's house. You'll no get any sense out of him."

"He seems to know what –"

"We knew there'd be trouble when he set that place up. Ye cannae just bankrupt a sports bar one minute then open an estate agency the next. I told Mrs Frazer so." He slammed the brown envelope into my hand and left with a, "You'll no be wanting a petition."

He exchanged a few unheard words with Darren as they passed on the path.

"Well that went better than I thought it would," I said as I watched him shuffle down the path.

***

Darren eventually gave up trying to persuade me to have his radio telescope on my roof and agreed to set up a TVOIP, whatever that was. He assured me there would be no dishes as everything came through the internet. Although apparently the resolution wasn't up to satellite and I wouldn't be able to differentiate between blades of grass on the Wembley pitch. He set off into town to collect the necessary kit and I headed up to the roof terrace to survey the damage.

The rear of the villa sported views of the nearly completed championship golf course. Which would probably have impressed me had I been even the slightest bit inclined towards golf. As it was, my only interest in small balls was the little silver one that flew around the pins and bumpers of my genuine 1950's Balley pinball machine that would hopefully be arriving with the rest of our possessions later this morning. Karen had insisted we had a view of the golf course and had great hopes for me taking up the sport. "It will give you something to do," she'd said.

Darren had clearly made a brave attempt to attach the dish to the roof and the plethora of small holes in the masonry looked like a bad day in Downtown Beirut. I added Polyfilla to my mental shopping list. I checked the time, it was only just after nine. Even if the van made good time it would still not be here before midday; plenty of time to get some basic supplies.

We unloaded the contents of the car then went down to the nearby Eroski Hypermarket at Velez Malaga. Eroski covers an area the size of the Isle of Wight (I refuse to think in football pitches). How did we ever arrive at a situation where we measure area in football pitches and height in double decker buses? Next we'll be using EastEnders episodes as units of time and cans of lager as volume.

Eroski is everything Tesco wants to be when it grows up. One can buy anything from a packet of butter to a huge American walk-in fridge in which to put it. The place is so vast that there are rumours of a Romanian family who went missing whilst in search of tinned sauerkraut. It's said that on the night of the full moon, when the wind is in just the right direction –

"Pink or blue?" Karen's voice snapped me back to the horror of my surroundings.

"What?"

"Pink or blue? The toilet paper, should we get pink or blue?"

"Would it be wrong if I said I didn't have a firm opinion?"

"It's just that our en-suite is blue but the family bathroom is pink."

"Well, get a pack of each?" I ran my hand over a leather recliner that offered Body Forming comfort and vital point heated massage panels.

"They come in packs of twenty," she said. "We don't need forty rolls. That would be silly."

"How about green?"

"I don't know why I bother asking your opinion." She threw a pack of pink rolls into the trolley and blustered away up the aisle. I went in search of Polyfilla and beer then caught up with her at the cheese counter. My rudimentary Spanish did not yet extend to cheese conversations so I just pointed at a few interesting looking specimens and ordered a quarto of each. It was far too much of course but quarto was the only fraction word I knew how to say.

With our overflowing and belligerent trolley we made our way to the cashiers. The girls at the checkouts were pleasant and phenomenally efficient. We found ourselves packed and bagged so quickly I was left feeling slightly dazed.

"Well, that was an experience," Karen said as we loaded the car.

"I'm already missing Sainsbury's home delivery."

Just as we arrived back at the house my mobile phone rang. It was Stuart.

"Slight problem, Mr England."

I knew it wasn't going to be a slight problem. Nobody ever uses my surname with good news. Right from the days of my first teachers in primary school. "What's the meaning of this, England?" No, use of my surname never announces anything pleasant.

"What slight problem?"

"It's the Town Hall. They've all buggered off for the weekend."

"But it's only Thursday."

"I know," he said. "But Friday is a regional holiday. Some saint or other."

"But today's Thursday. How does that work?"

"Oh, they do this all the time here. You'll get used to it. They always add an extra day or two to any public holidays. This is Spain. They'll have a fiesta to celebrate finding a parking space."

"But what about the deeds to my house?"

"I'll get onto the Notary as soon as they reopen on Tuesday."

"Tuesday?"

"Don't worry, Terry. Relax. You'll soon get used to the way things work!"

I put the phone on the kitchen work surface and decided Spain and I were probably going to have some negotiating to do.

***

Deciding I couldn't venture too far lest the furniture

appeared while my back was turned, we decided to explore the urbanisation. Calle del Mar was just one of a handful of wide avenues that made up this community of some two hundred villas which sat in the remains of the orange groves that once dominated this area. Tastefully thought out by expensive architects, hastily approved by equally expensive town hall officials and nearly built by the lowest bidding builders. We had been assured that one day ornamental gardens would replace the pile of rubble on a piece of wasteland in the centre of the community and that the big hole would transform itself into a swimming pool. We picked our way along the unmade Calle Buena Vista and quite by accident found ourselves at The 'Expats', the urbanisation's only bar and community focal point until such time as the promised sports centre arrives. The terrace was pleasantly shaded by vines that broke the fierceness of the midday sun. I left Karen at one of the small tables overlooking the main road along which the furniture would arrive and went to the bar.

The barman appeared from behind a beaded curtain. "Qué quieres?"

I'd been carefully rehearsing my Spanish for 'Could I see the menu of the day?' as I approached the bar but it left me just as my mouth opened. I gave a good impersonation of a goldfish for a few seconds then lamely asked, "Habla Ingles?"

"Que?"

"Menu del dia?

"Que?"

"Do you speak English?"

The barmen visibly relaxed and in a thick Birmingham accent, "Course I speak English, this is an English bar. What were you expecting me to speak, Hungarian?"

"I thought you were Spanish."

"Well, I thought you were a foreigner too! We get a lot of foreigners around here. That's why I try to pick up a bit of the lingo. You know, make them feel welcome. Always pays to try and blend with the locals. What can I do you for?"

"A beer and a margarita and do you have a lunch menu?"

"Right there." He pointed to a chalkboard behind the bar and drew the beer from a Foster's pump.

The menu consisted of various roast dinners or permutations on bacon, fried fish, pizza or chips. I ordered two of the seafood medleys and returned to our table with the drinks.

"Seems like a nice place," said Karen as I sat down.

"They serve Foster's beer and bottled margaritas," I said, slightly bemused.

"That's nice then."

We received polite nods and little waves from the other customers as they drifted in and out. An elderly couple at the next table introduced themselves as Jim and Diane.

"You must be Karen and Terry," Jim said. "Welcome to our little paradise."

"Word gets around?" I said.

"Oh, you'll find there are no secrets here." He smiled. "We're all very friendly. We live at Casa del Sol, just a few doors down from you."

"You must come round for our housewarming barbecue," said Karen, much to my surprise as this was the first I'd heard of a housewarming barbecue.

Our food arrived with an alarming rapidity that spoke of freezer and deep fat fryer.

"I see you've discovered the best food in Andalucía," said Diane. "They do a lovely roast beef and Yorkshires."

"Heard about your run-in with old Campbell Frazer," said Jim. "You don't want to pay no mind to him. All bluster and grump mostly."

"Yes, it appears there was a mix up at the estate agents." I poked at the seafood medley trying to discern what, if anything, lay underneath the batter.

"Ah yes, Pat told us about that," Diane said. "Stuart's a well-meaning sort but he's a bit clueless really."

"Who's Pat?" I asked.

"Pat?" said Jim. "Over there, at the bar. This is his place. That's why it's called the Expats. Sort of a play on words. Clever, huh?"

"Anyway, Stuart says he'll have it sorted soon. I understand this sort of mix-up is normal for Spain though," I said.

"Nope," said Jim, he took a deep pull on his beer. "Normal for Stuart perhaps. Boy's a born idiot. But that's what you get when you buy an estate agency off the internet."

A low rumble in the road caught my attention and I looked up to see a Shifter's Removals van creeping up the calle.

I sank the last of my beer and picked up a couple of chips. "Come on, Karen. That looks like our furniture."

We caught up with the van right outside our villa.

I knocked on the cab door and the driver wound down the window. "You looking for Terry England? Number twenty three?"

He checked his clipboard. "No, I have twenty nine, Mr Stuart Alinson."

"Ah, Stuart Alinson is the estate agent. He was just coordinating things this end. It's me you want, England."

"No England on here, mate." The driver tapped at his clipboard.

"Where's George? The driver who picked up the load in England?"

"George? Oh he don't do the continent no more. He's dyslexic. Has trouble with his lefts and rights. Got a forty tonner stuck on a roundabout in Dieppe once. Rush hour it was, took them two hours to sort it out, never driven abroad since. He drives to Plymouth and we pick it up and do the foreign leg."

"Oh, I see. Anyway that's my house." I pointed to our villa.

"That's as maybe, mate. But I have to deliver this lot to Mr Alinson at number twenty nine and you appear to be neither he nor residing at twenty nine. It wouldn't do to have somebody's worldlies delivered to the wrong house now."

He climbed down from the cab and marched up the garden path to Frazer's house. He knocked on the door with the tone only over-officious jobsworths can achieve. He waited a moment then knocked again. "Nobody home," he announced as he headed back to the cab.

"What's happening?" asked Karen.

"They've got the wrong address," I said. "What now?" I asked the driver.

"We wait," he said as he started rolling a cigarette. "Can't do nothing until Mr Alinson is here."

I contemplated briefly offering a bribe but decided that would probably make matters worse. I also contemplated unloading the van myself or dragging him out of the cab and hiding his body under the nearly finished community swimming pool. In the end I decided the only way to resolve this was to get Stuart here.

I rang his office and the answering machine assured me my call was important. I rang his mobile twice before he answered.

"Stuart? It's Terry England. You anywhere close to my place?"

"Sorry, mate. I'm up in Sayalonga. Just taken on a cracking place here. You can see Morocco on a clear day. You're not interested in a country house with Moroccan views by any chance?"

"The movers won't deliver my furniture to my house because of the number mix-up."

"Hang on a minute." I heard him mumble to somebody else, *"Should be able to shift this in a couple of weeks... five percent.* Terry? Terry?"

"Still here."

"Why don't you just tell them it's a screw up at the Town Hall?"

"Oh, I didn't think of that. Of course I told them that but they won't listen because it's your name all over the bloody paperwork!"

"Ah, I can see how that would be a problem."

"How soon can you get down here?"

"I've got to take these lovely people back to the office to sort out the finer details. I can meet you there in about an hour?"

I looked at the driver. "An hour?" I said.

"Up to you, mate. We're on the clock, got a load to pick up in Malaga first thing."

"I'll be as quick as I can."

***

Of course Stuart wasn't there when I arrived. I rang his mobile but no answer. After half an hour of pacing up and down outside his office he finally appeared.

"Sorry, Terry. Stopped off for a coffee to seal the deal." He fumbled with the keys before finding the right one. "Lovely people. German couple been living here –"

"Look, Stuart, I'm in a rush. Are you coming with me now?"

"I need to stay here. Got some people coming to look at a nice little finca in Frigiliana. It's got a sun terrace that looks out over..." He caught my look. "I'll give you a letter. That'll do the job."

We waited five minutes while his computer started up and then another ten while Windows updated.

"I'm sure handwritten would've done." I looked at my watch, I'd been gone an hour and a half already.

"More official this way." He picked at the keys of his computer. "To whom it may concern... Hereby solemnly declare that the statement I am about to make... Without just cause or impedi... Imped... How do you spell impediment?"

I spelled it out for him with a calm that belied my desire to reach across his desk and gently squeeze his throat until he stopped talking. I could go a full year without ever using the word 'impediment'.

He finished typing with a self satisfied, "There we go! All nice and legal." He hit print and the printer in the corner gave a whinging crunching noise then spat out a crumpled and shredded sheet of paper. "Oh, bollocks. It always does that."

While I waited for him to sort out the paper jam I tried to remain calm by staring at the walls of his office. In amongst the property display boards a small certificate caught my eye. A five-star diploma from the University of Real Estate in Swamp Creek, Wisconsin.

A loud clatter and another, "Bollocks," from the direction of the printer. I turned to look and Stuart was holding a large piece of plastic in one ink-stained hand and more crumpled paper in the other. "This might take a moment," he said.

My phone rang. Karen.

"Terry? Where... Going... I can't cope..." Dead line. I stared at the phone. A full five bars, it must have been Karen's phone breaking up. I stabbed redial. A very nice Spanish voice apologised that my call couldn't be connected. Or at least I assumed that's what was being said.

"Got it!" Stuart announced and the printer finally spat out a serviceable letter. Slightly crumpled, slightly ink-stained but it would have to do.

I took it from Stuart's hand, declining the offer of an envelope and ran to my car.

I knew I was too late as I saw the Shifter's Removals van heading in the opposite direction as I neared our calle. The uselessly optimistic part of me hoped they were just going for a cup of tea but when I pulled up outside our house that faint hope faded. Our furniture was piled neatly onto Frazer's lawn and Karen walked in manic circles on the pavement.

"I didn't know what to do," she said as I pulled up. "They said it was either this or they take it all to their depot in Malaga and I couldn't reach you."

"It's okay. It's not your fault." I stared at the pile of furniture. Fortunately there wasn't a huge load. We'd been ruthless with our possessions prior to The Grand Move. I'd calculated that the cost of moving was around a hundred pounds per cubic metre; therefore we'd left behind anything we could replace at a lower cost. But it was still enough to create a sense of the overwhelming.

"We can't do this ourselves." Karen started to sob. "It'll take us all night."

"Then it will take us all night." I picked up the packing case that held my hi-fi system. "We've all the time in the world now."

We were about half an hour in to the task and already feeling the strain when a huge white Range Rover pulled up.

A deeply tanned face appeared as the window slid down.

"You need a hand, mate?" The voice was pure East London.

"Oh, no," I said. "We'll manage."

"We'd love a hand," Karen said as she placed a standard lamp on the pavement near the Range Rover.

The man jumped out of the vehicle. He stood around six two and his straining tee-shirt told of hours in the gym and probably a liberal supply of steroids.

"No problem," he said. "Name's Billy. Billy Gibson. Live just up there." He waved his hand towards the end of the calle. "Last house in the road."

"Casa Grande?" I'd noticed it when we viewed our house. A huge villa with a remote controlled iron gates and CCTV cameras.

"That's the one. Modest pile but we call it home. What happed here?"

"Idiot estate agent, muddle at the Town Hall, cantankerous removal men."

"Ah," Billy said as he lifted a huge crate of books as if it were empty. "I guess you've run into Idiot Boy Stuart down at Costa Casas?"

"How did you guess?" I followed Billy into the house. "Just drop it over there. We'll sort it later."

We did a few more trips to and fro and it looked like we were winning when a Seat Marbella pulled into the Frazers' drive.

Frazer struggled out of the car and strutted over to me. "What the hell're ye doin' here, man?" He stared at the chaos on his lawn. "You've wrecked my lawn. That took me three years. D'ya ken how hard it is to grow a lawn in this furnace? It's not enough that ye try to snatch a man's house from under him but now you want to destroy it and all."

"Don't get your sporran in a twist, Jock." Billy tucked a box marked 'China Fragile' under his arm. "I'll send Manuel round with his roller. He'll have it sorted in no time." He looked to me, "He's magic, that boy. He could grow primroses in the Sahara. If you ever want any bougainvillea for your gazebo just let me know."

Frazer marched up his path and slammed the door shut.

"I don't think I got off to a good start with him," I said.

"Oh, pay no mind to Jock. He's just a miserable old git. Never 'appy unless he's got something to moan about. You've probably made his week."

We continued to march our possessions into our house and eventually Frazer's lawn was empty. A bit muddy and churned but empty.

We stood in the kitchen surrounded by boxes. I handed Billy a can of San Miguel. "I think you've earned that. Thanks. We'd never have managed."

"Think nothing of it." He sank the beer in one. "Community spirit, we're all here to help each other. Know what I mean? We're having a barbecue tomorrow, you ought to come. Be a chance to meet the neighbours."

"We'd love to, thank you."

We stood at the door as we watched Billy take the Range Rover up the calle.

"He seems like a nice man," said Karen.

"Hmm. Come on. We'd better get back to the hotel. You've got cats and a mother to feed."

Chapter Five

The hotel provided a huge selection at their buffet breakfast. Cold meats, cheese, a huge variety of cereals and perfectly cooked bacon and eggs. Something for every nationality, religion and palate. We sat at a table by the window and watched the sun pierce through the palm trees that lined the avenida.

"You ought to try one of these croissants, Mum. They're delicious." Karen tried to persuade a dollop of marmalade to balance on the remains of her crumbling croissant.

"Foreign rubbish," Dot said. "They're just empty pasties." She emptied the contents of three tomato ketchup packets over her fried egg.

I'd selected a few cheeses and meats that I didn't recognise but they tasted bland and processed. The restaurant bustled with activity and a myriad of languages babbled around us like a busy stream over pebbles. It reminded me of the places in which I used to stay during my times on set. A highly efficient and homogenised machine providing home comforts and snippets of familiarity to the international traveller.

"Have you packed, Dot?" I asked.

"What's to pack?" Dot dabbed a piece of toast at the remains of the ketchup on her plate. "They lost it all."

"Don't exaggerate, Mum. It was only your hair curlers."

"I felt proper violated. Brutes like that rummaging around in my unmentionables."

"Have you packed yet, Mother?" Karen repeated with an air of gentle firmness.

"What little I've got. Comes to something when seventy years goes into a suitcase with room to spare."

"What about those huge boxes we spent half of last night lugging –" I started.

"Terry, shut up. You're not helping."

We finished breakfast and loaded the car. In the end we

still had to make two journeys to transport Dot, her luggage and five cats with all their cat essentials. The much rehearsed feline exfil from car to villa went like clockwork, shaming my disastrous efforts in England.

Manuel stopped rolling Frazer's lawn for a moment and watched the operation with great interest. He waved to greet us. "Hola Señor y Señora. Buenas dias. Welcome to España."

"Hola," I returned with a small wave and even smaller attempt at Spanish.

"You bring cats?" he asked, with an air of surprise.

"Yes," I replied. "We have four, quatro." I held up four fingers.

"Five," corrected Karen. "Remember?"

"Oh, yes. Five." I added the last finger. "Cinqo."

"Five?" Manuel looked genuinely puzzled. "Ay, so many. Why you bring cats? You know we have cats already here? We have many cats in España."

"Yes, but these are special," Karen said. "My babies."

"Muchos gatos." Manuel shook his head and returned to his rolling.

I looked at our villa, our new home. The whitewashed walls, an attempt at the traditional, broken by the natural wood shutters that flanked each double glazed window. A row of six young palm trees stood sentry each side of the path leading up to a set of wrought iron double doors.

"So, what are we going to call it?" I said.

"I was thinking Morse," said Karen.

"Morse? You can't call a house Morse? That's... Oh, I see... you meant the cat."

"Or Poirot. But I was never very keen on Poirot. He was always too pompous for me. That ridiculous moustache."

"Morse it is then."

We set about unpacking the essentials. The kitchen cupboards remained capacious even after consuming the contents of every box marked 'Kitchen'. We had been particularly ruthless with aging crockery and utensils. As I found homes for the electrical equipment I mentally counted the number of new plugs we would need.

After several hours work we left Dot listening to The Archers on my laptop and adjourned for lunch.

We found a shady table at The Expats and our beers arrived along with a pair of miniature bacon sandwiches.

"Tapas," Pat explained, obviously catching my surprise. "Traditional in Andalucía."

We drank our beer and sampled Pat's Traditional Tapas. The sunshade gave little opposition to the sun but we waited until Dot arrived then retreated to the comfort of the air conditioned bar.

"How are the Archers?" I asked. "All well in Ambridge?"

"Some consortium trying to buy Bridge Farm to put windmills all over it. There's a meeting tomorrow in the Village Hall."

"Oh dear. I'll get some drinks in. Tea?"

"Ask them if they can make proper tea. PG Tips in a cup. Not in bits."

Pat wasn't there so I was served by a young English woman. She wore a flimsy white cotton dress that betrayed her dislike of underwear.

"You must be Terry," she said. "I'm Tracey."

"Hello, Tracey. Word gets around."

"Small community here." She placed the drinks on the bar. "What do you think of the place?"

"It's very... very English. A bit like Bournemouth I suppose. Only hot. Very hot."

"I know!" Her brilliant blue eyes sparkled with enthusiasm. "Isn't it just perfect?"

"Depends how you feel about Bournemouth, I suppose."

I'd just juggled all three drinks into a suitable carrying position when a tall, slim man in a white suit approached from the other end of the bar.

"Hello," he said. He held a glass of something with lots of fruit in one hand and a cigar in the other. "I'm Simon, Simon Farrington. You must be the newcomers everybody's talking about." He extinguished the cigar in an ashtray and held his hand out. I replaced the drinks on the bar and shook his hand.

"So it appears," I said. "I'm Terry and that's my wife over there, Karen, and her mother Dot." I nodded towards our table. Karen and Dot were in deep conversation and appeared not to notice me.

He patted my back. "Come, you must introduce me." He headed for the table so I picked up the drinks and followed him.

"Señoritas guapas," Simon greeted as he approached the table. "Bienvenidos a España." He took each of their hands in turn and kissed them.

Dot giggled and Karen said, "Hola." She fluffed her hair.

"Ah, you speak Spanish already," he praised. "How wonderful."

"Just a poco," Karen said.

"This is Simon Farrington," I said. "Simon, this is my wife, Karen, and her mother, Dot."

"Really? I thought you must be sisters." He pulled a chair from a nearby table. "May I join you?"

"Oh, yes," Karen said. "Are you here on holiday?"

"Unfortunately not, my dear. Would that I had the opportunity for holidays."

"What do you do?" Karen asked.

"All very boring. I'm a mere functionary for the political machinery of Europe. A glorified civil servant really."

Pat had returned and brought over four small plates of cheese cubes and pickled onions.

Simon ordered more drinks for us all before we could protest.

"Which department are you with?" I asked.

"Europe. I'm the Conservative Euro MEP for Stockwood and Hamsdown. A humble task but when one is called to serve one must put aside one's personal ambitions. Noblesse Oblige."

"I see," I said, not really seeing. "But I thought the Tories were against Europe in the last election?"

"Ah, mischievous nonsense disseminated by the tabloids. We embrace Europe. Indeed, we used to own most of it. Most of us have our second homes in Europe. I myself have a little retreat in the Dordogne."

"You don't live here then?"

"Temporarily assigned here by Brussels," he said. "I have

my constituency house here. One of the few perks of an otherwise thankless job. I'm here on a Fact Finding Mission to study the impact of mini roundabouts on small communities."

"Mini roundabouts? Is there a problem with mini roundabouts in Bahía Blanca?"

"Of course not, dear boy." He laughed. "That's why I chose this place! No point in studying somewhere that already has a problem, is there? What would be the point of that?" He examined a piece of cheese before popping it in his mouth.

"Of course. How long have you been here?" I realised I had two almost full beer glasses in front of me and set about rectifying the issue.

"Fifteen years."

"Fifteen years?"

"I know." He sipped slowly at his fruit laden drink. "These studies do take time. It's often tempting to make pre-emptive decisions but it in the final analysis it always pays to make a full and comprehensive study of all the potential implications before instigating wide-reaching and dramatic changes on communities. I mean, just look at Milton Keynes. We can't in all conscience allow that sort of thing to happen again. So it falls to my humble desk to stand as the final arbiter and guardian of the public good to ensure due process is observed before giving in to the desires for quick fix solutions to the detriment of my protectorate." He picked at the cheese. "But enough of me, what brings you and these delightful ladies to this particular forgotten corner of the European Dream?"

"He lost his job so he decided to drag us all halfway round the world," Dot offered.

"He didn't lose his job, Mother," Karen said. "He just got outsourced."

"I'm a... I was a Special Effects Consultant. Blowing up trains and buildings for Hollywood mostly. Then along came CGI and now any thirteen-year-old with an iPad can do in five minutes what it took me three months and half a million pounds to set up. So I decided to retire."

"Ah, the headlong rush for progress catches us all in our pyjamas eventually. I say, you don't fancy making up a four for golf tomorrow, do you? I was due to partner Charles but he's had to fly back to England. Sudden by-election in Godalming."

"I'm not sure." I scraped for an excuse. "I don't think I've got any clubs."

"Yes you have," said Karen, helpfully. "I bought you a set for your birthday. Remember?"

"Excellent!" Simon stood and patted me on the back. "That's set then. I'll pick you up outside here at ten." He turned to Dot and kissed her on both cheeks. She giggled and blushed like a sixteen-year-old. "You will have to learn the Latin ways, my dears." He repeated the procedure with Karen. "Ladies as beautiful as you will soon find yourselves the subject of much attention." He walked over to the bar and planted a note in Pat's hand, giving a casual wave towards our table. I assumed he'd just taken care of the bill.

"What a delightful man," said Karen. "See, Terry, you're making friends already. And important people too!"

"Oh good."

We finished our drinks and traditional Andalucían tapas then headed back to the villa to do battle with the rest of the boxes.

***

By five o'clock we'd broken the back of the unpacking and headed up the calle to Casa Grande. The sounds of Duran Duran greeted us as we approached the iron gates. I pressed the call button and the gates swung open. A slight upward slope to the paved driveway swept round in a crescent to arrive at a set of marble steps leading to the front doors. Billy appeared in the doorway. He wore an unbuttoned white silk shirt, grey shorts and blue flip-flops. A gold chain round his neck complemented the Rolex on his wrist. He held a can of Alhambra Especial.

"Ah, you made it! Fantastic. Come and meet everybody."

As we followed him through the house I noticed Karen

taking everything in with acquisitive eyes and no doubt compiling a very expensive shopping list. We were led through a large set of patio doors and into the garden area. The smell of barbecuing meats greeted me and the noise of chatter and eighties electronic pop seemed perfectly balanced. A tall, deeply tanned blonde woman noticed us, waved a glass she held and headed in our direction.

"Ah, darling," Billy said as she approached. "These are our new neighbours. Meet Dot, Karen and Terry." He introduced each of us in turn. "This is Junie, my wife."

Junie wore a brightly coloured sarong and a blue bikini top that barely contained a set of double Ds of which no doubt her surgeon was very proud.

"Lovely!" Junie said. She gave each of us exaggerated air kisses near both cheeks. "So nice of you to come."

She led us to a large wooden table that offered a selection of spirits, wines and dozens of bottles of Moet & Chandon. A waiter poured each of us a glass of the champagne.

Billy led us through the guests, throwing out introductions as we went. The barrage of names and faces slipped through my memory faster than the champagne flowed through my glass. He deposited us in front of a huge gas fired barbecue with a, "Phil will look after you. I'll catch up later." He slipped into the group of revellers and disappeared.

"What'll it be?" Phil stood behind the sizzling monster with spatula and tongs in eager readiness.

I took a burger that was three sizes too big for the bread roll and helped myself to a side salad. Karen and Dot took a pork chop and baked potato.

"That's the job," Dot said as she covered the chop in ketchup. "Proper English food."

"Hello!" a voice from behind us greeted. I turned to see a couple in their early sixties, both deeply tanned. "You must be the Englands?"

"Yes," I said. "We seem to be famous already!"

"Small community here. We tend to stick together and it's nice to see new people from the Old Land." He laughed at his joke. "I'm Peter, this is my wife, Joan. We live at Casa Rivendell, just down from you. The one with the blue gates?"

"Ah, yes. We're at number nineteen. Or fourteen... or twenty three. Depends who you ask."

"Oh, yes." Peter roared with forced laughter and slapped my shoulder. "We heard all about your troubles. Poor Campbell got himself in such a state."

"Campbell?"

"Campbell Frazer, your neighbour? You bought his house?" He laughed again.

"Stuart's sorting it out on Tuesday apparently." I tried to manoeuvre myself into the gap between Peter and Karen to make a break for freedom. Peter shifted his position and I was thwarted in my attempt.

"Stuart, yes. Nice boy but a bit clueless. Used to have a sports bar on the parade." He put his arm around my shoulder. "Look, if he doesn't sort it you should have a word with Billy."

"Billy?" I slipped free of the embrace as I turned to face him.

"Billy knows people. Did you know this whole estate was deemed illegal by the regional government? They issued demolition orders and everything."

"No?" I felt a twinge of panic squeeze at my insides. "That appears to be something else that slipped Stuart's mind. What's happening?"

"Oh, nothing to worry about now. Billy sorted it all out. He never said how, but within two weeks we'd all received an apology from the Town Hall and a notice waiving our property taxes for three years as compensation for our emotional distress."

A loud shout and a splash from the pool grabbed our attention and gave the opportunity to escape. We moved closer to see what was happening. Two young women and three young men were splashing in the pool. Several others jumped in after them. They were all completely naked.

"Oh, Good Lord!" exclaimed Karen.

Dot adjusted her glasses. "Are they naked? Well I never. That's disgraceful. Does he have no shame? You can see his..." she paused while she adjusted her glasses again and strained towards the pool. "He's a big lad, isn't he?"

"Mother!"

"Well, I'm just saying."

"I think we should be going," Karen said.

"Don't be silly," Dot snatched another glass of champagne from a passing waiter. "Things are just beginning to warm up."

I slipped away from Karen and Dot and headed for the nibbles table. I took a paper plate and collected some crisps and nuts. I noticed Billy by the patio doors. He was deep in conversation with two men, they wore jeans and white shirts and seemed somewhat overdressed. Billy patted one of them on the shoulder and they slipped into the house. Billy returned to the party. He spotted me watching him and came over to me.

"Ah, Tel, how's it going? Are they looking after you alright?" He waved a hand towards a waiter and indicated my glass. It was swiftly topped up. "I try to hold these little soirées from time to time. Nice to keep a sense of community."

"Have you been here long?" I juggled my plate and drink.

"About ten years. Had a place in Marbella but it got too up its own arse so we moved up here. Quieter, more...discreet. What brings you here?"

"Early retirement. I used to run a Special Effects company. You know, films? Want somebody to explode a helicopter over the White House or sink a cruise ship then I'm your man." I took a thoughtful sip of champagne. It was remarkably nice. And punchy. "Or I was," I added. "What about you? What do you do?"

"Oh, a bit of this, a bit of that. Just doing my bit to keep the wheels of commerce turning and inject a little currency into one of the poorest regions in Europe." He nodded towards the hot tub at the far end of the pool. "Looks like your mother's having fun."

"Mother? Oh, you mean Dot." I noticed much splashing and laughing from the group in the tub. "Oh hell! Must go. Catch you later."

I peeled Karen away from the attentions of an Antonio Banderas lookalike and headed for the hot tub.

"Mother!" Karen exclaimed at the sight of her mother in the tub with three middle aged men. "What do you think you're doing?"

"Oh, don't be such a fuss pot," Dot said and turned for a conspiratorial giggle with her hot tub companions.

Karen looked a bit more closely at the scene in front of her. "Mother, are you... You're not.... Heavens above, you're naked!"

"As the day I was born." Dot wobbled a glass of champagne to her lips. Nearly missing. She reached underneath the bubbles and the man next to her jumped and they all giggled.

"You can't... I mean you're..." Karen struggled for words to do the scene justice and finished lamely with, "What will the neighbours say?"

The man next to Dot grinned and said, "Oh, I shouldn't worry about that."

"And why ever not?"

"Because we *are* the neighbours!" They all erupted into more giggles and I nudged Karen away from the scene.

"Come on, love. She's just having a bit of fun."

"Fun? That's not fun! Bridge is fun. Listening to The Afternoon Play on the BBC is fun. That's... That's..." Words escaped her again. "I don't know what *that* is."

I herded her towards the nibbles table as a distraction and ensured her champagne glass remained fully charged.

The afternoon drifted into early evening and more people seemed inclined towards removing their clothes. The alcohol in my system reduced inhibitions, the unrelenting heat drove motivation and before long, I too was naked in the swimming pool. Much to Karen's disgust. The pool felt refreshingly cool and the nakedness refreshingly liberating. I hadn't been skinny-dipping since my stag night. And that had been many years ago on Minehead beach at midnight in October. Definitely a different sensation. Following the lead of other guests I simply wrapped a towel round my waist after leaving the pool, although many didn't bother with even that token of modesty. I chatted with other guests, some wrapped in towels, some fully dressed and some naked. It didn't seem to matter anymore. Karen remained stubbornly dressed and studiously tried to only converse with those still fully attired.

The clear blue sky gradually darkened, the Milky Way straddled the blackness above and the music slowed. The guests started to form small groups. Sometimes twos and threes, occasionally fours. I realised events were beginning to take a slightly different turn and decided it was probably time to take our leave. I tracked down Karen who was sat with another couple round a small table. At first she was reluctant to leave until I gently encouraged her to look around. Realisation dawned and she stood quickly.

"Sorry, we must go now," she said. "We've got to... I left... Umm...The cats! They'll be wondering what's happened. It's been lovely meeting you."

The other couple looked slightly disappointed as we left.

"They seemed nice," I said as we headed across the patio to where we'd last seen Dot.

"Humph!"

Dot was nowhere to be found. We asked around but eventually I persuaded Karen that she had more than likely left earlier and would probably be tucked up in bed listening to Book at Bedtime by now. We said our goodbyes and thank-yous and made our way down the drive. The security gates slid aside for us as we approached then closed behind us with a firm clunk.

Much to Karen's concern there was no sign of Dot when we returned. I assured her she could come to no harm as Billy's place was like a fortress and she'd probably just fallen asleep in a corner somewhere.

Chapter Six

A clattering from the kitchen startled us awake. I glanced at the clock, just after four. I slipped out of bed and picked up the only weapon I could find, a shoe. I heard Karen stir.

"Just going to check," I said. "Probably a cat."

Poking my head round the kitchen door the light from the open fridge gave an eerie cast to the room.

"Dot?"

"Ah," she said. "Just making a cup of tea." She turned, showing me the milk carton in her hand.

"At four o'clock in the morning?"

Karen appeared from behind me. "Mother? What are you doing?"

"Why's everybody making such a fuss? It's only a cup of tea. Can't I make a cup of tea when I want one? It's not like they're easy to come by in this infernal country."

"It's just that it's so early for you," I said. "You're not usually up until eight. And you're dressed already."

"And in the same clothes you went out in last night!" exclaimed Karen. "Oh, I can't bear it. My own mother doing the Walk of Shame. And at your age."

"I don't know what you're getting your knickers in a twist about." Dot shuffled the milk carton over to the side and emptied it into the kettle.

"Well at least I kept mine on," Karen said.

I took the kettle from Dot before she could switch it on and emptied the milk into the sink. "I'll make your tea, Dot. Why don't you go and have a shower."

Dot stared at me for a moment. "Ah, Terry? Where did you come from? Be a good boy and put the tea on the kettle, I think I'm going to have a little lie down." She leaned backwards against the marble work surface then slid slowly down until she was sitting on the floor in a movement that vaguely resembled a burial at sea. She gave a small hiccup then closed her eyes.

"Great," said Karen. "Goodness knows what she's been up to. You know we'll never be able to go back there again, don't you?"

I managed to carry Dot into her bed and Karen arranged the bedclothes around her. I slipped back into bed and tried to get another hour's sleep before morning.

***

The alarm woke me at seven and I checked Dot on the way to the kitchen. She was still fast asleep.

A breakfast of tea and toast followed by a quick shower and I was ready and fully armed with my virgin golf clubs outside The Expats by the time Simon arrived. He drove a brand new white Mercedes SLR Coupe.

"Fantastic," he said as the boot slowly lifted for me. "Just drop your clubs in the back, we're meeting the others at the clubhouse."

The white leather-clad interior still smelled of the showroom. The Mercedes slid through the morning traffic with the grace of a stalking panther. Once clear of the town the open roads greeted us and the Mercedes gave a slight roar of pleasure as Simon let her off the leash and the seat pressed into my back.

"Nice car," I said. "Is it new?"

"A couple of weeks. They give me new one each year."

"They?"

"Brussels. All a bit of a pain really. Just get used to one and they go and change it. Mind you, this is more comfortable than the BMW."

We swept through a series of mountain edged curves with barely a shift in sensation.

"Financial Crisis not having too much effect on the EU transport budgets then?" I queried.

"They did a study. Apparently it's more cost effective this way than sending me everywhere by rail or air. I don't involve myself in the financial nonsense, I just try to make the best of the lot they give me."

"But you do get a choice of car?"

"Within reason. Pretty much anything as long as it's German."

We pulled into a gravelled drive where a sign welcomed us to 'Palm Oasis. Andalucía's Premiere Professional Golf Course'. The car park wouldn't have disgraced any Knightsbridge prestige car dealership.

Inside the clubhouse Simon introduced me to his companions. "This is Julian." A tall man with sun-bleached blond hair and a deep tan. "He's in banking."

Julian held out his hand. "Retired actually," he said with a smile. "Got out just before the big pooh storm of oh-eight."

"Some would say it was your final bonus that caused the pooh storm," Simon said with a smile.

"Nonsense, dear boy. It was your colleagues' drinks bills!"

They both laughed very loudly at their obviously much familiar banter.

"And this is Vernon," Simon indicated a smaller man with dark hair. "Vernon's with the Inland Revenue."

Those words always brought a chill to my blood. No matter how perfect my accounts the words 'Inland Revenue' always triggered a strange fear. Taxmanaphobia?

"Oh," I said. "On holiday?"

"No, we have an office here. Investigative branch," said Vernon. "Keeping an eye on the expats," he added with a smile.

"He's a lovely chap really," said Julian. "Very helpful. If ever you need any help with Her Majesty's Highwaymen he's your man."

We headed for the first tee and it didn't take me long to show my complete incompetence with the game. I'd had a few lessons, Karen had included them with the golf set she'd given me for my fortieth, but that was a long way off now and I hadn't touched them since. My first attempt sent the ball rolling gently to settle not ten metres from the tee. My second go created some spectacular backspin effect and the ball actually ended up behind the point from where I'd started.

"That's unusual," commented Simon in a very measured tone. "I've not seen that done before."

They waited with great patience while I nudged the ball gradually towards the first pin with a series of missed strikes, chips and slices.

"Haven't played for a while," I said lamely as I retrieved my ball from the hole.

The second tee wasn't much better. I lost one ball in a pond and another just mysteriously disappeared altogether. I'd hit it well and been really proud of my success but when we'd gone to look for it, it had vanished.

"Just drop another one here," Julian indicated a point not one metre from the pin. "That's about where it went, I'm sure."

"Are you sure?" I said. "I didn't think it was anywhere near that close. I thought it went back there somewhere." I waved my club towards the edge of the green.

"No!" Julian said with a note of panic. "Here, really. It was nearly in. I remember. Remarkable shot."

I potted the ball with my next attempt and felt a slight glow of pleasure. However the third hole took twelve goes, partly due to the fact that at one point I lost track of which pin I was aiming at and landed the ball neatly on the eighth green.

As we plodded round the course I was struck by the dramatic contrast between the cultured, well watered greens and the stark, arid landscape just beyond. The morning sun shone a harsh light on the folded mountains behind us, highlighting the rust coloured slopes dotted with the deep greens of the pine forests further up. And in the distance, at the furthest reaches of the mountains, the brilliant white of the snow capped peaks. All the seasons of the year laid out in one sweeping vista. I wished I could capture the beauty. I had a top-end Nikon at the villa, I should have brought it. Or painting. Maybe I could learn to paint. I couldn't be any worse at it than this pointless nonsense.

My game actually improved as we progressed but not enough to prevent Simon paying over a wedge of Euro notes to Julian at the end of it.

"I didn't realise we had a bet," I said. "I should pay half."

"Nonsense," said Simon. "Just a silly little flutter.

Anyway, keeps his spirits up if I let him win once in a while!"

As we drove back Simon recounted golfing stories and had I had my Number Two Iron close at hand I would probably have beaten him with it until he stopped talking. As it was I just nodded and laughed when it seemed appropriate. He dropped me off back at the Expats and I took my clubs and threw them in the back of the garage. Hopefully they wouldn't be disturbed again for a very long time.

Dot was sat at the kitchen table, her head in her hands. In front of her sat a plate of toast and an untouched cup of tea. She gave a low level grumble as she half opened one eye in my direction.

"Morning, Dot," I announced with exaggerated enthusiasm. "Good night last night?"

Another low grumble and an unsteady hand reached towards the tea, missed the handle and knocked the contents onto the plate of toast. As if with a mind of its own, the hand patted at the table until it landed in the soggy toast where it came to rest. She collapsed into her arms with a long deflated sigh.

"How was the golf?" Karen asked as she moved her mother's hand from the soggy mess and cleared the table.

"I feel it might not be my natural sport." I loaded the coffee machine with fresh beans and pressed the button for espresso. Its enthusiastic munching and squishing noises provoked another groan from Dot.

"Oh, you'll soon get the hang of it. And it's such a good way to make new friends."

I thought about my trio of golfing partners. "I think I'm going to learn to paint," I said.

"Don't be silly, dear." Karen poured a fresh tea in Dot's mug. "We can always get a little Spanish man in for that when it needs doing. No need to give up your golf, you know how much you enjoy it."

"What? Oh, no. I didn't mean –"

A knock at the front door thankfully diverted what was certainly heading to be a pointless conversation.

Darren greeted me as I opened the door.

"I've got your TVOIP," he announced with a big grin and handed me a large box. "It's the latest version."

"TVOIP?" I stared at the box but the Chinese characters that covered the box gave no clues.

"Telly box. TV through the internet. No dish?"

"Oh, right." I vaguely remembered him saying something about that.

"I'll have it up in time for The Big Match this evening." He breezed into the house. "Where's your telly?"

"Over there." I pointed to a large flat package which leaned against the wall at the far end of the lounge.

"Okie dokie. Want me to put that on the wall for you as well?"

I remembered the hole spattered remains of his attempts to fix the satellite dish. "No, I can do that later."

"You sure?" He dumped his toolbox on my handmade silk Chinese rug and commenced scattering tools. "Only it's no trouble while I've got the drill going."

I hadn't figured on drilling. I thought he'd just be plugging bits in. I pondered for a moment. "Okay, probably best just have one lot of mess I suppose."

"That's the job. Where do you want it?"

Darren was very helpful, holding the TV against the wall in various positions while Karen and I did 'Left a bit, right a bit' before finally settling on a position. We marked the wall and left Darren to his drilling. I didn't want to see.

"Where's Dot?" I asked as I went back into the kitchen.

"Gone back to bed," Karen answered.

"Come on, let's go to Expats for lunch. I don't want to be here when this all goes horribly wrong."

Karen prised Dot from her bed for a second time and we headed up the calle, leaving the sounds of drilling behind.

We settled at a table under the vines. Jim and Diane, the couple we'd met at our first visit, sat at the next table.

"Buenos dias," greeted Jim.

"Good morning," I returned.

"See you can't keep away from the place," Diane said. "It's so lovely here."

"It's the only place to get English tea," grumbled Dot.

"Proper English tea where I don't have to make it myself."

"Yes, Mother," said Karen. "I'm sure they know about English tea."

"Don't know what's so difficult to do," Dot continued unabated. "And why do they always bring it in bits? A cup of warm water, a glass of milk and a tiny teabag on a piece of string? That's not a cup of tea, that's a recipe."

Diane smiled politely. "I know what you mean."

Oh dear, I thought. There'll be no stopping her now. One should never feed The Grump.

Encouraged by her newly discovered camaraderie, Dot railed further to her subject. "I mean, I have to do all the work and they still expect a tip!"

Karen patted her mother's hand. "Okay, Mum."

Dot fell silent for a moment but just as I was about to speak she burst forth once more.

"What if I ordered a roast dinner? What would they do then? Bring me a live sheep and an axe and expect me to sort it out from there, shouldn't wonder."

"Oh, Lord," I said.

Tracey arrived with two beers and a pot of tea. "Did I get it right?"

"Spot on," I said with a smile.

Dot was still in full flight. "It's Ikea started all this, with their build it yourself nonsense. Now you can't buy anything finished anymore."

I sipped at my beer and felt the day smooth out a little.

"Your tea's here, Mother." Karen pushed the teapot towards Dot. "Nice English tea, in a pot."

"They do make a good pot of tea here," Diane said. "PG Tips, I believe."

"Britmart," said Jim.

"Britmart?" I queried.

"British supermarket in town. Get anything there. Teabags, bacon, Radio Times, you name it. Even proper English coffee."

"There you go, Mother." Karen said. "That's not so bad is it?"

No reply. I glanced at Dot. She appeared to be studying

something in her lap. I touched her shoulder gently. Nothing, she'd fallen asleep.

We had second beers and Tracey brought tapas of miniature pork pies and pickled onions.

Jim and Diane continued to brief us on the best places to visit in the area.

"There's a lovely restaurant down near the harbour, Ole's. On Saturdays they have flamenco with paella and sangria. All very colourful."

"That sounds nice," said Karen. "Doesn't it, Terry? We ought to give it a try."

"We're going down there tonight actually," said Jim. "Why don't you come along?"

We arranged to meet up later, finished our drinks and headed back to the villa. I wondered how long it would be before I thought of it as home.

Darren was just packing up his tools when we arrived back. "All done, Tel." he stabbed the remote control and the television sprang into life.

I glanced around the room looking for random holes or piles of rubble but all was clean and tidy.

"Fantastic, thanks."

"You just go to Aux 1." He pressed a button on the remote and we were presented with a welcome screen asking us to select our language. He scrolled through the options until he found 'Inglish'. I was beginning to worry. Another screen welcoming us to The Transatlantic Hotel Malaga confirmed my fears.

"Umm, Darren..."

"Oh, that. That's nothing. Just... er... generic... default configuration protocols. Technical stuff."

He poked at another option and we were treated to a video featuring views of a swimming pool and five star restaurant.

"Whoops, don't want that. Hang on, I've got this." He poked randomly at the remote and a list of channels appeared. "There we go!"

The channels scrolled through a bewildering variety of choices. All the expected BBC and ITV channels were there along with some slightly unusual options such as the

Transatlantic What's On Channel, Tonight's Menu in the Conquistador Restaurant and a selection of Adult channels.

"Are we hooked in to this hotel's entertainment system?" I asked.

"Depends how you define 'hooked in'. Are you familiar with I.P. routing configurations through proxy tunnelling servers peer to peer?"

"No."

"Well, it's sort of that."

"You mean we're stealing a television feed from the Hotel Transatlantic in Malaga?"

"No! Not really stealing. Stealing is taking something with intent to deprive the legitimate owner of it." He recited that with remarkable fluidity. "This is not depriving nobody of nothing. Ipso facto, can't be stealing!" He chose Sky Sports and suddenly my television was full of football. "Cool! That'll be the Arsenal. Who do you support?"

"I hate football," I said.

Karen appeared with a mug of tea which she handed to Darren. "Will it get Strictly?"

Darren reluctantly moved away from the football and found the BBC. Celebrity Bargain Hunt or something was showing. A faded girl-power bimbo was looking pleased with her valuation of a silver snuff box. "See, BBC One. No worries. What time's it on?"

"Six o'clock, I think," Karen said. "Oh, you are wonderful." She took the remote control from him and turned up the volume.

"We can't keep it," I said. "It's not legal."

"Don't be such a fuss pot," Karen said. "If Darren says it's alright then I'm sure it is. Anyway, you're the one who didn't want the dish."

"It's only signal leakage we're collecting," Darren explained. "Overspill that nobody cares about. It's sort of fallen off the back of a transponder!" He laughed conspiratorially with Karen.

"I give up."

Karen settled down to watch the television while I paid Darren.

"You know what you need there, don't you?" Darren nodded towards the patio.

"No," I said hesitantly.

"A terrace cooler."

What's that?"

"Um, it's a bit like a patio heater, only in reverse. About three metres high and makes a curtain of cold air. I can get you a good deal on one at the moment. Mate of mine has a contact."

"Why on earth would I want one of those?"

"It gets very hot here in the summer. You'll be glad of it then."

"I could always just go inside?"

"No worries," he said cheerily. "But they're all the rage in Dubai."

"So are gold Ferraris."

***

We met Jim and Diane in the car park near the harbour and walked through the bustling early evening streets. Night had just fallen and the bright lights of the shops spilled out onto the pavements. Jewellery and fashion shops were the predominant species but they were interspersed with ice cream parlours, restaurants and bars. Ole's Flamenco Bar was located at the end of a narrow pedestrian street. We threaded our way through the outside tables and into the main restaurant.

A waitress greeted Jim and Diane like long lost friends and showed us to our table. "There you are," she said. "Managed to get your favourite table."

No sooner had we sat down than another waitress brought two bottles of wine and a basket of bread. "Qué desea tomar?" she asked.

I gazed blankly at her and she sensed my confusion. "To drink? Qué quieren?"

I ordered beers for us with a warning glance at Dot not to even think about tea.

"It's a fixed menu for the Flamenco Nights," explained

Diane. "But I'm sure they'd let you choose off the main menu if you really wanted."

We settled for the fixed menu and the first course arrived promptly, a salad with cheese and ham. It looked delicious.

Dot poked at the ham with her fork. "This bacon's raw," she announced after careful examination.

"That's the local ham," said Jim. "It's air dried in the Alpujarras."

Dot looked at him quizzically then flipped a piece of the ham over with her fork. "You can't eat raw bacon. It'll give you worms!"

"Shush, Mother," Karen whispered as she hooked the ham from Dot's plate and dropped it on her own.

A group of three young Spanish girls arrived at the small raised area at the end of the restaurant and set a CD player going. The sounds of furious Spanish guitar filled the room and the girls' heels fired off the platform in the staccato bursts of the flamenco dance. All three were probably in their early teens and dressed in spectacular tiered dresses.

We finished the first course and the Spanish waitress brought the paella in a huge dish and placed it in the middle of the table. "Buen provecho," she said.

"I'm not eating that," Dot, right on cue. "It's got too many legs!"

"Legs?" I said.

Dot pointed to the paella dish. "Look at it! Those prawn things have still got all their legs. And octopus legs. Ugh!" She gave a little shiver.

The English waitress heard the complaints and came over. "Is everything all right?"

"My mother's not very keen on paella," Karen said. "Do you think you could do something different? A bit more plain?"

"Of course." She turned to Dot. "What would you like? A nice tuna salad or something?"

"Fish and chips."

"This is a Spanish restaurant, Mother. Can't you be just a little bit more adventurous? It's amazing you ever came off rusks!"

"I'm sure we can do something," the waitress said. "I'll ask the chef."

The paella was rich and varied. Every type of fish and meat imaginable. Chicken and mutton I recognised, spicy chorizo, and white fish. But other meats I did not know, possibly rabbit or goat.

A few minutes later the waitress returned with a plate of fried fish and chips and placed it in front of Dot.

"It's got eyes! I'm not going to eat something that's watching at me."

Karen slid Dot's plate towards her and removed the head from the fish. "There you go, Mother." She slid the plate back. "Harry Ramsden couldn't have done it better."

As the evening progressed, the dancing grew more frenetic, the drinks flowed freely and Dot eventually mellowed. She even sampled the liqueurs presented at the end of the meal.

The dancing ended to appreciative applause from the diners and the sounds of animated chatter filled the room. As designated driver, I'd stuck to mineral water all evening and found the alcohol-fuelled noise increasingly grating. We left shortly after the tables had been cleared and thanked Jim and Diane for showing us their little bit of 'Real Spain'.

As soon as we arrived home I opened a bottle of twelve year old Speyside and fell asleep in front of 'Once Upon A Time In The West'.

Chapter Seven

Sunday morning didn't bring the hoped-for peace and quiet. I attempted to take a book out to the terrace but was driven back inside by the sounds of hedge cutters and leaf blowers. Whoever thought leaf blowers were a good idea? Probably the most pointless invention since the electronic egg-boiler.

Karen always chose Sunday morning for the Big Clean and the house smelled faintly of bleach. She paused mid-polish as she watched me settle in the armchair. "I was just about to hoover there," she said.

I dropped my book on the chair and picked my keys off the table. "Just going out for a bit of a walk."

"Well don't forget we're booked for Sunday lunch at the Expats."

I had forgotten. In fact now I distinctly remembered purposely trying to forget that as soon as I'd been informed it was happening. I walked past Casa Grande and through a cut at the end of the calle. The path was well worn but still rugged. The sounds of unnecessary garden machinery seeped into the background then disappeared completely. I had no particular idea where I was going, I just wanted quiet. And space. Mostly I wanted space. Since I'd arrived in Spain everything had been so frenetic and claustrophobic. A very odd feeling considering the size of the country and general sparsity of the population.

Each time I was presented with a choice of direction I chose the path that led upwards and before long I was looking down at our estate, or 'urbanisation' as everybody insisted on calling it. Our particular urbanisation was one of several that surrounded Bahía Blanca. It drew a stark line between township and wilderness. From this vantage point it looked somewhat like modern version of a medieval walled town. The purposely twisting roads threaded through houses of all different shapes and sizes, all cunningly laid out to provide a sealed perimeter, the only road access to our urbanisation being through a pair of mock Roman pillars and up the main calle. The brilliant blue of the Mediterranean lay beyond Bahía Blanca and was so bright in the morning sun it hurt my eyes. I turned to look at the mountains, stark and impassive against the morning sky. I continued upwards.

After half an hour of steady climbing I stopped to take in my surroundings. The town had receded to a mosaic of colour nestled against the sea and in the other direction the mountains remained unchanged. No nearer and no less impassive. I sat for a while on a rock and pondered that it had probably been there longer than man has walked this planet. I realised that once again I'd neglected to bring a camera with me. The sun burned through my shirt and it dawned on me that I'd probably been out longer than I'd intended.

I stumbled back along the track until it became more worn and stable then eventually deposited me in the calle.

"Morning, Tel!" I heard from behind me. I turned to see Billy just behind his gates. "Been meaning to try to catch you. Couldn't do me a little favour, could you?"

"Sure, no problem. What do you need?"

"It's Junie's birthday on...um... Next week. I've got a package... a present and she might find it. Want it to be a surprise, like. You couldn't look after it for a couple of days for me, could you?"

"Sure. Do you want me to take it now?"

"What? No. I'll drop it round later. When it's dark. In case she sees."

"Okay, I'm in all evening."

"Thanks, mate. You're a pal."

***

Sunday lunch at the Expats was everything I expected it to be and everything I'd feared. I'm actually rather partial to roast dinners, pork being my favourite but never in restaurants. Restaurants are never able to present a roast dinner the way in which a home kitchen can. It's always too long from oven to table. However Dot was in her element. Her roast beef swam in gravy and horseradish sauce.

"Now that's proper food," she said. "None of your garlic and funny sauces."

My pork was passable and augmented with a couple of ice cold beers. I indulged in a sticky toffee pudding for desert and Pat brought a small dish of complimentary mints.

We sat and chatted for a while enjoying the sunshine and relative quiet. Once back at the villa I took a book to the garden with my MP3 player to drown out the garden machinery.

I awoke with a start and realised the sun had disappeared behind the mountains. I gathered my book and MP3 player and headed inside.

Dot was watching Celebrity Big Brother Does Cooking on Ice. I picked up a copy of The Sentinella, the English language magazine for the area, and settled in my armchair. An interesting article on Lanjarón caught my attention. Apparently it had just been recognised by the World Health Organisation as having the highest longevity in Europe. I heard a bing-bong noise from the television and figured some celebrity had just been executed. The Lanjarón locals put their exceptional longevity down to the local spring water. They ship it all over the world. Bing-bong. I glanced up involuntarily to the television. A flashing box at the top of the screen said 'Message Waiting'. The World Health Organisation had a slightly more prosaic view to the Lanjarón longevity though and put it down to the Mediterranean diet and exceptional air quality. Bing-bong.

"What *is* that?" I asked Dot.

"Dunno," she said. "Keeps happening." She reached for another chocolate digestive.

I looked at the screen. The flashing box was shaped like an envelope and flashed 'Message Waiting' constantly. I realised it didn't actually appear to be part of the programme. Email? I hadn't paid an awful lot of attention when I'd bought the television so it was possible it may have an email facility of some sort. But surely I'd have needed to set it up first?

I reached for the remote control.

"You're not going to change the channel are you?" Dot looked alarmed. "Jordan's just about to show off her soufflé to the housemates." I hoped that wasn't a euphemism.

I could find nothing on the television remote control that related to messaging of any sort. The remote to Darren's TVOIP box had lots of coloured buttons and I tried several of those, much to Dot's distress when I accidently switched channels and instead of celebrities cooking on ice, we were confronted with celebrities cooking in the jungle. A short, high-pitched squeal from Dot persuaded me to change back quickly. After a few more random button stabbings and two more Dot squeals I finally found a button that opened the message. 'Mr Olbatain, welcome to the Hotel Transatlantic, Malaga.'

I closed the message and it disappeared. Once more we had the full undisturbed beauty of some fading actor juggling with the remains of something which had probably once been a duck. The doorbell ringing saved me from seeing the outcome of the tussle.

"You're a star, mate." Billy greeted me as I opened the door. He held a parcel about the size of a microwave oven.

"Sure, glad to help. When's her birthday?"

"Who?"

"Junie. Her birthday?"

"What? Oh, yes. Junie... um next... Not sure yet." He dumped the parcel in my arms. I sank slightly under the weight. "I'll let you know." He gave a wave and disappeared down the path.

I gazed at the parcel as I took it through to the kitchen. It was almost completely covered in brown parcel tape with no markings or labels of any kind.

"What's that?" Karen asked as I placed it on the table.

"Birthday present for Junie. I think. We're looking after it for Billy so she doesn't find it."

"That's nice, we should get her a card." She handed me a mug of tea. "Take that through to Mum."

I'd just settled with my book when the doorbell rang again. I opened it to find an elderly man standing on the doorstep. He wore a pair of three quarter length trousers, a tee-shirt that said 'Looking Good' and a straw hat.

"Yes?" I said.

"Is Dot in? I said I'd pop round."

"You are?"

"Walter!" he said as if it was perfectly obvious he was Walter.

"Walter?"

"From Billy's party the other night. We met in the hot tub, me and your mother. Little minx she is. You know –"

"I don't think I want to, and she's not my mother," I said. I shuddered. "Come in, she's watching Celebrity something or other."

I left them to it in the lounge and headed off to the garden with my book. I was asleep before I'd finished the first page despite the steady drone of garden machinery in the background.

***

I spent Monday morning hanging things on walls and setting up my hi-fi. After lunch, Karen said she was going to join Diane and Jim for a Bridge afternoon while I went into town to explore. In reality, I'd been given a shopping list and sent to the supermarket but I seized the opportunity to wander. Bahía Blanca is a pleasant town with wide, tree-lined avenues creating a feel of openness and space. However in the older quarter, near the harbour, the roads become narrow and twisting with a myriad of pedestrian walkways. I stopped for beer and tapas in a seafront bar and watched the afternoon drift by. It was fun trying to spot the nationalities. The two largest contingents appeared to be English and German but listening to the conversations as they passed by I heard Dutch, French and a collection of Eastern European dialects which I couldn't place.

Pleasantly anesthetised, I decided I was ready to brave the local Mercadona Supermercado. Armed with my wonky trolley and Karen's detailed and fully annotated shopping list I entered through the automatic doors and was immediately launched into the fruit and vegetable aisles. Three onions, six tomatoes, two peppers (one red & one green). I carefully selected and bagged the listed items. Three pounds of potatoes. That was a bit more complicated as it involved the weighing machine and mental arithmetic. The selection of bread overwhelmed me momentarily but I managed find a nice baguette with seeds and headed off for the tinned food section. The aisle to the tinned fruits was blocked at both ends by clutches of elderly women who seemed to be conducting very important, and noisy, meetings. I abandoned my trolley at the end of the aisle and ferried the tins in my arms. Mandarins, peaches, strawberries, I ticked off the items on the list. It looked like we were having fruit salad. The frozen food section caused problems as nothing related to Karen's list. No McCain's Battered Fish although I did find something called merluza which looked close. But 'those lovely Sainsbury's tuna and chilli fishcakes' defeated me completely so I substituted with fish fingers.

The cleaning and washing aisles caused panic as I could find nothing that resembled anything on Karen's list. No Clarins Wrinkle Cream or Boots Number 57 chestnut hair dye. I bought a bottle labelled 'champu' as I was reasonably confident that was shampoo and a tube of something I really hoped was toothpaste and fled to the beer section.

The checkouts were five deep by the time I arrived with my laden trolley. Eventually I loaded my shopping on the conveyer belt feeling pleased with my conquest of this particular corner of Spain. That was until my fresh vegetables arrived in the cashier's hands. She held up my bag of three onions and jabbered furiously at me. Clearly I had committed some heinous crime but for the life of me I couldn't see what was wrong with attempting to buy three onions. The cashier quickly realised she was dealing with a Mercadona virgin and called for help. I had a momentary panic as I had visions of being ejected by security for my crimes against onions but it turned out to be a helpful girl who transported my bags of vegetables to the nearest weighing machine and applied little labels to each. It seems one is supposed to weigh and apply these labels before reaching the cashier. I turned to the rest of the queue and gave a big smile and shoulder shrug which I hoped conveyed my apologies. I was met by stony faces.

Having loaded my shopping in the car, I shut the door and sat quietly, trying to remember to breathe. I was either going to have to learn more Spanish or persuade Sainsbury's to extend their Home Delivery network.

On my return to the villa, my shopping went through an inspection worthy of the most enthusiastic Heathrow Customs Officer.

"That's not McCain's?" Karen held up the packet of merluza. "I don't even know what this is."

"That was the closest –"

"Mum won't eat that, it's in Spanish. And you forgot the PG Tips tea bags."

"They didn't have any. Only Spanish tea bags. Or fruit tea bags, they had lots of fruit tea bags."

"You could have got Typhoo, that's not as good as PG Tips but it would have done."

"They didn't have –"

"And where's the bacon?"

"They didn't... Never mind. How was Bridge?"

"Very pleasant. That nice Mr Farrington made up the fourth. He's such a charmer. What's this?" She held up a packet of cheese.

"It's a local cheese. I thought we might like to try it."

"It's got a picture of a goat on it."

I slid into the lounge with a beer. Dot was watching 'Get that Celebrity out of My F***ing Kitchen', Gordon Ramsey's latest prime time offering on BBC. He had twenty seven minutes to teach a footballer how to make beans on toast. I noticed there was another little envelope shape in the top left corner of the screen.

"How long's that been there, Dot?"

"What? Oh that, ever since I switched it on."

I took the remote and opened the message, 'Mr Olbatain, you have a guest waiting in reception, a Miss Domina.'

I deleted the message and settled down in my chair. Five minutes of Gordon Ramsey's berating and I was actually beginning to feel sorry for the footballer. I was also beginning to feel my brains bleeding out of my ears so I picked up my book.

The doorbell snatched me from the brink of dozing off. The porch light shone on a tall, gangly-looking man in his early thirties. He wore jeans three sizes too big, an Iron Maiden tee-shirt and woolly cap. I kept my distance from him as I opened the door.

"Billy sent me," he said, his body moving to the rhythm of the words.

"Okay?"

"You got a package?" He moved constantly as though he was on a rolling boat.

"You mean Junie's birthday present?"

"What? Yeah, what Billy said. Junie's present."

"I didn't think it was yet?" I queried.

"No, yeah. It's like now. You know what I mean? It's all now."

"Hang on," I said and retrieved the parcel from the kitchen.

"Cool, man," he said as he took it. "You're the dude."

I closed the door after watching him disappear into the dark. I hoped I'd done the right thing.

Chapter Eight

By Tuesday afternoon I still hadn't heard anything from Stuart so I rang his office.

"Ah, Mr England," he greeted. "I was just about to ring you. Good news."

"It's all sorted?"

"Well, not quite. But I have found out how to sort it."

"Go on." I settled on a kitchen stool, feeling drained already.

"We just need to arrange a compraventa between you and Mr Frazer for the transfer then we all pop along to the Notary and there you go, all nice and dandy!"

"Sounds easy enough, when?"

"It will take a few days to prepare a compraventa and then –"

"A few days?" I interrupted. "I need this sorted now or Frazer's going to start with the barbed wire and machine gun posts."

"Well, I suppose if I just used the old compraventa then swapped the names and house details you could sign it today. That should work."

I couldn't see anything at all going wrong with that idea. "And is that the point at which I end up buying the local police station?"

"Huh? Oh, no. No, you worry too much. That couldn't possibly happen."

With his assurances still ringing hollowly I gave a brief précis to Karen and headed for my car.

"Give my love to Stuart," she called after me.

I was just unlocking the door when Billy pulled up alongside me in his white Range Rover.

The tinted window slid down and Billy's face appeared. "You alright, Tel? Thanks for looking after that package for me. Forgot to tell you Jason would be by for it."

"That's okay," I said. "Did she like it?"

"Who?" Billy looked puzzled.

"Junie? Her birthday present?"

"Oh, yeah. Loved it, mate. What you up to then?"

"Got to sort out this house business. Stuart's going to do something clever with some paperwork to put it all right."

"Stuart? Clever? We are talking about that idiot down at Costa Properties, aren't we? Only you don't very often hear the word 'clever' in a sentence involving Stuart."

I gave Billy a quick rundown as to what Stuart was planning to do.

"And you couldn't see anything wrong with that plan?" he asked. "Hop in." He swung the passenger door open for me. "I'll take you down there, we'll sort it out."

Billy swung the Range Rover round and we headed off into town. The interior smelled of new leather mixed with a slight metallic undertone of air conditioning.

"So what did you get her?" I asked.

"Who?"

"Junie? Her birthday? The package?"

"Oh, yeah, erm, an MP3 player. Latest thing with multi... mega...something."

"In that huge box?"

"Well, you know Amazon and their zealous packaging." He slammed his foot to the floor as we overtook a little red Fiat. "Bloody tourists." Billy had clearly decided that subject was closed and I decided I probably didn't need to know what was actually in the box.

We stopped half on the pavement outside Costa Properties and Billy left the hazard lights going.

"Oh, hi, Billy, Terry," Stuart said as we entered his office. "I printed out the old compraventa and crossed out the old names, look." He rummaged in a pile of papers on his desk. "Somewhere.... Ah, here you go."

Billy intercepted the paper before I could take it. He scanned it quickly. "This won't work," he announced. "Who's paying the taxes?"

"What taxes?" I asked.

"Genius's little plan here involves you selling back Frazer's house and you buying your house again. That's another two lots of taxes for the government. Two times eight percent of the value of the two properties."

"What? Stuart, you didn't tell me anything about the taxes." I measured the distance between myself and Stuart and looked for something heavy. Fortunately for Stuart I could find nothing. "When were you going to tell me about the taxes?"

"Well, I thought –"

"That'll be a new one," Billy interrupted. "Give me the original paperwork."

Stuart pulled a thick file from behind the desk and meekly handed it over.

Billy scanned through the sheaves, quickly locating the one he was looking for. He fished his mobile phone from his pocket, scrolled through the names and hit 'Call'.

"Hola, José. Soy yo. Cómo está su esposa e hijos?... Bien, bien." He continued jabbering, he'd lost me at 'Hola'. At one point he held the paper in front of him and read off some details. "Si...si... Bueno...bueno..." A moment later I heard Stuart's name being mentioned accompanied by much laughing, then, "Muchas gracias, José. Dar mi amor a Conche." He put the paper on the desk and turned to me. "Sorted," he said.

"Who? What?" I said.

"Just had a word with José, the mayor. He'll re-register everything properly tomorrow." He turned to Stuart. "You ever thought about a different career?"

"Thanks, I really appreciate that," I said as we left Stuart's office. "But I don't understand –"

"Oh, no problem. He owed me a favour anyway." He threaded the Range Rover smoothly into the traffic and we headed back.

Two days later I received an official looking letter and spent a half hour typing it into Google Translate. Apparently the house was now correctly registered in my name and Frazer's house returned to him. I took a bottle of ten-year-old Laphroaig from my whiskey collection as a peace offering.

"Ye've nae got a Speyside then?" was his response.

On Friday I found myself being propelled towards yet another shopping trip. This time at the insistence of Dot who had demanded we go to Britmart for our shopping. Britmart sat on the outskirts of Bahía Blanca. It was a large, grey industrial building with a huge Union Flag banner draped across the front. Inside it felt more like a warehouse than a supermarket. Cases of Heinz Baked Beans or HP Sauce piled high on metal racking lining narrow passages. I tried to ignore the horror as Dot and Karen cooed with delight at all the luxuries they'd missed for the last couple of weeks. Our trolley gradually filled with Typhoo tea bags, Branston Pickle, bacon, treacle puddings and chocolate digestives. There was much delight at discovering a pack of Ginster's Cornish Pasties although I could never recall either of them ever eating one before.

We returned home and I headed to the lounge with a much-needed beer, leaving Karen and Dot to find cupboard space for the piles of tins and boxes. At least if the Zombie Apocalypse came we would not be short of baked beans or tea bags. Zombie Apocalypse? Where had that idea come from? Harley, that was it. Everybody has to have a Zombie Apocalypse plan.

I flicked on the television to find a movie. The now familiar little envelope in the top left corner greeted me. For a while I tried to ignore it but after a while it began to irritate. I opened it.

'Mr Olbatain, we regret your bed sheets were damaged beyond normal usage expectations therefore we have had to add the cost of replacements to your account. Have a nice day.'

I deleted the message and returned to The Great Escape.

For the next couple of weeks we settled in to our new environment, getting used to the heat and the slower way of life. My Spanish was gradually improving with the help of an online course and I could now buy a ballpoint pen and ask for directions to the nearest hospital. My endeavours to formally import my car however had met with an impenetrable wall of bureaucracy and circuitous paper trails. Eventually I employed a local paralegal firm to help who took care of most of the details. Apparently I had to arrange an ITV certificate, the Spanish equivalent of an MOT. I had been told that the best ITV station to avoid lengthy queues was at Órgiva, as it was new and the locals didn't trust it yet.

I found the place on a map; it was actually in Los Tablones, a small village just outside Órgiva. Sara at the paralegal office had booked my appointment for ten thirty so I set off at nine to enjoy a leisurely drive along the coast road rather than the autovia. The roads were clear and even the ubiquitous road works at Salobreña flowed freely. The morning sun carved stark shapes into the mountains as the motorway snaked northwards. At one point I noticed brake lights coming on about a mile ahead and I slowed down. As I approached the cause of the problem I noticed two men on the central reservation, each holding a paint pot and brush. I gave them wide berth as I passed but other cars seemed to pay little attention. The men painted, dodged and painted some more as the cars flew by. No traffic lights, cones or speed cameras. In England, one man digs a small hole near a country lane and he needs a six man support team complete with Mobile Incident Unit. Two different approaches to dealing with the problems of excess staff, I supposed.

I turned off the motorway and took the Órgiva road that wound through the Alpujarras. Sharp rock faces on ones side of me and a sheer drop on the other tempered my desire to let the Stag have her head on the mountain roads. James Bond would have to wait. The road wasn't busy but what traffic there was seemed to have little regard for lane etiquette or precipitous drops and frequently headed straight for me on the wrong side. Usually on a blind bend with the unprotected sheer drop on my side. The few crash barriers that were in place seemed quite random. In some places they were solid affairs and supported by drifted earth but in others quite flimsy or missing altogether. About every kilometre the weather-stained barrier was broken by a shiny new section that told of somebody's over optimistic driving skills.

As I rounded one particular corner a yellow Seat headed straight at me and I swerved into a gravel track between two steep hills. I came to a halt in a cloud of dust and panic. I turned off the engine and gathered my thoughts and my breathing. First check the obvious, I am in Spain therefore we drive on the right. Check. This is not a dual carriageway with me in the wrong lane. Check. Conclusion, lunatic drivers. Check. As I settled my adrenaline, my gaze drifted over the view. In my concentration to stay on the road and avoid the kamikaze dodgems that had been hurtling at me like some manic video game I'd not noticed the stunning scenery. A flat, green valley spread out between tall mountains topped with brilliant white snow. I breathed in the fresh, clean air and my soul felt lighter.

Gathering my courage I eased the Stag back onto the twisty mountain road. I had a moment of panic as my brain seized; momentarily I couldn't remember on which side of the road I was meant to be. I was brutally reminded by a large frozen food lorry thundering towards me on what I'd hoped was my side. A quick lane change, another flush of adrenaline and swift prayer of thanks for the Stag's responsive steering.

The ITV station was a huge, brand new building in a small village just outside Órgiva. Exactly as I'd been told, it was very quiet. In fact to all appearances it seemed deserted. I drove round the building looking for the entrance. It was a huge glass and chrome building with a massive sign in front giving thanks to the EEC for the funding that made it possible. The three acre car park was neatly painted with direction symbols, parking bays and give way signs. It was also completely empty. I parked randomly in one of the bays and headed for the entrance. Rows of deserted seats fronted the office. There were several machines that resembled large ATMs and a line of desks which cut the foyer in two. A bored looking girl sat behind one of the desks. I headed over to her and in my tortured Spanish explained I was importing my car and needed an ITV certificate. She looked up from her magazine long enough to point towards the row of machines.

"Necesita tomar un boleto," she said.

I'd understood the word 'ticket', so headed over to the machines. Helpfully I had the option of using the machine in twelve different languages. I chose English. Enter car details, take the provided ticket and await your turn. It gave me ticket 'Number Two' and I found an empty seat from which to watch one of the four computer screens that I assumed were any minute going to announce my ticket number.

After half an hour the receptionist was still focused on her magazine and the computer screens still stubbornly displayed zero. I was just about to go over to her desk and try to find out what was happening when a man walked in and headed straight for the machines. He nodded in my direction with an accompanying 'Hola' as he passed. He was deeply tanned, with sun-bleached hair and equally sun-bleached Metallica T- shirt. He sat a few seats away from me clutching his ticket. A moment later the computer screens gave a loud buzz, blinked on and off a few times then announced Boleto 1. I was out of my seat before I noticed the mistake. The man smiled and marched over to the desk and I returned to my seat.

He retrieved a pile of paper from the girl and headed out of the door. I waited. After ten minutes I wandered out the front to stretch my legs. The man was sitting in an ancient Landrover Defender and staring at another huge information screen that announced 'Espere', Wait. The Defender had a large covered trailer behind it, reminiscent of a Wild West covered wagon.

I went back inside, to the cool. The screen still displayed Boleto 1. Twenty minutes later the man came back inside and headed over to a large window that took up the opposite wall. He sat in a seat opposite the window watching. I wandered over. The window gave a view of a cavernous workshop. It was pristine clean and clearly well stocked with every piece of equipment necessary for vehicle testing. And all of it looked brand new. On a rolling road in the centre of the workshop sat the Defender and trailer. A mechanic in clean and neatly pressed overalls put the vehicle through its paces. Although he did seem unduly focused on the trailer.

"Es beuno," I exhausted my Spanish.

"Si," he replied. "You English?"

"Yes," I said, relieved. "They seem thorough."

"Thorough's not the word for it." His accent was English, somewhere within the M25. "They're trying to find a reason to condemn it. I'm Andy." He held out his hand and I took it.

"Terry. Why would they condemn it?" It seemed slightly paranoid. "It looks in good shape."

"It's the trailer they want off the road." He tapped the glass in the direction of the trailer. "They want me out of the fiesta tomorrow."

"Who?"

"The Mayor." He turned to look at me as if I was a stupid child. "You new here?"

"Yes, well... I don't live here. I live down on the coast. Bahía Blanca?"

"Ah," he said with an air that said now he understood. "Costa Expat! What brings you up here?"

"Getting an MOT for my car. They told me it was quicker here as nobody uses this station."

"That'll be right." He turned his attention back to the mechanic who was at this moment in a pit below the trailer. "It's new. Spanish don't trust new. They think it's all a German plot."

"Why does the Mayor want your trailer out of the fiesta?"

"Because I win every year. His granddaughter and her mates dance on a huge float, all flamenco and fireworks. To be honest, I can understand why he's pissed off when they come second every year. But that's life."

"So what float do you have?"

"That's her, there." He pointed at his trailer. "That's my baby. Wins every fiesta we go to." He gave a big grin.

"That?" I looked at the trailer. "What do you do to it?" I assumed it would be adorned in bunting and regalia.

"I put a beer keg in the back."

"A beer keg? That's it?"

"Yup! Wins every time. Free beer for the judges and the marshals. And of course the Policia."

"And now the Mayor wants you out of it?"

"Oh, that's nothing new. He tries something each year. Last time he tried to change the start point without telling me. You ought to come up, it's a great laugh."

"Here?" I asked. "Órgiva?"

"No. Órgiva's later in the year. Tomorrow it's San Tadeo, up in the hills. It's only a small fiesta, this one, but a good laugh. Just head towards Trevelez and you'll see the signs off to the right. Got to go, looks like he's finished."

I watched as the mechanic drove the vehicle out of the workshop then settled back in my seat. Fifteen minutes later my number came up on the screen and I went over to the desk. The girl was actually very helpful and had enough English to explain that I had to wait in the car until the signs told me which lane to follow. I did as I was told. While I sat in my car watching the announcement board I realised there was actually only one lane. It was number 15. Ten minutes later my registration number appeared on the board along with 'Carril 15'.

I followed Lane 15 until it led me into the workshop where the mechanic took my keys and pointed to the waiting room window. I watched through the window as he went through his tests. They seemed far less thorough than those afforded the trailer before me. Fifteen minutes later I had my ITV sticker and another pile of paper.

As I drove out of the village I checked my watch. Just after twelve. I remembered Harley talking about Órgiva and figured that as I was here I might as well go have a look.

I drove along the main road that led into the town, avoiding the meanderings of little white vans that seemed to make up ninety percent of the vehicles. Each van had almost identical scrapes along the side and small dents in the wings. It also seemed compulsory to drive with one arm hanging out of the window. Maybe these two things were connected? They idly drifted across the road, reversed into my path or stopped randomly to talk to somebody by the side of the road. The other vehicles consisted mostly of battered 4X4s, old saloons and the occasional horse. At one point I even saw a rotavator with an elderly man and two small children riding on it. They parked outside Dia, a small supermarket.

As the traffic became increasingly unpredictable I feared for the virginity of the Stag's paintwork and found a quiet side street in which to park. I continued to walk into town, all the time watching in bemusement at the mild chaos all around as cars continued to show total disregard for the most basic traffic conventions such as on which side of the road to drive, traffic lights or pedestrian crossings. After the orderly roads and disciplined traffic of Bahía Blanca this all seemed vaguely anarchic.

The main road was lined with small shops and bars. Each bar had staked a claim to the walkways outside their premises with a collection of tables and chairs, making pedestrian progress convoluted. A selection of tempting smells drifted out of their open doorways inviting one to stop and sample their tapas. I eventually succumbed to the call of beer and food at Sástago's, a small bar in the Plaza. The waiter brought a chilled beer and a small plate of paella. The Plaza was an area of calm with a collection of shops and a small fountain near the bar. A police 4X4 was parked nearby. It seemed as battered as every other vehicle I'd seen in the town. The voices from the surrounding tables represented an eclectic mix of nationalities. I watched the people drifting across the Plaza. There was a pronounced eclectiveness to them, much more than I'd seen in any other town. There seemed to be little consideration towards convention or norms with people seeming to be totally comfortable in expressing their individuality with their dress. Smart business types mingled with hippies and young families gathered with the elderly. Overall there existed a vibrancy and an odd sense of tranquillity amidst the bustle.

The beer went down easily and I felt a sense of peace as the sun warmed me and I settled further back in my chair, enjoying the view of the mountains towering in the background. The waiter brought more beer and a delicious seafood salad. Certainly a much tastier fare than tinned sardines that the Expats favoured.

The day was in danger of slipping peacefully from my grasp so I gathered my resolve, paid the ridiculously small bill and went to retrieve my car. On the way I happened by an estate agent's and accidently looked in the window. My eyes absentmindedly tripped over a little house just outside San Tadeo, the village Andy had mentioned. Ten minutes later I was back outside the estate agent's clutching a piece of paper with the details. How had that happened?

The drive back to Bahía Blanca seemed like a return to a different world as the traffic became more organised and at least had a predictability in its carelessness.

I returned to the house having slipped the house details into the car paperwork. I felt like a teenager smuggling in pornography.

"Terry? That you?" Karen called from the kitchen as I shut the front door behind me. "You're late."

I went through to find her reorganising the cupboards again.

"There was a bit of a wait and then I popped in to look over the town."

"Oh, that's nice," she said as she moved pots of Marmite from one cupboard to another. "We've been invited to dinner with Jim and Diane. Just the two of us, Mum's got a date with Walter. Diane's picked up a lovely piece of New Zealand lamb from Britmart."

"Oh," I said. "I'm just going to... erm, file the car paperwork."

In the smallest bedroom assigned the tag 'Office', I dumped the car paperwork in the drawer and placed the house details on the desk by the computer. What on earth had induced me to pick them up? It was a white single storey building set in a three hectare grove of olive, almond and fruit trees. The details told of three good sized bedrooms, kitchen, bathroom and proudly announced it even enjoyed good views. It was the price that I found most intriguing. What sort of house could one buy for €80,000? That's around £70,000! Must be a complete wreck. For want of nothing better to do I idly pulled up Google Earth on the computer and scanned the area. Mostly nothing but hills, woods and a small river. San Tadeo itself seemed to consist of one main road and a few narrow side streets, all hanging precariously on the side of a steep drop into a wooded valley. Ridiculous place to live. I shut the computer down, slipped the papers in the drawer and headed downstairs.

**

Jim and Diane were the perfect hosts. Their villa lay on the edge of the urbanisation with views over the golf course. I remembered when buying our place that golf course views came at a premium. A slightly different layout to our own house with different tiles and kitchen units but in essence the same. Like buying a Ford car then selecting colours and optional extras to make it appear different to everybody else's Ford car.

Jim opened a bottle of Loire Valley Muscadet.

"We pop over to Saint-Nazair a couple of times a year," he said. "Always bring a few cases of this back with us."

"There's a lovely little restaurant near the bridge that serves the most delicious trout meuniere," said Diane.

"Tell me about the car, Terry." Jim touched my shoulder, indicating we were to adjourn to the lounge and leave the women in the kitchen.

I related the story about the ITV station with its array of waiting ticket machines and empty Lane Fifteen.

Jim laughed. "Bloody typical. Millions of our money wasted and they still can't even finish the coastal motorway."

I listened to him telling tales of Spanish incompetence and laziness while all the time resisting the temptation to punch him on the nose. I glanced through the open kitchen door. Karen and Diane appeared to be involved in deep conspiratorial whispering.

The roast lamb when it arrived was tasty and suitably dressed with roast potatoes, gravy and mint sauce. Jim kept the wine glasses topped up and I felt myself relaxing. A little too much.

"I stopped off in Órgiva after I'd sorted the car," I said. "Lovely town. So... I don't know... so real."

I might just as well have said "Did you know the Pope's a lesbian?" for the effect it had.

"Órgiva?" said Jim with a puzzled look on his face. "You do mean the Órgiva up in the Alpujarras? Where all the hippies and mountain people live?"

"Err... yes. Quiet little town. There's a lovely bar in the Plaza that...that..." I watched the tumbleweed drift through the dining room. "Nice tapas," I finished lamely.

"How lovely," said Diane with a face that said "How dreadful."

"We're thinking of starting an am-dram for the community," said Jim. "Eric, you know Eric? Down at Casa Camelot? Anyway, he used to tread the boards in the Basingstoke New Players. Well known for his Horatio."

"Terry did a good Widow Twanky a couple of years ago," Karen volunteered.

"That was fifteen years ago," I said. "And I was only a stand in for Reverend Fothergill when he broke his wrist on that jet-ski."

We finished our meal then repaired to the terrace to watch the sunset over the golf course. Jim kept our glasses full and Diane brought a tray of chocolates she'd made in her Bahía Blanca Ladies Group.

"Not so many Brits out there these days." Jim nodded towards the darkening greens. "Things are much more expensive here than they used to be. Particularly if they cut the Winter Fuel Allowance."

We escaped around midnight and made our way back to our house. Dot was asleep in her chair. One shoe was missing and she had grass in her hair. We let her be.

"There's a fiesta tomorrow in one of the villages up near Órgiva," I said as we got ready for bed. "Thought we might give it a try. You know, a little local colour? Might be fun."

"If you like, dear. Don't know what Diane did to that poor lamb. It was so dry, didn't you think?"

Chapter Nine

Saturday morning brought a ringing on the doorbell before I'd even finished my first coffee. I was seriously considering dismantling that. Darren's eternally cheerful grin greeted me.

"Morning, Tel," he greeted. "How you keeping?"

"Great," I said with a degree of uncertainty.

"Fantastic. I got you one of those internet radios you wanted." He picked up the box that was at his feet. It was covered in Chinese writing.

"Internet radios?" I said. "I don't remember wanting an internet radio?"

"What? Oh, maybe it was your lovely lady. Said she was missing Radio Four. I'll have it set up in a jiffy." He bustled past me and into the lounge. "I guess you want it here?"

"Karen!" I yelled towards the bedroom. "Do you know anything about internet radios?"

"Internet radio?" She appeared in the hall in a dressing gown. "What's that?"

"Morning, Karen," Darren called from the lounge.

"Oh, hello, Darren. Let me just get decent." She headed back to the bedroom.

"No need to get decent on my account," Darren said and I heard Karen giggle from the bedroom.

I followed her in. "Internet radio?"

"I remember now. He popped round while you were out yesterday. Said he'd got a job lot of them and did we want one."

"Well, no, we didn't want one."

"How was I to know?" She shuffled herself into a floral print dress. "You weren't here to ask, were you?"

I went back into the lounge to find bits of polystyrene packing lying around and Darren fiddling with a large black box and a jungle of wires.

"I'm not sure about this," I said.

"No worries. You'll wonder how you ever did without it. It's as easy as the TVOIP box."

"Oh good. That fills me with confidence."

"He said I can get The Archers without having to set up the laptop," Karen said as she came in.

"You'll be able to get The Archers in Swahili on this." Darren draped a piece of wire across the lounge. "This is just to get it working. All be Wi-Fi when it's set up."

I left them to it and went to the kitchen to make a fresh coffee. I settled with my laptop to scan the newspapers. Eventually I heard, "All working now, Tel," from the lounge and headed back.

BBC Radio Four sounded clearly from the black box. Gardener's Question Time or something. I was actually quite impressed.

Darren went through the controls and explained how we could listen to a million different radio stations around the world and in any language we wanted. It all seemed a bit overkill for The Archers but if it kept Karen happy then it was probably worth it.

"Can't I have it in the kitchen?" Karen asked. "That's where I like to listen to The Archers."

"Anywhere you like." Darren unplugged the box and transported it through to the kitchen.

"Just over there." Karen pointed to the window ledge.

Darren plugged it in and lights started to blink in sequence. "Takes a moment to go through its start up," he explained.

A few seconds later the radio burst into life. "...and the glorious people's army have once more again making help the peoples of our heritage lands with the support and generosity of our loyal..."

"What the hell is that?" I asked.

"Oh, that. Ah..." said Darren as he stabbed at random buttons on the unit. "That's just the default station. I think it's the Chinese National Radio for the West. Not sure how to reset it. It'll be in the instructions somewhere, I expect." He handed me a booklet the size of a small novel. It was all in Chinese. A few more random buttons and Gardener's Question Time returned. "There you go!"

I paid Darren and escorted him to the front door.

"You had any more thoughts about the patio cooler, Tel?"

"No."

"Well, if you do just give me a bell. I've still got a few left." He gave a cheerful wave and headed back to his van.

We went over to the Expats for a lunchtime beer and tapas of cheesy puffs.

"You fancy going up to San Tadeo for the fiesta then?" I asked.

"What's it about?" Karen said idly nibbling a cheesy puff while she watched a young couple at a table in the far corner of the terrace. They were clearly having a heated row but trying to keep it quiet.

"I'm not sure. Floats and things I expect. Be a bit of fun. Local culture."

"Not sure," she said. "There's the final episode of Downton Abbey on tonight. And I don't know what time Mum's getting back. I ought to wait in for her. You go if you like. It's more your sort of thing."

The table in the corner suddenly erupted into shouts as the woman stood up and stormed off.

"Well, as long as you don't mind..."

"I expect they'll have some fireworks. You'll like that. What do you think that was all about?"

Back at the house I checked the maps for the best route to San Tadeo, grabbed my camera and at Karen's suggestion, an overnight bag. Just in case I didn't fancy the mountain roads back late at night.

"A break will do you good, dear," she said. "You've been looking stressed."

As an afterthought I picked up the house details. I wasn't quite sure why.

The road to Órgiva seemed slightly less traumatic this time round. Perhaps it was because I anticipated the kamikaze Seats to appear like guided missiles at any moment so I was more ready for them when they came. From Órgiva the road drifted upwards once more and I followed the signs for San Tadeo. A narrow bridge over a deep tree-lined ravine marked the beginning of the village. High up above the village a wind turbine turned lazily. It appeared to be the first of a line of about a dozen snaking into the distance across the mountains. A line of giants standing guard to the entrance of the Alpujarras.

Yellow barriers blocked the main road with diversion signs pointing to either a detour around or parking for the fiesta. I found the make-shift car park on a piece of barren land about three hundred metres from the village. There were only twenty or so vehicles there. I checked my watch, just after five so early yet. The short walk to the main road threaded through some quiet back streets lined with white houses and neatly maintained trees. The centre of San Tadeo was defined by a large Plaza surrounded by shops, bars and palm trees. A few deserted food stands stood awaiting the commencement of festivities. Candy floss, sweets, baked potatoes and barbecue. The bars of the Plaza had spread their tables and chairs out in anticipation and the shops appeared to be reopening for the evening shift. I sat at one of the tables and ordered a beer. The late afternoon sun was still warm enough to induce me to sit in the shade. The house details appeared on the table in front of me just at the same time as my second beer. £70,000? In Somerset one might find a one bedroom flat with views over a chicken farm for that. I was curious as to just how run down the house would have to be. Estate agents are very good at taking photographs. When we'd bought our place in Bahía Blanca it had all been a bit of a rush, we hadn't looked at anything else. Let alone somewhere as off-the-track as this. It would be interesting to see though, just for comparison. Sort of a cultural exploration of my adopted land.

Alpujarra Properties answered straight away. They were based in Órgiva but Maria, the manager, offered to come up to meet me and show me round. It seemed impolite to refuse her obvious enthusiasm. I didn't remember ordering another beer but it appeared anyway along with a seafood salad. The Plaza was starting to come alive in preparation for the evening's festivities. The food stands were creating tasty smells and the traders set out their stalls.

"Terry?" a voice called.

A tall slim woman with dark hair approached. She held a leather portfolio so I guessed it was Maria, the estate agent. We did the double kiss, I was getting the hang of those now. Feeling slightly guilty at bringing her up here on a fool's errand I offered her a drink. She obviously knew the waiter and greeted him like a long-lost friend.

"What do you think of San Tadeo?" she asked as she settled at the table.

"It's quite beautiful," I said. "Certainly a different feel to Bahía Blanca."

The waiter brought a glass of vino tinto for Maria and another beer for me.

"Gracias, José," she said. "So, Terry, what brings you up here?"

"I'm not really sure. It just sort of tripped me over as I was passing."

"Ah, yes. Órgiva will do that."

We chatted for a while then she checked her watch. "We should go while there is still good light."

We took Maria's car, a white Berlingo with the requisite scrapes along the side. We drove back down the road I'd taken for about a mile then turned right into a well laid gravel track. The track continued for about a hundred metres where we parked in an area of olive trees.

"Not much chance of passing visitors here," I said.

"Muy tranquilo." Maria led the way along the path between the trees.

Casa de las Estrellas appeared from between a small grove of orange trees. Clean white-painted stone walls surrounded a patio area that led to a wrought iron and glass doorway. Grape vines spread up the walls and snaked across some wooden beams above.

Maria opened the door and we found ourselves in an open lounge area. A large, brightly coloured rug lay on the natural marble floor. A sofa and a couple of chairs faced a large log burner in the corner.

Maria pushed open the window shutters and the early evening sunlight streamed in, filling the room with a warm red glow. She led me through to a small but efficiently planned kitchen then into the dining room which opened onto a patio on the other side of the house. She indicated a wicker chair and we sat for a moment taking in the view. From here the valley spread out below us and the Rio Guadalfeo meandered its way through the wide riverbed on its way to the Mediterranean.

"Come, let me show you the rest."

The bedrooms, although on the smallish side, were light and airy with stunning views over the valley. Each consisted of a simple bed, wooden wardrobe and chest of drawers.

The bathroom was clean and compact and fairly dated. Outside she led me into the terraced garden that fell away from the house. A selection of different fruit trees surrounded a small tiled area. We sat for a moment by a small glass table and watched as the sun tipped the mountain, casting red shafts across the clear sky.

"It'll be easy to keep the zombies at bay up here," I said.

"Zombies?"

"When the zombie apocalypse comes."

"Of course. What do you think of the view?" she asked.

"It's quite beautiful." I realised I was giving buying signals and needed to stop this. "But I expect it gets very windy up here." After all, it was just idle curiosity and I didn't want to give here the wrong impression.

"Yes," she said. "Fortunately there is a nice cooling breeze at times. You'll need it in the summer."

She drove us back to the Plaza and she ordered more drinks. The square was now a bustle of activity as the people were emerging for the evening's fun.

"Are you staying for the fiesta?" she asked.

"I was planning to stay a while then go back."

"That will be a late drive? José has some rooms here. Do you want me to ask him?"

At that moment José arrived with a glass of beer and a vino tinto for Maria. They chatted rapidly for a moment. Too fast for me to understand but I caught enough words to realise she was setting up a room for me for the night.

"José would be pleased to have you stay as his guest," she said to me.

"Oh, okay," I hadn't really thought this through. "How much?" I asked her.

"No," she said. "As his guest. He is my friend of many years. Enjoy the evening."

"I can't... I mean... Oh, that's very kind of him. Will you tell him that's very kind of him?"

She smiled and said, "Of course I will."

We chatted about the fiesta for a while and Maria explained this was just one of the minor events of the year.

"The best one is the Town Patron Saint's Day in October," she said. "That always used to be a huge affair."

"Used to be?"

"Since the financial problems and the bad unemployment in Andalucía they are not able to make any more the big fiesta. Did you like Casa de las Estrellas?"

"What?" That was a sudden conversational switch. "Oh, yes. It's..." *Be non committal, Terry.* "Nice."

She smiled. "Good."

"What does it mean? Casa de las Estrellas?"

"House of the Stars. Lovely name do you think?"

I agreed in my best non-interested way and tried to turn my attention to the gathering activities. A small group of children marched up the main road banging drums and blowing a variety of wind instruments. What they lacked in musical ability was more than made up for with enthusiasm.

"I think the owners may be acceptable to an offer," she said. Clearly my diversionary tactics were not working.

"I think it's far too much for me at the moment," I said. Best to be honest and upfront. "It's more than I could raise now. Maybe in a year... or two." That should do it.

"How much more?" She looked at me over her wine glass as she brought it to her lips. The brilliant red of the wine and the lights of the fiesta flashed in her eyes and she broke into my defences.

"Huh? Oh, I see..." *Stall. Make it look like you're considering it then act disappointed.* "Um... It's about... all things considered at the moment I could raise... I suppose..." *Put in a silly figure. Stop this dead.* "I suppose at the moment I could really only go to... about... €60,000. Perhaps next year..."

"Oh, I see," she said.

There, that did it. That was close. Could have been in a bit of trouble there. Nicely handled, Terry.

"Sorry," I said. "I've got a pension coming out next year. I'll have a look then to see what's about."

"I understand," she said. "It's such a shame, I could see you loved it."

"I did. It was perfect. But just too much. Never mind."

"I'll put your offer to the owners."

"What?"

"Your offer. €60,000? I'll let the owners know that's what you're offering. I think they are quite keen to sell."

"Oh good," I said. *Oh hell,* I thought.

Maria said she had to leave so we did our air kisses and she promised to let me know what the vendors said.

Feeling slightly woozy from the conversation and the beer I figured Maria was right and I ought to stay the night. I collected my overnight bag from the car and José showed me the room. It was at the back of the building and faced onto a quiet street. The room was small but clean and a small en suite bathroom had been squeezed into what was once probably a broom cupboard.

I sat on the bed for a moment plucking up the courage for the phone call to come.

The phone rang for several minutes without answer. I called her mobile and she answered immediately.

"Hi, Karen? It's me."

"I knew that," she replied. "Your name comes up, you idiot!"

"Of course. I tried the house phone."

"Really? Oh, I was out. Outside, that is. I'm in the garden. Didn't hear it."

"Ah, I've decided to stop over. I'm feeling a bit tired and I don't want to risk the mountain roads at night when I'm tired."

"Thought you might," she said. I could hear the smirk. "How's the local beer?"

"Hmm, yes. It's not bad," I admitted. "I'm staying in the local... um... bed and breakfast place."

"Okay, well you have fun. We're all okay here although Mum's not back yet."

"Really?"

"Oh, she did ring though. They're going to a karaoke bar or something."

"Your mother?"

"I know. It's like having a teenager!"

We said the familiar goodbyes we'd grown used to all the years I'd been on far-flung film sets. I had a quick wash and headed out to see what was happening.

The fiesta wasn't a large affair but seemed spread out around the village. It held an odd feel about it. Unlike the fairs in England which seemed to be dominated by teenagers and boom-boom music, here was an eclectic mix representing all generations. Children, adults and the elderly all mingled together as if it were some enormous family function. The overwhelming sound was excited chatter mingled with laughter. The smells of the food stalls called to me and I felt spoiled for choice. Baked potatoes, kebabs, pancakes. I would endeavour to do justice to their hard work and sample as much as possible. I started with churros, a sort of long doughnut filled with chocolate.

Picking my way through the revellers whilst trying to keep melted chocolate from dripping down my shirt proved tricky. I found a clear space just as a group of drummers started playing. There were around fifteen of them, mostly young women, dressed in ethnic clothes. They beat a surprisingly melodic rhythm that stirred something primal that made me realise the power of this simple instrument. The people around me were enthralled by the energy and passion as the drummers moved up the street.

Following them came a flatbed truck with some children dressed in flamenco costumes. They danced enthusiastically to music blaring from a set of over-driven speakers attached to the truck's roof. I guessed the Mayor's granddaughter was somewhere in the group.

A trio of horses followed close behind ridden by young men in leather cowboy hats. Just after them came Andy's 4X4 with the supposedly now legal trailer behind. As described, a huge beer keg sat on the back and as it passed people crowded round the trailer taking the plastic cups of beer that three very attractive, and skimpily dressed, young women distributed with amazing speed and dexterity. Andy's was certainly the most popular float and attracted not only fiesta goers but several police officers as well. Andy spotted me and waved me over.

"Here you go, son," he shouted above the din. "Have one on the 'ouse!" He thrust a beer into my hand just before the crowd closed around me and the procession moved on.

A few other trucks went by including one with a huge crucifix held high, adorned in flowers and colourful silk drapes. After they had all wended their way up the street I turned to have a look at the handful of artisan stalls scattered around the side streets. I bought a pair of leather sandals that felt really comfortable and a braided wrist band for no reason whatsoever. Thinking I really ought to buy Karen something I found a wooden box with multiple drawers. Be nice for her to keep her teas in. Although it had probably been created with an entirely different purpose in mind.

As the evening drew on the younger and older generations thinned, leaving the rest to carry the flag of the festivities through the night. My energy finally gave out around one o'clock and I headed for my room.

***

I was awoken by my phone's insistent ringing.

"Huh?" I greeted as I propped myself up, eyes squinting against the unwelcome sunlight crashing through the window.

The phone rang loudly against my ear. I'd forgotten to press answer. I peered at the keypad, located the correct key and carefully aimed a finger at it. Maria's voice filled my head with chatter. I held the phone at distance from my head that induced less pain.

"Spoke to owners... disappointed with offer... yada-yada."

I made what I hoped were appropriate noises as I fumbled for the glass of water by the bed.

"They're back in England now," she went on.

"I see." My hands refused my brains instructions to hold the water steady and dribbled it down my front. "Damnit!"

"What's that?" Maria asked.

"What? Oh, sorry. Just spilt something."

"So they want a quick sale."

"I imagine they would." I mopped at the water with a tissue from a box on the side. "Never mind. That's life I suppose."

"So," said Maria. "I'll arrange a compraventa."

"Jolly good." I clicked the phone off and slid back under the bedclothes.

I awoke sometime later, showered and stumbled out into the bright light. It wasn't until I was on my second coffee that the fug started to clear and I began to get an uneasy feeling I'd probably done something very stupid last night but I couldn't for the life of me think what.

I'd woken up on my own in bed so that was a good start. I still appeared to have a full set of limbs, all of which seemed free of tattoos.

José brought a toasted cheese and tomato slice out to my table. "Una buena noche, si?"

"Si," I said "Muy buena."

I gazed around the Plaza, now quiet in the morning sun. There was surprisingly little mess but then I had remembered street cleaners busy at work during the festivities. Very organised.

I checked my wallet. Maybe I'd bought something expensive? I had a tendency to do that sometimes when I'd had a bit to drink. A quick count of the notes revealed a definite decline in funds but nothing dramatic. I started to relax. Whatever I'd done couldn't be that bad, probably just a bit of a hangover. I called José for another coffee.

I decided I should ring Karen and let her know I'd be back shortly. Telephone? I patted my pockets. Damn, where was that. I then remembered placing it on the bedside table. After talking to Maria. Maria, the attractive woman I'd met last night. Maria, the estate agent. That was it, she'd woken me this morning jabbering on about something. What was that?

Compraventa, she'd said. What was that word? I remembered that from somewhere. Stuart? Stuart was talking about a compraventa or some such when I was trying to buy the villa back from Frazer. Why would I need a compraventa? "Oh, bugger!" I said out loud as enough of this morning's phone call reassembled itself to begin to make sense. I played back in my mind those bits I could recall. They'd been disappointed with the offer? Wanted a quick sale?

I thrust a ten euro note at José on my way through the bar and dashed upstairs to my room. I grabbed the phone and called up the last number. Maria. I hit dial.

"Hola, Terry." My name must be in her phone. That's not a good sign.

"Hi, er... just wanted to touch base. I was a bit sleepy this morning when you rang."

"No problem. Was a good fiesta, no?"

"Yes, very good. Lots of... um... music and dancing. Very colourful."

"I'm pleased you enjoyed. Is good news about Casa de las Estrellas. You are very fortunate."

"I guess. Just go over it again for me. You know so I'm clear about... the erm... the details."

"No problem!"

So she went over the details again. About my offer of €60,000 being disappointing but as the owners were back in England and keen to sell they'd reluctantly accepted. She reinforced how lucky I was. Funny, I didn't feel particularly lucky. Then she explained she'd have the compraventa ready by tomorrow, so could I call in then to sign it. I lamely agreed.

I hung up the phone with a mental resolution to stop talking to estate agents after a few drinks.

Chapter Ten

I took the drive back at a steady pace. I needed time to gather my thoughts. Órgiva presented me with the now familiar challenges of loose dogs and randomly reversing cars. One car actually reversed straight across the main road right in front of me and carried on into a side street. A car behind me hit his horn the moment I stopped. I was beginning to get the hang of horn conventions in this part of the world. It is rarely used as a warning; its prime function seems to be as a test of reaction speeds for the driver. How quickly can he sound it when the traffic lights turn green? The other function is as a greeting to the driver's friend on the opposite side of the road. This one is often accompanied by a sudden stop in the middle of the road whilst pleasantries are exchanged.

Once I'd left the casual chaos of Órgiva's traffic the twisty mountain roads occupied my mind so it was not until I reached the motorway did I once again ponder the problems of explaining this to Karen.

"You'll never guess what happened last night, you'll laugh when I tell you." Hmm, probably not.

"I bought you a surprise." No, not since the last time. My track record with surprise gifts after a few drinks was not altogether sound. It was the set of antlers I'd discovered in a junkshop after a liquid lunch with the film crew that had finally clinched it. So, no more surprise gifts. Best say nothing for the moment. Sneak it in to a conversation at some future time.

I arrived back at the villa around midday. Karen was in the kitchen baking something or other and Dot was settled in front of the television watching Celebrity Prison Camp. The usual little envelope icon blinked at the top of the screen. Curiosity compelled me to open it.

'Mr and Mrs Smith, welcome to the Hotel Transatlantic, Malaga.' Here we go again.

"So, come and tell me all about the fiesta," Karen called.

I proceeded to tell her about the procession and the beer wagon. I left out the bit about buying a house and told her what a good host José was. I presented her with the wooden box.

"What's this?" she said as she pushed it to one side to make room for a tray of scones that had just emerged from the oven.

"It's a tea box," I explained. "You can put all your different teas in it."

"But I only have PG Tips."

"Or you can fill it with paper clips and rubber bands."

"Well, it's lovely and I'm sure I'll find a use for it. Make yourself useful and fetch that cake rack."

I picked up what I thought was a cake rack. "This?"

"That's a teapot rack, idiot! Out of the way. Why don't you make Mum a nice cup of tea?"

I did as bidden and settled in the lounge just in time for the repeat of last night's EastEnders. After ten minutes of the usual shouting, traumas and arguing I was thankfully pulled away by the doorbell.

Billy stood on the doorstep, another large parcel in his arms.

"You wouldn't be a diamond and look after this for me, would you? It's a... a..."

"Present for Junie?" I offered.

"Yes. It's for... err... our... you know."

I took the box from him. "No problem. I'll keep it safe."

"You're a pal. Sorry we can't make it for tea. Got a little business to attend to down Malaga. Maybe next time?" He gave a casual wave and headed down the path.

I put the package down in the hall then headed into the kitchen. "Billy said they can't make it for tea?"

Karen had the tablecloths out. That was never a good sign. "Oh, that's a shame," she said as she set about arranging chocolate biscuits on a silver tray.

"What tea?" I asked.

"Oh, forgot to mention it, but you were in such a rush. We've invited a few friends round for afternoon tea."

"We have?"

"You wouldn't be an angel and wipe down the patio table, would you? It gets so dusty."

I went outside and lined up the garden furniture then turned the hose on each piece in turn. More efficient than messing around with dishcloths.

"Yo, Tel!" I turned to see Darren coming up the path. "Couldn't make anybody hear from the front."

"Oh, hi, Darren." I turned the hose to point at the flowerbeds. "What can I do for you?"

"You know I mentioned that windmill?"

"No."

"Well, I've been able to get hold of a few on a sort of a test basis."

"That's nice." I gave the pink stuff a good soaking. Bougainvillea, I seemed to remember somebody calling it.

"Great discount, less than half price. All you've got to do is keep records of what it makes."

"I'm not very good with records, Darren. Might be best to count me out of this one."

"But it can save you a fortune on your electric bill, they're all the rage in Wales now."

"But they're ugly great things. Don't they kill birds or something?"

"No, not these. These are domestic ones. Sits on your roof, you'll never notice it."

And another good way of annoying the neighbourhood, I thought. I eventually managed to convince Darren I had no need of his domestic windmill then upended the garden furniture to let it dry out.

***

Afternoon tea turned out to be a master class in transposing English fine culture to Spain. The white napkins and cucumber sandwiches presented an irresistible temptation to Andalucía's fly population. The few friends turned out to be Jim, Diane, Simon Farrington and Dot's beau, Walter.

We chatted about Bridge, in which I had absolutely no interest, golf, same as, and Downton Abbey, ditto. Karen played perfect hostess keeping plates piled high and tea cups or wine glasses fresh. The conversation shifted to films so for a while I had a voice.

"Tell me," asked Simon. "How did they smash that train through the wall in Skyfall? I assume it was computers?"

"No, we actually did that. It was a real train. The James Bond series always try for the real thing. The Broccolis have great pride in the realism."

"Jim had a train set in England," said Diane.

"It wasn't a train set," protested Jim. "It was a miniature railway based on the Aln Valley Railway in Northumberland."

"I had a train set once," said Walter. "Hornby double-O it was. Also had a Tri-Ang London bus. But I swapped it with Charlie Briggs for a packet of Player's Navy Cut. My dad tanned my arse so hard for that I thought I'd never sit again!" He giggled wheezily until it turned into a coughing fit.

Karen tried to head off the conversation, "Simon, what did you think of Jayéd's performance in Strictly? I thought she was very brave... considering."

I opened a San Miguel and the late afternoon took a slightly softer feel. I wondered what it would be like in my little house at the moment. Parts of the valley would already be falling into long shadows about now. Maybe it hadn't been a mistake after all? The conversation around me drifted through Kate and William's various shenanigans and onto Jamie Oliver's latest recipe book. Something to do with wild mushrooms and yams. The chatter faded with the light and eventually the group dissipated. I helped Karen clear up.

"Well, that was nice," she said. "Shame Billy and Junie couldn't make it though."

"Maybe next time. I've got a bit of work to do in the office."

I sat at the small desk in the bedroom assigned as the office and fired up the computer. While I was waiting for Windows to load all of its critical updates my eyes wandered through the window to the neatly kept lawns and shrubbery area that would one day adjoin the community swimming pool. But for now it adjoined a hole in the ground and a yellow digger that hadn't moved since we'd first looked at the house nine months ago. Windows finally played me a triumphant little tune and announced with great pride it had finished an important upgrade and would now allow me access to my computer.

I tapped into my bank and trawled through the various accounts. The house sale in England had left a good surplus over the cost of the villa here so I had sufficient funds to pay the deposit and leave enough for extras. My private pension fund would allow me to take a lump sum. That would reduce my future income marginally but not significantly. I had a few shares that had been left to me by Great Aunt Katherine. I'd kept them for sentimental reasons, silly really. I clicked a few buttons and numbers started moving from one place to another. Okay, I could do it without major trauma and more importantly without Karen realising. I deserved it, I reasoned. I'd worked bloody hard all my life. I'd spent years in film set caravans, and often tents, in some of the most unpleasant places in the world. Why did directors always want the most complicated effects in the most uncomfortable places to work? I shut the computer down with a slight tinge of guilt. I wasn't quite sure why, perhaps it was because I was keeping it from Karen? I'd tell her later. When the time was right.

We spent the last of the evening watching something on the television which I immediately forgot as soon as it finished. I pondered again the problem of explaining my house to Karen. Maybe if I could get her to fall in love with the area? To see the rugged beauty I'd found.

"I fancy driving up into the mountains tomorrow," I said. "You know, visit the area in daylight. Fancy coming?"

"Oh, I was thinking about taking a picnic to the beach."

"I think I've had enough sun for the moment," I said, hoping the relief didn't show. "Bit headachy. That's why I thought of going somewhere cooler. But you go to the beach with your mum. She'll like that. It'll be nice for you both." Phew!

"Hmm... On the other hand... It might make a change. It's time we left Bahía Blanca for a day."

Oh, hell! This was going to prove tricky.

***

Karen and Dot were fine all along the coast and up the Granada motorway. Lots of oohing and aahing at the snow topped mountains in the distance. However as soon as we left the motorway and joined the Órgiva road the sounds of appreciative novelty changed to uneasy murmurings. We hadn't been on the road for more than a couple of kilometres when Dot started complaining from the back seat.

"Why can't they make these roads straight? It's making me feel sick."

"They can't make them straight, Mother," said Karen. "They have to go round the sides of the mountains."

"Well, they could cut the mountains a bit. They did that with the M5 at Bristol. I need a cup of tea. Can we stop for a cup of tea?"

"There's nowhere to stop here," I said. "We'll be there soon."

"Can't you just slow down a bit, Terry?" asked Karen.

"It'll just take longer."

"Humour her, please."

I slowed the pace a bit and we collected a couple of cars behind us. The road started to climb into the Alpujarras and twisted high along the edge of the mountains. I glanced at Karen. She'd gone very quiet and was holding tight onto her seatbelt. The rear seat was silent, I glanced in the mirror. Dot looked white. Her arms were outstretched holding the seat at both sides of her. Her eyes wide and staring steadfastly forwards.

"Terry?" Karen's tone was overly calm and measured. "Do you think we could slow down a bit. Please. Terry?"

"I'm only doing twenty now." I checked the mirrors. We had collected a little trail of cars.

I rounded a particularly sharp hairpin with a sheer drop to our left. This elicited a strange little squeal from the back seat.

"Terry!" Karen, more insistent now. "Please slow down. It's dangerous."

I reduced speed to around fifteen miles an hour. Every so often somebody would whip past us but in the main we just continued to collect traffic. Lots of it. Cars, vans, articulated lorries, I couldn't see the end of it. I wanted to slide down in my seat and hide. Who, me? Not me, it's not me driving like a ninety-year-old mouse with timidity issues. I found a cut in which to stop to allow the trail of vehicles to pass. We sat there and watched them as they went by. It took ten minutes. There was even a group of cyclists tangled up in the melee.

We eventually made it to the Seven Eye bridge on the outskirts of Órgiva. A bridge just wide enough for one car. A bridge which has priority signs from the south in an attempt to prevent cars meeting in the middle but in reality just encourages drivers to drive as quickly as possible onto the bridge to stake their claim.

As we drove through the town, Karen and Dot forgot their terror of the mountain roads and watched in bewilderment at the gentle chaos that is Órgiva.

"Look out," squeaked Karen as a car reversed into the main road.

"Mind that dog. Dogs. Why are all these dogs running loose across the road?"

"Look at those children on that tractor! There must be... there must be six of them!"

"There's a horse. Somebody's parked a horse outside that bar!"

I found a parking space and we ambled through the town centre. I ignored Alpujarra Properties as we passed and tried not to see Maria waving at me from inside. She had a telephone to her ear so I knew she wouldn't come out. I still didn't know how I was going to be able get away long enough to sign the papers without being noticed.

"There's a nice bar up here," I said. "In the Plaza, if it's not too busy."

It was busy but we still managed to find a table near the little fountain.

"Is this where they had the fiesta you came to?" Karen asked.

"No, that's a smaller village, up there." I pointed vaguely in the direction of San Tadeo. "We can go up and have a look if you like? It's very nice. Fantastic views."

"Is it straight roads?" Karen asked, looking at her mother.

"No, it gets a bit twisty turny up there."

"I think we've done enough twisty turny for today. Mum's looking decidedly peaky."

The waiter arrived and I ordered two beers and a sherry.

"Don't know why you dragged us out here," Dot announced. "Place is full of hippies."

"They're not hippies," I said. "They're... They're people, individuals expressing their... err... individuality."

A couple of young women wandered over to our table. They both wore sun-faded cotton skirts and flimsy tie-dyed tops that almost concealed but not quite. One of them unfolded a blue velvet cloth on the table to expose a selection of leather bracelets, necklaces and hair clips. I bought another leather braided wrist band. And they wandered off to the next table.

"Well," I said. "Perhaps *they* were hippies. But mostly it's just people being different. I like it."

"I noticed," said Karen with that look. "What on earth did you buy that thing for?"

The waiter brought the drinks and tapas.

"What's that?" Dot poked a fork at the plate.

"Not sure," I said. "Looks like little fishes, peppers and some sort of rice. No, might be couscous. Don't know. But it looks very nice." I tasted the couscous, which it wasn't, but I was still none the wiser.

"I'm not eating something I don't what it is. It could be anything."

"I'll order some chips," I said.

The bar customers were an eclectic mix. Business types, young people, families and some definitely alternative types all seemed to mix together. English seemed to be the most prolific language being spoken but with a variety of accents. I realised there were many different nationalities here and

English was being used as a common second language. The waiter brought the large plate of chips which I'd ordered and three more drinks which I hadn't.

I drank mine quickly then announced I was going to pop down to a hardware shop I'd noticed. I needed a new spare key for the Stag, I'd lost the other one. I figured as they had a large plate of chips and a pair of nearly full drinks, they probably wouldn't be interested in coming with me. I figured right.

"We'll wait here," said Karen "I think Mum's a bit tired. You know, after the journey."

I hurried down to the estate agents. Maria had the file on her desk already.

"Ah, here you are. I have the compraventa ready for you. Is very simple and normal. We have a date on this for final transfer at the Notary of the twenty first. Is that suitable?"

"But that's next week?"

"It is too quick? I can ask to delay if you prefer?"

I did a quick mental calculation. The money was ready, that wouldn't be a problem. No, the biggest difficulty would be giving Karen the slip again. Assuming I hadn't come clean by then of course.

"No, that will be fine, the twenty first. "

"We meet here and I'll take you to the Notary. But now you must sign this," she pushed the document towards me and thrust a pen in my hand.

I signed where indicated.

"How do you wish to pay the deposit?" she asked.

"Deposit?"

"Ten percent. It is normal. You can ring your bank and make a transfer?"

I borrowed her computer and logged into my bank then transferred the deposit to Alpujarra Properties. Ten minutes later I was back at the bar.

"Did you get your key?" asked Karen.

"Key? Oh, no. They didn't have that type. Worth a try though. What's that?" I pointed to a brightly coloured plastic parrot in a gaudy plastic cage.

"It's a talking parrot," Dot said.

"I see," I said. "Why?"

"This man came round selling stuff. He had knife sets, torches and these," Dot said.

"And you needed a talking parrot?"

"I didn't," Dot grumbled. "I explained I didn't want anything."

"Apparently 'sod off' translates as 'I want a talking parrot'," said Karen with a grin.

"I'm sure he spoke English," said Dot. "He was just being a git."

"Are we stopping for another one?" I asked.

We had another drink then wandered the town a bit more. I found a bottle of Embrujo, a very rare local single malt. Karen found a straw hat and Dot a shop selling PG Tips.

"So, what did you think of Órgiva?" I asked as we climbed back into the car.

"Odd little place," said Karen. "Felt like going back fifty years."

"I know. That's what I like about it," I said. "No big chain shops. No McDonalds or Next."

"No decent food neither," said Dot. "Can't get a proper fish and chips anywhere."

We drove back round the mountain road at a sedate fifteen miles an hour, stopping every few miles to let the build up pass. Karen and Dot sat in terrified silence as we snaked higher, leaving the Guadalfeo valley far below. It gave me time to think. I wasn't used to deceiving Karen. It felt wrong. But her reaction to Órgiva had been so hostile that I daren't own up now. It came as a bit of a shock. I'd thought she'd love the place with its old fashioned charm and stunning scenery. I then realised that of course Karen hadn't travelled very much at all. She'd always stayed fairly close to the town in which she'd grown up. It was me who'd been everywhere. Everywhere a spectacular explosion was needed or a fight on top of a cable car, that's where you'd find me. We'd probably lived apart more than we'd lived together. That was a strange thought. Maybe we had done the wrong thing moving to Spain? On the other hand, Karen had adjusted remarkably quickly. Perhaps that was because the English community where we lived was so familiar? Nothing much had changed for her. I was the one having to adjust and it appeared I wasn't making a very good job of it.

A white van overtook us on a blind one-eighty degree bend reminding me I needed to pull over once again to let the accumulated traffic pass me. How I longed to let the Stag have her head on these roads. This was what she was made for.

Once we hit the motorway Karen and Dot relaxed although they remained subdued. Apart from some appreciative noises as we passed Lidl's at Solabreña.

Chapter Eleven

The noise of leaf blowers and hedge trimmers woke me. It must be Sunday again. The coffee machine made its friendly crunchy gurgling noises as it prepared my morning kick-start and the toaster threw a slice of Britmart's finest white onto my plate. Karen greeted me as she headed to Dot's room with a cup of PG Tips and the Spanish edition of the Mail on Sunday. Another fine day in paradise. I vowed today would be the day I'd tell Karen about the house. We'd never had secrets and this was stupid. She'd understand. I hoped.

I drank my coffee on the patio while trying to work out how best to broach the subject. Radio Four dribbled in the background and I caught snippets between bouts of garden machinery noises. Apparently some of the banks had been caught selling mythical bits of paper to each other again. New financial crisis, we were all doomed. House prices were set to plummet and the price of bananas was set to go through the roof. But on a positive note, Jayéd had announced she would return to Strictly Come Dancing next year. All was normal in the world. I still couldn't work out a way of spinning my news so in the end I decided head-on would be the best way. I headed into the kitchen, full of resolve.

"Karen..."

"Oh, be a love and pass me that salad bowl, would you?"

I looked at where she was indicating. A selection of different bowls teased me from inside the glass fronted cabinet.

Karen sensed my confusion. "The Nigella Lawson one," she said, helpfully.

I grabbed a medium sized white bowl and handed it to her.

Karen looked at it. "Okay, that one will do." She returned to chopping apples and grapes.

"Karen," I tried again. "You'll never guess what happened..."

"Do you think I should add some chopped almonds?"

"Huh?"

"You know how it is with nut allergies these days. Don't want somebody getting anaphylactic shock over a fruit salad."

"No, I suppose not. I popped into an estate agent the other day."

"Oh, that's nice. Is there any cling film in that drawer? Only this bowl hasn't got a matching lid."

I found the cling film and handed it to her. "There was this funny little house... What are you making?"

"Fruit salad. For this afternoon? You haven't forgotten we're going out this afternoon, have you?"

"Out?"

"Simon's garden party? Oh, for goodness sake. I swear you don't pay any attention to anything I say."

"Sorry, I completely forgot. Anyway, I went to see it. It was really out of the way, up in the hills. Stunning views."

"I'm sure it was lovely. Did you remember to put the wine in the fridge?"

"Which wine was that?"

"The Chardonnay? Oh really, Terry. Pop it in the freezer, we can't take a warm Chardonnay to a garden party."

I found the bottle of wine and tucked it in the freezer alongside a bag of McCain's Oven Chips. "So, I put in this ridiculous offer. You know, really low. Just taking a wild punt, sort of... See what would happen."

"Well, I'm sure you know what's best. Do you think I should wear my new hat?"

"Yes. No. I don't know. So, they only went and accepted it. Who'd have thought?"

"It doesn't go with my Laura Ashley though."

"Well, the upshot is, it seems I've bought a house." Well there it was, I'd told her. I waited for the storm.

"I suppose I could wear my Stella McCartney. I've not worn that for ages. What do you think? "

"I think I'm going to the bar."

"Well don't be too long, we're due at Simon's at four and it's eleven already."

110

***

The Expats was quiet for a Sunday morning. Just a couple from down the road I'd noticed before. We'd never spoken but we are on nodding terms. I nodded and they nodded then returned to their newspapers.

Tracey brought me a beer without asking. "You on your own today then, Tel?"

"Yes, I'm in a bit of trouble I think. Or at least I will be when she realises."

"Not been playing away have you, you old rascal?"

"No, heavens. Nothing like that. I've bought another house."

"Oh! I'd have thought you had enough of those already, what with your place and then Jock's as well." She punched my arm in a playful way.

"Yes, you'd think, wouldn't you?"

I sat for a while soaking in the sun and the sound of birds. The garden machinery noises had abated for a while. I needed to talk to somebody. I pulled out my phone and scrolled through the numbers.

Gerry. Gerry Fenchurch. We'd worked together on many films; he was the best armourer in the business. When a director needed a Martini Henry mark three rifle or an Abrams Tank then Gerry was the man. He was probably the closest I had to what could be called an 'Old Friend'.

He answered on the second ring. "Tel! We were just talking about you. How's retirement?"

"Driving me nuts. How's business?"

"Cracking, I've been contracted to supply the hardware for the next film in the Who Dares series. They've been looking for locations for a mountain car chase or something. I think Southern Spain was on their list. I mentioned you were down that way. Anyway, what brings you into my day?"

"You remember when you packed up the movie business for a while and tried for a normal job. What did you do? Logistics for Tesco's or something, wasn't it?"

"Sainsbury's actually. How can I forget. Stuck behind a desk most of the time. Big mistake that one, not for me. Why do you ask?"

"How did you and Trish get on? You know, suddenly spending all that time together?"

"I went back to the movies after six months. Does that answer your question?" He laughed.

"I see," I said thoughtfully. "I think it probably does."

"Sound like you need a hobby," he said. "Ever thought of golf?"

"Yes, thanks. Didn't work, I wasn't allowed to blow anything up."

"Well, you take care, Tel. I got to go, trying to find a Bushmaster M4A3."

We made noises about meeting up for a beer one day then said our goodbyes. I pondered the phone call over a second beer. We'd shared many jobs over the years and I suppose he was the nearest I'd ever got to having a best friend.

I took my time ambling back to the villa. Karen was waiting.

"What do you mean you've bought a house? Are you completely off your head?"

Ah, it seems the penny's dropped.

"As I said. it was –"

"What happened? Were you drunk or something?"

"Not really. I thought it would be an investment. I thought we –"

"And just where is the money coming from for this lunacy?"

"Well, I moved –"

"We'll talk about this later. I don't want to go out all upset." She bustled off into the kitchen leaving me standing in the hall. Well that went better than I thought it would.

**

Simon's garden party was a modest affair. The grounds of his house were extensive and beautifully manicured. Set near the huge oval swimming pool, a couple of large tables carried an assortment of bottles and nibbles. I put the bottle of frozen Chardonnay on the table.

"I'd give that a minute to thaw out," I said to the Spanish waitress stood behind the table.

Karen scowled at me. "I knew you couldn't be trusted with the wine. You didn't think it was... Ah, Simon! How lovely of you to invite us." Her conversation switched immediately on seeing our host arrive.

"Karen," Simon greeted. "As beautiful as ever." He kissed her on both cheeks. "And Dot, how *do* you stay so young?"

Dot giggled and Simon turned to me. "Terry, good to see you, old man. Really must make time for another round."

A waitress brought a plate of nibbles and as I took a couple of canapés I noticed Karen and Simon drift slightly from Dot and I while they chatted.

"What's this then?" Dot peered at an anchovy pâté canapé held tentatively between her fingers.

"Fish paste on toast," I said.

"Oh, I like fish paste." She popped it in her mouth with an, "Mmmm."

Simon came over to me and patted my shoulder. "Well done, old chap. Wise move."

"Huh?"

"Your lovely wife was telling me about your little investment."

"She was?" I stared at Karen.

"Bang on! Now's the time," continued Simon. "I was at a conference in Malaga only the other day. I have to say the mood was very bullish. Definitely the right time to be investing. Been looking for a home for a little nest egg of my own."

Karen's face held a painted smile.

"Good, that's what I thought," I said and slid off to track down something cold.

The party dragged painfully into the early evening. The only other people I recognised were Julian and Vernon from the golf course. We nodded at each other as we passed. I mumbled to Karen about having a headache, too much sun, and managed to slip away.

Just as I was heading out of the gate I heard behind me, "Here, wait on." It was Dot chasing after me. "You ain't leaving me with that lot."

"How do you fancy stopping off at the Expats for fish and chips and a nice cup of tea?" I suggested.

"You read my mind."

***

I spent the next few days in a state of mild excitement. The sort of thrill I'd not felt for a long time. Now I'd come clean about the house and Simon's approval even had Karen thinking it was a good idea, I wanted to get up there again and explore. Maybe buy a couple of pictures or something. Maria had told me that all the furniture would remain, apparently that was quite normal in Spain, so that would make life easier. I didn't quite know what I was going to do with the place yet. Karen clearly thought I was going to rent it out or something, maybe holiday lets. I might do that. But probably not.

Karen seemed to keep up an endless trail of Bridge, garden parties and meals out. Mostly I managed to avoid these but I did join in on an organised walk which I thought might be of interest as it included a Roman aqueduct. As it turned out, the walk was only one kilometre with a distant view of the aqueduct and terminated in a visit to Charlie's Traditional English Bar on the seafront.

On Tuesday Maria rang and told me that on Friday the Notary would be in attendance in Órgiva and we would be signing the final papers for Casa de las Estrellas.

I went into town to buy bits and pieces I thought I might need in the house. Electric kettle, some mugs and cutlery. As I passed an art shop, an easel and canvas set in the window snagged my attention. That was an idea, I was going to learn to paint. I visualised myself sitting on the patio painting the sunset. The German woman in the shop provided me with everything I'd need to start out on my artistic path. Including a book, *Painting for Dummies*.

I increased my time with Rosetta Stone Spanish. My

vocabulary was steadily improving but the grammar still evaded me.

Karen brought me a cup of tea while I wrestled with subjunctives. "I don't know why you torture yourself with that," she said. "Everybody speaks English round here anyway."

"It's good to try to communicate. Hey, I'm going up to Órgiva on Friday, fancy coming up? You can have a look at the house?"

"I'd love to but I've got Book Group. We're doing Jamaica Inn round at Jane's."

"Jane?"

"You know Jane. You met her at Simon's. They have the house with the black gates and the lions?"

"Lions?"

"On the gateposts. The one with their initials in the ironwork. You remember, he has all those nursing homes in Brighton."

"Oh, yes," I lied and returned to my subjunctives.

***

On Friday morning I set out early for Órgiva. Way too early. I arrived with two hours to kill before the meeting with the Notary. I settled in the Plaza outside the Bar Sástago with a coffee. At one end some men were erecting a stage. I asked the waiter if he knew what was happening. I was pleased with myself for being able to ask the question, slightly less pleased that I didn't understand his answer. But I think the gist of it was that he didn't have the faintest idea, only that it would mean lots of people and therefore more work for him.

A man wandered over to my table and held his hand out. He gave a good attempt at looking hungry and pathetic but as he was distinctly overweight and had a bottle of wine stuffed in his pocket I wasn't fooled. I shooed him away only for a man selling fake perfumes and DVDs to take his place. I wondered if I had 'Punter' tattooed on my forehead. A busker struck up just under the trees. He hammered his battered guitar and bewailed the loss of his Liverpool Lass.

I checked my watch and wandered down to the estate agents. Maria had the papers on her desk, she took me through them briefly and we made our way to the Notary's office. The whole process was over in less than twenty minutes. The vendors had assigned power of attorney to a local solicitor and we all stood in front of the Notary as she read out the documents. Maria translated for me. Basically the vendors agreed to sell, I agreed to buy, banker's draft exchanged and I was the proud owner of Casa de las Estrellas. We all shook hands and Maria took me across the road to a small café where we sat and enjoyed a celebratory beer.

I drove up to San Tadeo in a state of slight bemusement. I owned a house up here, on the edge of these mountains. In the Sierra Nevadas. I nudged the car down the gravel track; I would probably need something more gravel track friendly at some point. I pushed the vines away from the door and fiddled for the lock. The door swung open and the morning sunshine struggled into the dark lounge. I opened the window shutters and sunlight bounced from the white walls. I wandered from room to room taking stock of what was there. The furniture was serviceable. In the kitchen a fridge, freezer and cooker all seemed in reasonable shape although I couldn't get any of them to work. In fact the electricity appeared to be off. I found the switchbox for the electrics and moved the switch to the on position. Still nothing, not surprising, I suppose. I turned the water tap, nothing. Okay, no gas, electricity or water. As a cup of coffee was clearly out of the question I opened a beer and contemplated the problem. I should probably have checked this out before. I would need to contact the electricity, gas and water people to switch me on. Only of course I hadn't the faintest idea who supplied the services here. Even assuming I had the language skills necessary. Come to think of it I barely had the language skills to deal with Wessex Water or Southern Electricity back in England. They all spoke in utility double-speak designed to confuse and I hadn't reached the utility company jargon module on Rosetta Stone yet.

I pulled up Maria's phone number on my mobile, she would be a good place to start. Or she would be if I had a mobile signal. I hopped into the car and drove up the road until I had a clear signal.

"Maria?"

"Si, digame."

"It's Terry, Casa de las Estrellas?"

"Oh, hola, Terry. Are you at the house?"

"Yes, only I have a slight problem. I don't seem to have any electricity... or anything. Silly really. I should probably have sorted all this out earlier."

"Electricity, okay let me check. One moment."

I waited for a couple of minutes then she came back. "I don't know. We have no notes on the file. Have you tried the main switch?"

"Yes," I resisted the temptation to add, "Do you think I'm an idiot?"

"You will need to ring Endessa, the electric company. They may have to reconnect you."

"Right, okay."

"Do you need me to do that for you?" She clearly sensed my confusion.

"Oh, please. That would be a great help."

"No problem. I will ring you back." She hung up before I could explain about the lack of mobile signal.

I sat in the car for half an hour waiting for her to call back then decided to head into the village for lunch.

The Bar Mirador was busy but I found a table in the sunshine, the locals all clearly favoured the ones in the shade. José welcomed me like a long lost family member and brought beer without asking. I scanned the menu and ordered pork loin and patatas pobre, then settled back enjoying the scenery. The little square was quiet with only a few locals wandering around. Certainly different to the festivities of my last visit. The phone rang at the same time as my meal arrived.

"Hola, Terry," greeted Maria.

"Ah, Maria. Any news?"

"Yes, but it's not good."

"Oh?" I speared a piece of pork and nibbled at it. It dribbled garlic oil down my chin. "What's wrong?"

"Endessa cut the property off a year ago. There is a dispute over a debt."

"Well, okay but isn't that the vendor's problem? It's not my debt."

Maria hesitated. then, "In Spain the debt goes with the house. You did not know that?"

"How? I mean, why would I know that? How much is it?"

"Um... One thousand two hundred and thirty six euros forty two cents."

"WHAT?" I realised everybody around me had stopped talking and was looking in my direction. I continued more quietly. "How? I don't understand, how can a little place like that run up a bill of one thousand two hundred and thirty six euros?"

"And forty two cents," Maria added helpfully.

"How is that even possible?

"It includes the fines. And interest."

"Fines? What fines?"

"Hmm..." Maria hesitated again. I was learning fast that Maria's hesitations never precursored anything good. "Illegal use of Endessa's electricity. Apparently Casa de las Estrellas was hooked up to a nearby pylon without permission."

I let the patatas pobre tumble from my fork. "Stealing? And you didn't know this?"

"It's not something we check for. It's the...errr..." more hesitation. "It's usually the buyer who checks this."

"I see. So what do I do?"

"Well if you pay the bill... and the fine then that clears the debt."

"And then they reconnect the house?"

"Not necessarily. It was never actually connected. Not as far as they knew. So they cannot simply reconnect."

"Oh, wonderful. So I pay somebody else's bills and fines and I still don't have electricity?"

"But then you can apply for a supply," she said with a slightly more cheerful note to her voice.

"And how long does that take?"

"They send out a surveyor to see if it's possible to connect you first. That might take a while. Two, maybe three months."

"Surveyor? But it *was* connected so surely they know it's possible?"

"But not legally. To connect legally they have to survey first."

"Two months," I said.

"Maybe three. The man wasn't sure. He said they're very busy. Do you want me to arrange it? They'll need the debt cleared first of course. And a deposit."

"A deposit? How much deposit?"

"I don't know, I can ask. It's because you are a bad risk. The house... not you."

"I'll need to think about it. What about the water? I suppose I owe money for that as well?"

"No! There's good news. It's not connected to the supply."

"How is that good news?"

"You have your own private water. Comes up from a well."

"Ah, oh, that is good. But there's nothing coming out of the tap?"

"Have you switched the pump on?" She paused then, "Oh dear, electric pump." She tried to stifle a giggle.

I clicked the phone off and ordered a second beer.

A voice off to my left said, "Mind if I join you? Only it's a bit busy today."

I looked up to see Andy. "Oh, hi, yes." I waved at the empty chair opposite.

"So, how's tricks?" he asked.

"Oh, well, I've just bought a house with no gas, electricity or water. Oh, and a fifteen hundred euro debt."

"Okay," he said. "Sounds about right for Spain." José appeared and Andy ordered a beer.

I explained the predicament and Andy listened as I ranted about estate agents.

"The problem is, Terry, you're in Spain now, not England."

"What do you mean?"

"Spain expects you to be a grown-up, England expects you to be a child."

"I don't understand?"

"Well, in England if you fall down a hole in the pavement they hunt down the nasty man who made the hole and, take his money and force him buy you sweets to make it all better. But in this country," he paused to sup deeply on his beer, "In this country, if you fall down a hole in the pavement everybody will assume you meant to do it all along. After all, anybody but an idiot could see there was a hole there!"

"Hmm, okay..."

"And if you buy a house with no electricity, everybody will assume that's what you wanted."

"I see," I said.

"Rule one, never assume anything. Don't assume the people selling you a house actually own it. In fact, don't assume it's even a house until you've checked."

"Well, at least I know it's a house. It's got a kitchen and everything."

"Ah, it may look like a house but don't assume."

"I don't understand?"

"It may look like a house, with its kitchen and all. But if the Town Hall have it down as a goat shed then it's a goat shed and any time they feel like it they can tell you to rip out your kitchen and put the goats back. Always check."

"I didn't check," I admitted.

"Where've you bought?"

"Casa de las Estrellas, just down the road." I waved an arm in the general direction.

"Oh, yeah. I know that place. Been there forever, that place. Probably alright. Tell you what you should do," he said. "You should put solar in and tell Endessa to go whistle."

"I hadn't thought of that," I said.

"Hang on," Andy said. He waved for José. They jabbered furiously in Spanish for a moment. Andy sounded like a native. He thanked José and ordered two more beers. "José's brother is an electrician. He's going to have a word with him for you."

I gave Andy my phone number to pass on and we chatted for a while longer. He had been here for nearly twenty years.

Apparently he came to the first Dragon Festival, a huge free music festival held in the valley, and stayed. He'd bought an old finca on the Órgiva to San Tadeo road and gradually refurbished it over the years.

We chatted a bit longer until I realised how late it was. I thanked him and promised to buy the beers next time we met.

I drove back to Bahía Blanca in somewhat of a daze. A lot had happened in the last few hours and I may just have bitten off more than I could chew.

Chapter Twelve

I spent the morning researching the internet for details on solar installations and private water supplies. Solar looked like the right choice. Once installed I'd be independent, bill-free and one step closer to Zombie Apocalypse survivability. When I'd looked around outside the San Tadeo house I'd managed to trace some lazy pipe work back to a small breeze block construction in the higher reaches of the garden. A wooden panel had fallen off under my examination. Inside was what appeared to be transformer of some description then some cable and plastic pipe disappeared into a hole in the floor of the tiny shelter. It had looked a bit like a fishpond pump setup. I guessed that was my fresh water well. It all looked simple enough, once I had electricity for the pump. Okay, not such a disaster.

My phone rang with an unknown number. I answered to be greeted by a flow of Spanish. I apologised for my minimal Spanish and asked the person to speak more slowly. He introduced himself as Paco, José's brother. He wanted to look at my house on Tuesday. We arranged to meet at ten. I spent the rest of the morning with Rosetta Stone then we went to the Expats for lunch.

The usual faces sat at their usual tables. I nodded at the nodding acquaintances and said hello to the speaking ones. The ham, egg and chips were all they were supposed to be and Dot made appreciative noises about the tea. All was well in the world, only suddenly it all felt very alien.

Karen jabbered on about some charity jumble sale that was being organised to help a dog sanctuary. I didn't pay a lot of attention until I caught, "You don't mind, do you? I mean I don't think I've ever seen you use it."

Whoops. I either had to own up to the fact I hadn't been listening to a word she'd been saying or agree to the unknown donation. *Go with the donation, it'll be less painful in the long run.*

"Well, if you think it will do any good," I said, wondering what to what I'd just agreed.

"Oh, good. Jane will drop by later pick up everything."

"I think I'm going to have to put solar electricity on the house in San Tadeo," I said.

"That will be nice. Sandy in Woking had it. You remember Sandy and Dennis, they had a holiday home in St Ives? We stayed there once, difficult parking. Oh, no, come to think of it, it wasn't solar, it might have been a Jacuzzi."

"Hmm? I think I'm going to take a stroll up the hill. Fancy coming?"

"No, Pride and Prejudice is on the BBC this afternoon. Mum and I have a cake."

My walk up the hill behind our urbanisation went slowly. The afternoon sun burnt through my clothes as if they weren't there and within twenty minutes I was a soggy mess. I sat on a rock at the peak of the first hill and stared out across the sprawl of buildings that spread from the coast and appeared almost animate as they made their way towards the hills. I had the distinct feeling that if I sat here too long they'd sneak up the hill and start nibbling at my feet. I turned to look towards the Alpujarras, the snow still capped the highest peaks and the valleys looked like folds in a crumpled green cloth. My house was up there somewhere, in one of those valleys. I heard footsteps behind me and turned to see a group of about a dozen walkers marching up the hill. They seemed to be mostly female and similarly dressed in grey shorts and white shirts. Most carried Nordic style walking sticks. They stopped just in front of me and the guide, a well-built woman in her sixties, explained some of the sites visible from this vantage point.

"The Phoenicians first landed over there, near Ikea, around 800BC. Then just last year Stefano Bertoni, the Manchester footballer, bought a villa just down there," she waved a hand, "next to the marina."

And so with three thousand years of Andalucían history neatly covered they moved off down the hill again.

I watched them for a moment as they threaded their way down the path back towards the sprawling conurbation. My eyes drifted towards the mountains in the opposite direction, taking in their impassive timelessness, a terrain that was old even before the Phoenicians had arrived. I headed off down the path with a new resolve.

I slipped through into cut that led behind the urbanisation and just as I was coming out onto the road near Billy's house I heard him call, "Oh, hey, Tel. Hoping to catch you." He beckoned me towards his gate and held it open for me.

"What's up?" We walked across his lawn towards a small group of trees. This was all very conspiratorial.

"You know these bangs you make?"

"Erm, yes."

"How easy are they to make? I mean if I wanted a bang, you know, bit of flash and smoke and stuff. Lots of noise. How hard would that be?"

"I can't, Billy. Sorry."

"Not to cause damage, like. Just a bang. Sort of a joke. A giggle, you know."

"It's really not something I can do. I'd like to help but that's a bit outside my comfort zone I think."

"Not to worry. Just thought I'd ask. Never hurts to ask, does it?" He clapped me on the back and we parted. I felt I'd narrowly escaped a pact with the devil.

"I think I'm going to stay in the San Tadeo house a while," I told Karen when I arrived back at the villa.

"Whatever you think best, dear," she replied. She dribbled water from a small watering can onto some potted plants on the window ledge.

"There's a lot to do and I think it's probably better if I'm on site."

"We'll manage. We always do. It will be just like before when you'd go off on your film trips."

This was way too easy but I wasn't about to push any harder at what seemed like an already open door.

"You should come up and see it," I suggested. "It's a lovely place. You can see for miles."

"Maybe when they do something about the roads."

***

I stopped off in Órgiva for no other reason than I just wanted to soak in the atmosphere once more. I sat at Bar Sástago in the Plaza with a cold beer and enjoyed the general bustle.

"I see you found Órgiva," a female voice approached from behind.

I turned to see Harley approaching. She wore a pair of faded jeans that were more holes than denim and a white shirt that was altogether too thin.

"Oh, hi!" I said. "Yes, quite by accident. I had to bring the car up here and... well... here I am."

"That'll be Órgiva." She settled at the table and the waiter appeared with a bottle of Alhambra beer. She noticed my surprise. "Fran knows me," she said by way of explanation.

"You didn't like Bahía Blanca then?" I said.

"Not my kind of place. Full of foreigners."

"Huh?"

"One square mile of English, one square mile of Germans, a Dutch Quarter, a French Quarter. All feels a bit like Berlin must have done after the war. All peeping out from behind their walls, frightened of the others. All very odd." She picked at the fish tapas. "Although come to think of it, I do understand why you'd want a wall around the French. Cussed gits, the French. Did you know they're taught English in school from the age of three yet you still can't get a waiter in a motorway services to understand 'One coffee please'?"

"You're not so keen on the French then?"

"Had a French boyfriend once, Claude, his name was. Had a degree in musical movement and spent his time stoned trying to be an anguished artist. The best he could manage was being a living statue outside the Louvre. He did a very good Joan of Arc though. That was until some drunk Liverpool supporter tried to set him on fire. After that he took his finger cymbals down into the Metro and I never saw him again."

"You seem broken hearted."

"Devastated. How are you finding life on the Costa del Expat? Cats all settled in?"

"Never see the cats, they're out all the time. I see the odd gecko without a tail so I guess they're still around somewhere."

"And your wife? Karen, isn't it?"

"Well, she doesn't chase the geckos but I don't see much more of her than the cats. Garden parties, Bridge clubs, reading circles." I watched a couple of dogs hurtle round the Plaza in pursuit of an orange. "I think she's having an affair." The words just suddenly appeared as if it hadn't been me that had spoken them. My beer disappeared, leaving a circle of condensation on the table and a warm glow in my head.

"That was quick!" Harley said.

"I was thirsty."

"I meant the affair. That doesn't usually happen for two years."

"Huh?"

"The Expat Bounce. Couples who've never actually spent any time together suddenly decide to move to a new life in the sun and then they realise they don't get on any more. Usually takes two years until one or the other screams and heads for home. You might have set a record."

Two more beers arrived unbidden.

"Órgiva's full of them," she continued. "Look around. People of a certain age, single."

I glanced around the tables nearby, she had a point. "I'll ask them to keep me a table."

"Who was it? The Pool Guy?"

"No, a Euro MP with an unnatural interest in mini roundabouts,"

"Oh, that's original, it's usually the Pool Guy."

"I haven't even got a pool,"

She appeared to be thinking for a moment, then, "No pool? You're not very good at this whole expat thing, are you?"

"It appears not."

Her hand reached across the table and she rested it briefly on top of mine. She smiled. "How do you feel? You don't exactly seem in a state of shock."

"I suppose it's a bit of a relief really, come to think of it. Strange. I haven't felt right since we moved here."

"Probably all the time you spent around all these big macho men with their big guns and explosions." She paused for a moment then, "You're not gay, are you?" she added with a mischievous smile.

I noticed the way the fierce sunlight made her white shirt almost transparent. "No," I said thoughtfully. "I'm fairly sure I'm not gay."

She gave my hand a quick comforting squeeze then reached for a piece of battered fish. "Well, Órgiva's waiting for you."

"I've already bought a house," I said, suddenly realising the full implications of that. "Not here, up in San Tadeo."

She turned to face me. "You really don't waste any time, do you? You seem intent on short-cutting the whole Expat Bounce thing."

A young woman appeared with a box of puppies.

I said, "No thank you, I've already eaten." So she put the box on the table. There were four of them in there, although it was difficult to be sure as they all sort of melded together in one bundle of fluff. I explained to her that I had cats and therefore a dog was out of the question. She removed one of the puppies and put it on the table in front of me. It was no bigger than a hamster and would probably make nothing more than a tasty snack for Holmes. I stroked its head with my finger. The fur was incredibly soft.

"I really can't," I said. I noticed Harley had turned from the table and was watching a child climbing into the fountain.

"He's a boy. The others are girls," the woman said. Her accent was probably Spanish but her English was excellent.

Huge blue puppy eyes looked up at me and the ball of fluff whimpered slightly then snuggled under my hand.

"He likes you," she said.

"The cats, you see..."

"I'll see you around. I can see you've got your hands full." Harley gave me the double kiss and wandered off across the Plaza.

"I'm sorry," I said as I picked him up to put him back in the box. "I have three... four cats and I'm not going back for a while. He's very cute but it would just be impossible."

And that was how I came to be a dog owner.

I sat at the table for a while totally bemused. The puppy immediately snuggled into my lap and promptly went to sleep. I felt trapped. Another beer arrived along with a tortilla tapas. A busker started to play a quite respectable Spanish flamenco guitar and people drifted across the Plaza, nobody seeming in any hurry. The puppy whimpered and I feared it might be hungry. What does one feed a puppy this size? I had no idea how old it was or what breed. For all I knew this might be a full grown example of some miniature breed. I broke off a tiny piece of tortilla and fed it to the puppy. It disappeared with lightning speed and two blue eyes blinked up at me. Is tortilla good food for one of these? I had nothing else so broke off another little piece. Puppy took it from my fingers and licked them clean. I gave it a few more bits before deciding fairly arbitrarily that was probably sufficient. The waiter helpfully supplied me with a saucer of water which the little ball of fluff managed to get all over me.

"Mastin," he said with a grin.

I hadn't the faintest idea what that meant so I just smiled and nodded. I needed puppy equipment. Bowls, a bed, a lead. And food. I'd noticed a shop at the bottom of town that seemed to sell most things so I settled the bill and headed down the road, puppy tucked into the crook of my arm.

Cami is one of those wonderful old fashioned hardware shops that England dispensed with many years ago. A helpful woman took one look at the puppy, and my probably slightly desperate expression, and took charge. Within ten minutes I had a full Puppy Kit consisting of carry basket, bed, collar and a variety of food and treats. I secured puppy in his carry basket, placed it on the back seat of the Stag and set out for San Tadeo.

Chapter Thirteen

I threw open all the doors and windows as soon as I arrived. The little house responded with bright light and the smell of wild rosemary. I'd bought a portable camping gas stove from Cami and some basic supplies from the nearby supermarket so with a degree of satisfaction I settled on the sun terrace with a cup of tea and a cheese baguette. Puppy slept in his basket at my feet and the overhead vines offered welcome shade from the midday sun. Cicadas chirruped from somewhere nearby, the only sound.

I could do this.

I spent the rest of the afternoon clearing out the rubbish left by the previous owners. The Spanish tradition is that when one moves, most of the furniture is left behind for the new owners. Quite a sensible approach and one which saves on removal costs. In this case however the previous owners had left everything. I had fifteen coffee jugs, a pile of crockery that would equip the complete Women's Institute of West London, six steam irons and a selection of tablecloths that could only be the result of somebody's manic, obsessive fixation. The furniture was a mixture of Alpujarran traditional and 1970s experimental flatpack. It would do for the moment, although a new bed moved to the top of the priority list when I moved yet another pile of tablecloths from the existing mattress and noticed the stains. It looked like somebody had used it as a workbench for rebuilding a tractor. I pondered for all of twenty seconds then dragged it outside onto the ever growing pile of detritus in front of the house. I put sleepy puppy back in his carry box, jumped in the car and headed for Órgiva. The furniture shop was simple. I wanted a new bed, they had a bed. If I'd wanted an internal cushioned titanium sprung memory foamed divan with a graduated firmness rating of medium resistive, I'd have been out of luck. But as all I wanted was a bed and they had one of those, we were in business. Better yet, they told me they could deliver it after they'd closed this evening for an extra ten euros. By the time I came back to the car puppy was awake and demanding something very loudly. I hadn't the faintest idea what he wanted but the volume that emanated from such a small ball of fluff was really quite extraordinary. I put a tablecloth over the top of the carry box in the vain hope that it might quieten him but clearly that only worked for parrots. Maybe he needed the toilet. I carefully put his collar and lead on, both five sizes too big though I'd been assured he'd soon grow into them. We stood together behind the car looking at each other from our respective ends of the lead. Puppy shivered and howled. An old man with a walking stick probably as old as himself shuffled to a halt in front of us. He spoke loudly at me in a dialect that was probably part rural Andalucían and part sixty a day. I didn't understand a word of what he was saying but he laughed a lot and waved his stick towards puppy. I did however recognise one word I'd heard before, "Mastin." He laughed again and shuffled off.

I gave up waiting for puppy to do its business and picked it up. He promptly stopped howling then urinated all over my shirt. Back at Casa de las Estrellas I continued dragging rubbish out of the house for another couple of hours. Why would anybody need three boxes of knives and forks? In the shed alongside the house I discovered a bicycle that was significantly older than me, a wooden chest of men's suits and a rusty old scythe that had probably once belonged to the Grim Reaper himself. The pile grew larger and I grew more exhausted. I shut the door on the house and puppy and went into the village in search of an early supper.

Bar Mirador already bustled with activity as the heat of the day began to subside. I ordered a portion of pork and chips for speed and simplicity. The meal arrived within ten minutes and José greeted me enthusiastically. We chatted briefly and as much as Level Two of Rosetta Stone allowed. He asked If I'd moved in yet and that if I needed any building work doing he had cousin who was very good. Or he might have been telling me he had a very nice mug he could lend me. I finished up and went back home. I heard puppy howling before I even opened the door. I let him out of his box and gave him a small portion of puppy food. Then another. I put him on his lead and took him out into the garden just as the Órgiva Muebles van arrived. I tied the dog to a post and helped the driver carry the bed through. He even assembled it for me. As he was leaving the driver made a fuss of the puppy, I heard the word "Mastin" again within the torrent of Spanish, only this time it was more in the form of a question. I shrugged and said, "No lo sé." I did however understand when he asked me what its name was. I said it didn't have one yet and he told me that was bad luck.

After the van had pulled away I threw some bedclothes in the general direction of the bed then took puppy and a beer out to the patio.

"So, little man, we need a name for you." I studied the ball of fluff as it tried to snuggle deeper into my lap. "Floyd? Do you look like a Floyd? Hmm, perhaps not. Jasper then." He buried his head under my arm. "Okay," I thought for a moment. "Sancho?" The little head popped out and the clearest blue eyes stared up at me. He gave a little bark. "Okay then, Sancho it is."

I pulled up the search function on my Smartphone and typed in Mastin. Traditional breed of Spanish sheepdog. There were some images but too small to see clearly on the tiny screen. Big floppy ears and sad eyes. I looked down at Sancho, yup, that was him. I gave him a few bits of the pork I'd saved from the bar and he gulped them down eagerly. We watched the sun go down and as I had no electricity or running water I took a wash with bottled water by torchlight and settled in for an early night.

The following morning I headed up to the bar for coffee and to make use of the bathroom then went back home to await Paco. He arrived just before ten and I showed him around. His sparse English and my Level Two Spanish combined to form a temporary hybrid language in which we could communicate reasonably effectively. He told me the wiring looked okay but a bit unusual. I wasn't sure I liked the thought of 'unusual' wiring but it would have to do. Unfortunately the roof wouldn't take solar panels. Something to do with the traditional build but I didn't fully understand what he was on about. He did however tell me there was an area on the slope behind the house that would be perfect. Apparently I would also need a bank of batteries and some other technical stuff that even my Smartphone failed to translate. We discussed money and timing and he said he could start next week. He also offered to lend me a generator to keep me going until then and promised to drop it round later in the day.

As we headed back towards his van he pointed to my rubbish pile. He jabbered at me and I caught enough words to understand he was asking me what I planned doing with it all. I waved my arms and joined together a few words to indicate it was rubbish and going out.

He pulled three of the electric irons out of the pile. "Qué quieres estos?"

I shrugged and told him he could have them. He pulled a few more electrical items from the heap and tossed them in the back of his van. I assumed he was going to pull them apart for spares. He drove off down the drive, waving as he went.

With the electricity in hand I now needed to tackle the gas supply. I had quite a nice looking gas oven but the supply was dead. I just hoped that wasn't another illegal hook-up that I would owe thousands for. I rang Maria. She seemed puzzled by my lack of gas.

"Have you checked the bottle?" she asked.

"Bottle? What bottle?"

"Umm... the gas bottle? It's probably empty."

"It's not a mains supply then?" I queried.

She actually laughed. "In Andalucía? Maybe in the cities but not in the campo. No, you need a bottle. Try the petrol garage, they will have them."

I thanked her and went to investigate outside. A short search turned up a gas bottle connected to a valve just outside the kitchen. I lifted it up and it felt empty. I gathered up the empty bottle and Sancho then we headed off to the nearest petrol station on the outskirts of Órgiva. On my return it only took a moment to figure out how it all connected and I had a working gas oven. I could cook! I proudly cooked myself a saucepan of boiling water and made a cup of tea. Okay, I could have done that with the camping gas stove but this was made with my cooker. I thought momentarily about how crazy all this was; just down the road I had a luxury kitchen, air conditioning, even electricity and running water.

The ringing of a bell caught me by surprise until I remembered seeing one hanging by the front door. I thought it must be Paco with the generator but when I went to the door I saw an elderly woman with a shopping trolley. Her accent was completely beyond the reach of Rosetta Stone but as she pulled various plastic bags from the trolley I realised she was selling vegetables. She gave me an empty bag to hold and while she jabbered unintelligibly she set about filling it with red peppers and tomatoes. I realised too late I was supposed to tell her when to stop. She let go of her end of the bag then announced in crystal clear Spanish that would be ten euros. I had a feeling I was probably paying over the odds but gave her the money and she headed off down the drive dragging the tartan trolley behind her.

Just as I was watching her go, Paco's little white van arrived. I helped him manhandle the generator down a makeshift ramp and we pulled it to the corner where the wires went into the house. It took him less than half an hour to make the necessary connections and another twenty minutes doing a rudimentary check of the wiring inside. The generator sprang into life with surprisingly little noise and I had electricity. I moved from room to room checking those lights that still had bulbs. The microwave worked just fine, the fridge light was on but when I tried the electric kettle I heard the generator struggle. Paco suggested I continue using the gas for heating water.

He explained he'd ordered the necessary equipment for the solar system and he should be able to fix it up next week. I walked back to his van with him and he reached inside for a huge plastic bag sat behind the seat. He handed it to me.

"Tomatoes. Tenemos demasiados," he said, they had too many. I gathered that he grew them but had far too many so he was happy to give them away.

"Muchas gracias," I said as he climbed back in his van.

"De nada, hasta luego." He eased the van down the drive.

I took the bag into the kitchen and placed it next to the other one. Well, I wasn't going to starve. I tried the kitchen tap. It gurgled, coughed then spat some brown sludge into the sink. For a moment I thought that was it then a slow trickle of clearer water started to flow. I left the tap running and headed for the bathroom. Best open all the taps and flush it through. I opened both the hot and cold taps and was pleasantly surprised when the hot tap actually produced hot water. A quick search and I discovered an aging and rust tinged gas boiler hanging precariously to the wall outside the bathroom. I dragged some vines from the ventilation fins. It seemed that this was somehow connected to the gas tank I'd installed. Bonus, I had hot and cold water, cooking facilities and at least some electricity. I left the water running for about half an hour, by which time it was running clear and fresh, although it did stop randomly from time to time. I risked a taste; it seemed fine although I'd probably stick with bottled water until I understood it better.

I sat on the veranda watching the sunset. A bottle of beer rested on the table next to me and Sancho lay curled up at my feet. I really should phone Karen. I pulled my phone from my pocket, scrolled through my list of numbers and dialled.

Gerry's eternally cheerful voice answered, "Hey, Tel, what can I do for you? Need an AK47 to cheer up the golf course? Just got my hands on a really nice M2 Browning if you prefer?"

"I think I've left Karen," I said.

"Okay, that's different. What happened, found a younger model? Usually a motorbike tends to be less trouble."

"No, nothing like that. I don't know what happened really. Perhaps nothing." I pondered that for a moment. "Yes, nothing. Nothing happened."

"Huh?"

"I suppose we've not really seen each other for... I don't know, feels like forever." I stared out across the valley without really seeing anything. "Then when we came here we were probably expecting... something to happen."

"Oh."

"I think it's just probably come to a sort of natural end. That'll be it. Yes. Thanks, Gerry, you've been a great help."

"Glad to be of assistance," said Gerry. "The machine gun's still on the table if it helps?"

I laughed. "No thanks. Although if you hear tales of a small explosion around Bahía Blanca and the simultaneous disappearance of a Euro MP, you know nothing."

"Roger that!"

We hung up and I watched an eagle wheeling across the treetops below. It suddenly fell like a missile and disappeared in between some pine trees. Time for the big one. I dialled the villa, it seemed to ring for ages then Dot answered.

"Bahhy Blanco ocho... I mean ochy.. uni... Oh, sod it. Hello?"

"Can I speak to Karen?" I asked.

"Who?"

"Karen? My wife Karen? Your daughter?"

"Oh, that Karen." Dot sounded flustered. "She's gone out. She's visiting... visiting... her mother. Yes, she's visiting her mother."

"Dot..." I paused wondering how to say this then, "You *are* her mother."

"What? Oh yes, silly me. I meant shopping. She's gone shopping. Shoes. She needed some shoes."

I looked at the sun just tipping the mountains in the west. Must be nearly nine. "Thanks, Dot. I'll catch her later."

"No, you won't catch her. She's not doing anything. Nothing, so you can't catch her."

"I meant figuratively. I'll catch up with her... never mind. Goodnight, Dot." I hung up.

I stared at the phone in my hand for a while then scrolled through to Karen's mobile number. It rang out then eventually switched to voicemail. I placed the phone carefully on the table then returned my attention to the setting sun.

Chapter Fourteen

I'd hung a tablecloth over the bedroom window as a makeshift curtain but the early morning sun exploded through it as though it were nothing. The everyday but much taken-for-granted combination of water and gas combined with my coffee granules to help start my day. Sancho nagged continually for something, I didn't know what. I tried water and biscuits yet still he nagged. I unhooked his lead from the back door. "Come on, boy. Let's explore."

We threaded our way through the scrubland that seemed to form most of my land. I could see no fence or any sort of demarcation forming my boundary but the ancient terracing stopped round about the point the estate agent had indicated so I guessed that was probably it. At the point at which the terracing ended the land fell away quite sharply. I didn't seem to have any neighbours so perhaps finely defined borders weren't important anyway. Sancho shuffled to and fro along a crumbly edge with a ten metre drop below. I kept the lead short as he turned my stomach with his antics. Something in the bushes just below seemed far more important than self preservation as he kicked scree down the hill. I encouraged him back from the edge and we headed up the slope.

We'd just reached the front door when I noticed somebody heading towards the house. He carried a spade in one hand and a canvas bag hung over his shoulder. He stopped when he saw us, a startled expression appeared on his face.

"Oh, whoa!" he said. He had long tangly hair that formed into natural dreadlocks as it fell across his shoulders. His skin was Caucasian but deeply tanned and weather beaten. He wore a multi coloured striped cotton shirt, shorts and sandals. "That's unnecessary."

"What's unnecessary?" I asked.

"You, man. I mean, cool and everything. But whoa."

My brave dog hid behind my legs, yapping.

"I'm sorry," I said. "You are?"

"I'm the gardener," he said, as if I should know that already.

"I didn't know I had a gardener," I said. "Nobody told me."

"You've got a gardener?" he said with a look of surprise.

"What? No. You said you were my gardener?"

"Hey, that's not cool. I'm not your gardener. I'm *The* Gardener."

"*The* Gardener? I see," I didn't. "What can I do for you?"

He looked me up and down. "Nothing," he said flatly and continued walking towards the side of the house.

"I mean, why are you here?" Hoping a slightly more direct question would help clear this up.

He paused and swung the spade across his shoulder. Sancho yapped once more.

"Mastin," The Gardener said, pointing at Sancho. "Cool dogs, mastins. They get a bit too horsey though."

"Horsey? You mean they cough?"

He gave me that puzzled look again. "No! I mean horsey, like a horse. Big, man." He held his hand above his head. "Huge."

Ah, that would explain why everybody laughed at me when they saw Sancho. "You were going to tell me why you're here?"

"I was? Doesn't sound like me. I don't know, who does? Did tangenital colour casting with my shaman once to answer that one."

"Tangenital? You mean tangential?"

"No, tangenital. He paints your genitals different colours to see which your aura responds to."

"And somehow this tells you why you are here in my garden." I felt I was beginning to lose track of this conversation.

"What? No, I know why I am here." He waved the spade around garden. "I mean why am I here." He held both arms up to encompass the universe.

I knew I was going to regret asking but I couldn't help

myself. "And what did your Tangenital Colour Shaman decide?"

"Best we came up with was blue."

"Blue?"

"See, you don't understand it either. I knew it wasn't just me. Yellow, now that makes sense. But blue?"

"Can we get back to why you're in my garden?"

The Gardener stood for a moment while he considered the question. I waited in fear of his response. He rummaged in his canvas bag and pulled out a bulging plastic carrier bag. He thrust it towards me. "I brought you these," he said.

I took the bag and peered inside. Tomatoes. "Well," I hesitated. "Thank you. Most thoughtful."

He shrugged his shoulders. "It's nothing. Well it's not nothing *really*. I mean nothing would be like a black hole that would probably suck us all in and –"

"You came here just to bring me tomatoes?"

"Huh? No. Yes. Tomatoes and gardening. Which I have to do now." He hoisted the spade over his shoulder and set off down the path behind Casa de las Estrellas. I thought of trying to stop him but my brain felt like it was full and just one more exchange with The Gardener would cause it to overflow and start to leak out through my ears. I took Sancho back inside and tried again with the puppy food. The expensive version with a picture of a terrier on the can with a bow in its hair. Seemed slightly incongruous now if The Gardener was right and this thing was going to grow into a horse. The tiny puppy ate hungrily then looked expectantly up at me.

"That's your lot. This place isn't big enough. No more growing." I wagged my finger at his nose in emphasis and he leapt up and started licking it.

I took coffee and puppy treats out to the veranda and settled down to watch the morning sun creep its way across the valley floor. The Gardener appeared to be doing something in the bottom right hand section of what I assumed was still my land. That area seemed especially green and although I couldn't actually see what he was doing from here, he did seem to be very busy.

Sancho fell asleep in the coolest place he could find and I set to work once more clearing the rooms of unwanted detritus. The pile in front of the house grew as the cupboards gave up their treasures. Two hours later I stood in front of the pile and heard a voice behind me.

"You chucking that out?"

I turned. The Gardener stood behind me, his spade over his shoulder now with the bulging canvas bag swinging from it like a Woodstock's refugee version of Puss in Boots. "Only it'll make a good gate for my plot." He pointed to the old bedstead buried halfway down the pile.

"Your plot?" I queried.

"Your plot, my plot. You're not getting all colonial on me are you? No point in throwing a good gate away."

"It's not a gate, it's an old bedstead."

"Most of the gates in Andalucía are bedsteads if you hadn't noticed. Just the same way most of the flower pots are water bottles and the village school bus is usually a moped with a plank." He didn't wait for agreement and just started dragging his prize from the pile. Along with the ancient scythe and an equally ancient telephone. "Never know when that'll come in handy. You know your water keeps cutting out?"

"My water?"

"Thought I'd use the hose today rather than wait for the acequia but it keeps cutting out."

"What's an acequia?" I asked.

He looked at me with a puzzled expression. "Your irrigation water. You get an allocation, all the houses round here do."

I softened slightly. Whether it was because I found this person totally bewildering or maybe I just needed company for a moment. "Fancy a beer?" I said.

"I haven't got any more tomatoes," he informed me with a slightly worried look on his face.

"That's okay," I said. "I think I've got enough to see me through."

We sat on the veranda with our beers.

"What are you actually doing down there?" I asked,

waving towards the corner in which he'd been so busy earlier.

He took a thoughtful sip of his beer, paused for a moment then said, "Gardening."

I tried a different approach. "What are you growing?"

"Oh, more deep questions. Always with the deep questions, man. You should chill. Doesn't do your soul any good to keep pondering shit like that. Trust me, I've seen it." He raised his beer as if in salute to the valley.

"Deep questions? I don't understand."

"Nobody does. That's why it's all so fucked up. I understand though. I can see cycle."

I presumed he wasn't talking about the old bicycle I'd thrown out. He went quiet and thoughtful again, his eyes defocused as if he'd just gone away.

"Cycle?" I prompted, after what seemed an age.

"The cycle of growth. It's the mystery. What do we ever truly grow? I put a hashish seed in the ground, you get tomatoes. Am I growing hashish or tomatoes?"

"You're growing hashish on my land?"

He looked at me in puzzlement. "Land ownership again? That's what you get from this? The farmer plants the wheat seed, what's he growing?"

"Wheat," I suggested.

"No! Nobody wants wheat. The mother wants a slice of bread to put in the toaster, the kid wants a pizza, Gordon Ramsey wants a ragliatelli or some such rubbish and wanker banker in Wall Street sees his new Porsche if only he can kidnap enough wheat and park it somewhere until every kid in Africa starves and they have to give him his ransom money. So what is the farmer growing?" He didn't wait for me to consider the question. "Porsches for wanker bankers, that's what he's growing. Or toasters."

"Toasters?"

"Toasters. No point in toasters if there's no wheat, is there? No wheat seeds planted, no toasters. It's the cycle. Nobody knows what they're growing until the cycle turns."

It took another couple of beers and another frustrating hour trying to untangle The Gardener's convoluted logic until

140

I thought I finally had a handle on what was happening. He grew hash which he traded for other stuff, such as tomatoes which he used to give to the previous owner as a token for use of the land. Then he also traded in that other stuff as well. Cheese, eggs, fake designer watches, macramé egg cups, the extent was quite impressive. It seemed that a local goat herder, Alejandro, did a nice line in homemade whisky. I suggested that might be preferable to tomatoes and The Gardener agreed to realign his cycles or something to divert the whiskey part of the cycle in my direction.

"But surely it's illegal to grow hashish?" I was suddenly concerned about having my land used for this.

"Illegal? There's nothing illegal in putting a seed in the ground. And what the ground then decides to do with that seed is not my responsibility. Any more than the woman who electrocutes her husband by chucking a toaster in the bath is the responsibility of the man who put the wheat seed in the ground."

He seemed content with his place the cycle but I doubted it would stand up in court.

"I'm Terry, what's your name? I can't keep calling you The Gardener."

"If it makes you more comfortable, you can call me..." he paused in deep thought, then, "You can call me Adam."

"That's your real name?"

"What's real? A name is just a label to identify an object. Like teapot. But Adam is a good label. Adam, the first. Like me. I'm the first of the new awakening."

Once Adam had gone I headed down into Órgiva to stock up the fridge and freezer. Electricity is such a wonderful commodity and so easily taken for granted. I raided the chilled section of Dia first, cheese, milk and pizza then I headed off to the main Plaza where a frozen food shop stood next to Bar Sástago. As I approached Fran, the waiter from the bar, waved at me.

"Cerveza?" he called.

I hesitated then, "Si," and pointed to an empty table. Oh well, I'd do the frozen food in a moment. Frozen chips are just food but a cool beer is a cool beer.

"Hi, Tel." I looked up to see Harley approaching. "He's grown already." She nodded at Sancho curled up by the table.

"Yes, it's a bit worrying," I said.

Fran arrived with a glass of beer for me and a bottle of Alhambra for Harley. She sat down at the table without asking. "How's the house? Got electricity yet?"

"Yes, temporary but at least I've got a fridge. Here to fill it up now." I pointed to the frozen food shop. "I'm having solar installed soon. Then I'm set for the zombies."

"What about water?" She sipped at the bottle playfully. "If they get to your water, you've had it."

"Ah, all sorted, I've got a well," I said with a smile. "Although the pump's playing up. It looks like an old fishpond pump. Any idea where I can get a new one?"

"I know somebody who's selling a windmill. They're moving. It's a proper setup for pumping water."

It seemed like a sensible idea. Diversified resources. Not that I believed in zombies but Harley had touched a nerve with me. It just seemed sensible that now I had the opportunity to start from scratch, building in contingency plans should be considered. Russian controlled gas pipelines, Middle Eastern oil and German money. The unthinkable was probably still almost unthinkable but it certainly wouldn't hurt to build in a bit of extra security.

We finished our drinks and Harley guided me down into the lower river region where traditional Andalucían houses nestled alongside yurts and tepees. Her friends, Niki and Tina, lived in a large log cabin in a field of olive and orange trees.

"I think I should warn you," Harley said.

I stiffened. "Hmm?"

"A lot of people in this area tend not to wear clothes much of the time. It's just too damned hot."

"Ah, okay." I wondered what I was getting myself into.

"Yoohoo!" Harley called as we approached the door. "It's only me."

As warned, Niki and Tina opened the door to us naked apart from sandals, a few bits of jewellery and a scattering of tattoos each. They welcomed me like a long lost friend and brought out iced fresh orange juice.

"Harley's told us all about you," said Niki. She was a tall willowy woman, probably in her early fifties but strikingly beautiful. Brilliant green eyes peered from a deeply tanned face. I tried to keep my focus on her face. "She tells me you've just found Órgiva?"

"I think Órgiva found me," I said. Sancho leapt from my grasp and landed on Tina's lap. "Sorry,"

"Not to worry." Tina tickled his ears. She was a degree shorter than Niki with short cropped sun bleached hair. "He's delightful. A Mastin?"

"So everybody tells me."

"They're lovely dogs, Great personalities. Hope you've got a big house?"

"Hmm, not really. But I have got a lot of outside."

We drank our orange juice then I was taken into their orchard to see the windmill. It stood around five metres high and was made of a wooden frame with two set of concentric blades in some sort of plastic. It looked as though it would have been more at home in the Wild West. They showed me how it collapsed down and how easy it was to set up. I just needed to line the well and install the piston and some other stuff I didn't understand and I would have water forever. It seemed like a great idea but this simple technology looked way beyond my abilities to install.

Harley laughed at my obvious mechanical distress. "Don't worry," she said. "They'll come out and fix it up for you."

"Oh, um. I'm sure I can..."

"No problem," said Tina with a mischievous grin. "We installed it here ourselves. Your male superiority is not in question, we just know how it works. We built it ourselves and we've been using it for years. We'll bring it up tomorrow?"

"Right, yes, okay."

We drank more orange juice and Tina produced some fig biscuits. We sat under a bamboo canopy and chatted for a while. Niki and Tina had been living here for twenty years. They'd had an organic smallholding in England which

143

became squeezed when the shops demanded lower prices while the local Council demanded higher rates.

As we continued chatting I suddenly realised I was no longer noticing that our hosts were naked. I learned about how the whole area had nearly been washed away by storms a few years ago.

"The water came down here like a tidal wave," said Tina. "When we went out in the morning there was a BMW in the olive grove."

"We kept chickens in it for months," said Niki. "Eventually somebody came to collect it."

We said our goodbyes and I felt ever so slightly awkward doing the double kiss thing with a pair of naked and not unattractive women.

Tina gave me a carrier bag of onions and tomatoes. "We've had a good year," she explained.

By the time we returned to the Plaza the frozen food shop was closed.

"You'll get the hang of it eventually," said Harley.

"What?"

"Siesta. The Great Spanish Tradition. Takes a while to get used to."

"But I didn't get my frozen food."

"But you did get a windmill."

"I can't eat a windmill."

"You got no food at all?"

"Bread, pasta, mushrooms, pizza. I've got lots of tomatoes."

"Sounds like a meal to me," she said. "Come on, I owe you a meal. Just show me where your kitchen is."

"It's up there." I pointed towards the mountains behind Órgiva.

Chapter Fifteen

Harley chopped and sliced. "Got any garlic?"

"I've got some powdered stuff somewhere." I moved jars around the cupboard.

"Powdered? Okay, I suppose that will do."

A few minutes later she was dishing out large quantities of pasta Bolognese. We settled on the veranda with the meal and a couple of beers.

"That's amazing," I said.

"Chef training in the School of Poverty and Scraps."

I rinsed the dishes under intermittent but hot water then made some tea.

"Very English," Harley said as I put the cups on the table.

"Always try to bring a bit of the Empire to even the darkest corners. Although I'm afraid I seem to have run out of marmalade muffins."

"Never mind, we have cheesy puffs." She fished a packet from her bag and put them on the table. "So how goes Bahía Blanca?"

"Don't know. Not been back." I nursed my tea as if it were a cold day and I needed the warmth. "Not even spoken to anybody. Well, apart from Dot but she doesn't count. "

"Dot?"

"Karen's mother. Completely potty. Seems to think we're living in some remote medieval time warp."

I heard a bell ringing and turned to see a flock of around a dozen goats ambling across my piece of rough land on the slopes. A great shaggy dog followed them lethargically and a few moments later a short, weather gnarled man passed into view. He waved an ancient walking stick in my direction, "Hola, buenos!" he called as he followed the animals down the slope and out of sight.

"Of course, she might have a point," I said.

"You have goats?" Harley said.

"Not that I know of."

"When do you plan on going back?" She dropped a cheesy puff into Sancho's expectant mouth.

I thought for a moment, casting my eyes over the green valley below. "I'm not sure I will. Seems like a different world. Karen's... Karen's..." I struggled to bring the words into the light. "She's happier this way." It wasn't quite what I wanted to say. I wanted to tell her how much it hurt.

"The universe turns and with each turn it takes and it gives."

I pondered her words. "That's very profound. Where's it from? Is it Buddhist or something?"

"No. Indian Steve. Somebody had just nicked his stash." She teased Sancho's twitching nose with a cheesy puff.

I closed the lid on my internal black box. "Come on, I'll give you the grand tour."

Casa de las Estrellas was a tangly house. Rooms had been added randomly over the years then knocked through or extended. The small windows and low ceilings gave the feel of a hobbit house.

The bedrooms were surprisingly large as they were clearly the results of previous 'knockings-through'. One room I'd designated as a spare room, although the likelihood of house guests seemed remote. Another room served as a store room for the bits and pieces I had yet to find homes for. I showed her my tablecloth collection and my tomato supplies.

She tugged a tablecloth free from my easel. "You paint?"

"Sort of. I'm learning." I showed her my copy of *Painting for Dummies*. "I'm on lesson two, how to stand your easel up without it falling over."

"I'll introduce you to Marco. He runs classes. I model for him sometimes."

My mind drifted into territories best left unexplored.

We wandered outside. Much of the land I had yet to explore myself. We crunched through dead grass and fallen olive branches.

"You should water this lot." Harley snapped a dead branch from an almond tree. "Looks like you get acequia." She indicated some overgrown channels in the ground.

"Adam said so but I'm not sure how it works."

146

"Adam?"

"The Gardener, he calls himself Adam for this cycle."

"Ah, he was Gandalf last time I met him."

Sancho scampered through the undergrowth, chasing butterflies and barking at fairies and other entities that only he could see. Every so often he'd run back to nudge our legs for reassurance. My land appeared to extend much further than I'd originally thought. Although there were no fences, the perimeter seemed marked by either natural features such as a sudden drop or the remains of small stone walls or tree lines.

"What are you going to do with all this?" Harley asked.

"I haven't the faintest idea. Chickens perhaps, I like eggs."

We came round to the front of the house where Harley stopped in front of my pile of out-throwings.

"What are you doing with this lot?" she asked.

"That's all rubbish. Need to find a tip."

She pulled an old wooden chair from the pile. "Why are you throwing out firewood? You'll only be buying it back again in a couple of months."

I hadn't thought of that. Together we separated the wooden furniture from the debris and set it to one side.

"You got a chainsaw?"

"No," I admitted. "I'll get one." I could see myself out there on my land doing lumberjack stuff. Cool!

"You've got quite a few dead trees out there you could take down."

We were just heading back inside when a white Berlingo bumped up the drive in a cloud of dust. For a moment I thought it was Paco but the car held three men. It seemed everybody round here drove white Berlingos.

We waited patiently as the men extracted themselves from the car. They all seemed to be in their seventies and dressed in suits that had probably been bought to celebrate Franco's rise to power.

Sancho barked furiously at the men then ran behind my legs and whimpered. The visitors arranged walking sticks and black trilby hats then the eldest of the trio greeted us in a thick mumbling local dialect that I found completely impenetrable. It all seemed very serious and I was wondering what I'd done to upset what I hoped wasn't the local mafia.

Harley came to my rescue. "They're from the Concejo Abierto, the local municipal Council," she said.

"What have I done?"

"I don't know, I'm having trouble with his Spanish."

"Glad it's not just me."

There was clearly much consternation amongst the group as they struggled to make Harley understand. I managed to catch the gist of what Harley was saying but the man's replies were beyond me completely.

"Apparently the Council is invalid," Harley informed me.

"Can you explain it's not my fault?" Their passion had me worried.

"I'm not sure, it's complicated. My Spanish is not really up to local politics."

More heated exchanges and it seemed Harley was making headway. She turned to me. "It seems they need you to take your place on the Council."

"What? That's absurd!"

"Don't ask me, I don't understand this stuff." Harley turned to the leader and persuaded the man to speak more slowly. He shook his head as if dealing with a child but then clearly made an effort to speak more clearly for the benefit of these stupid foreigners.

"Okay," said Harley. "I think I've got the hang of this. The Council needs two thirds of its members present to be valid and they're now below that margin. There's supposed to be six on the Council but they're down to three. Apparently that's not enough."

"What's that got to do with me?"

"It seems this house goes with a Council seat. That's how they choose the members here. Probably goes back to feudal times. Anyway, if you don't sit on the Council they're below the threshold and that makes it invalid or something. I don't know how it works."

"Did the previous owners sit on it?"

She conversed with the old man some more then turned to

me. "It appears not. The previous people were... I think 'awkward' is the best translation but not quite what he said. The Council hasn't sat for fifteen years."

The man tugged at her arm and spoke with as much clarity as he could. She turned to me. "He says they've got a bit behind with Council business."

My translated protestations had little effect on the three. Their minds were set on me sitting on the Council and they assured me that the fact I wouldn't understand what was being said was probably an advantage. They just needed my presence to make the Council valid. I reluctantly agreed and we all shook hands and hugged. They seemed relieved and I actually felt pleased I'd been able to help. One of them reached into the back of the car and pulled out a plastic carrier bag. He gave it to me. "Tomates," he said. "Muy buenos tomates." He smiled and patted my arm as I took the bag.

"I've already got –"

"Take them," Harley instructed sharply.

"Muchas gracias," I smiled and tried to look pleased with the gift.

One of them men pointed to my junk pile and mumbled something to Harley.

"He wants to know if you're intending to throw out that crockery."

"Tell him they can have it if it's any good to them."

The men sorted through the pile and gathered a selection of some of the undamaged pieces and placed them carefully in the back of the car.

After more hand shaking and hugs the men piled back into the car and drove away.

"Well, that was different," I said.

"Hmm, Councilman Terry. Has a sort of a ring I suppose."

"Wonder what I'm supposed to do?"

"Drink lots of red wine and smoke a pipe. I expect that's what happens in most town Council meetings."

"I suppose I'd better get you back," I said as we headed back inside.

"Oh, I see, I cook for you, do your translating for you then it's sod off?"

"No... I didn't mean... I just thought... Oh dear."

She laughed and pushed gently at my arm. "Just teasing. It's up to you. I have nowhere to be but if you need your space that's fine."

***

We went up into the village to explore. The last time I'd spent any time there I'd been slightly the worse for gin and the place had been full of revellers. Today it was quiet and at this time of day almost deserted. We stopped at the Bar Mirador and José greeted me enthusiastically. I introduced Harley and they chatted briefly then laughed at some joke I didn't catch.

"What did he say?" I asked as José went inside to collect the beers.

"He was telling me he was honoured to welcome the new councillor to his humble establishment."

"Hmm, word gets around fast."

We soaked in the peace of the Plaza for a while then went to explore. There wasn't a lot to the little town but it seemed well supplied with official buildings. There was a Policia Local office and what appeared to be two town halls. One of them was located in what I guessed was originally a small Moorish castle. They both flew the Andalucían flag alongside the Spanish state ensign and another green flag with a crossed axe and spear which I guessed was the town emblem. A scattering of shops provided a pharmacy, an ironmongers, the ubiquitous Chinese emporium and a small general food store. The ancient streets were mostly too narrow for cars although that didn't stop them trying. Every so often we had to take cover in a doorway to allow a battered Seat or white Berlingo passage. One particularly narrow street twisted through several hairpins as it descended to the lower reaches of the village. Suddenly the houses stopped and a paved area gave a spectacular view over the valley and mountains beyond. Just in the distance between two peaks the blue of the Mediterranean melted into the brilliant azure sky. A stone bench faced the view and we sat in silence taking in the sheer and unexpected beauty. We watched as an eagle hovered on a thermal, dipping occasionally to take a practise dive at some prey below.

"Thank you," I said after a while.

"What for?"

"This place. I'd never have found it if you hadn't mentioned it. I'd have come here, got the car done and gone back to Bahía Blanca without a second thought."

"You're welcome." She continued staring at the view but her hand reached across to mine and gave a momentary squeeze. Fleeting but electric. "Your soul would have died in that place."

I pulled a paper bag from my pocket. "Shrimp?"

"Huh?"

"Shrimp." I held the bag towards her. "Sugar shrimp things. Loved them as a kid and saw them in the supermarket. Want one?"

She smiled and took a shrimp. We returned to watching the mountains.

***

We returned to Casa de las Estrellas as the afternoon started to cool. Sancho settled on the veranda under the table and I poured chilled orange juice for us both.

"Sorry," I said. "It's only Dia's cheapy carton but I'll get a juicer thingy at some point." I stared out at my land. "And an orange tree," I added.

We chatted about nothing and we chatted about zombies. We pondered on the brevity of life, the fragility of dreams and the ethereal nature of hope. Harley tried asking me about Karen but I found that difficult so we went back to zombies.

"You'll need a shotgun, you know," she said. "Or a bow and arrows."

"I'd rather have a bow and arrows," I said. "Less chance of it going off in your face while you're cleaning it."

We chatted about places we had been and people we'd

met. Harley seemed impressed with the stars with whom I'd worked but her tales of the odd characters she'd encountered seemed way more interesting. She told me how Órgiva kept drawing her back. She was currently staying with friends in a yurt in the valley, picking olives in return for keep.

As the evening cut in I brought out some bread, cheese and a carrier bag of tomatoes.

"Supper?" I said as I placed it all on the wooden table.

"Perfect," she said.

The evening stars blinked into the darkening sky one at a time. First Venus then Polaris. One by one the sky lit up and Casa de las Estrellas lived up to its name.

As the evening chill tinged the air we went inside.

"Too late to take you back now," I said. "I'd better set up the spare room for you. You can be my first house guest."

We stood at the doorway of the spare room. It was littered with tablecloths and suitcases.

"Seems a shame to spoil it," Harley said. She turned to face me, her eyes danced across mine.

I felt an unaccountable warmth envelop me, like I'd just come in from the freezing cold. Harley took my hands and gently pinned them by my side. She raised herself on her toes until our faces were level. Her lips briefly brushed mine and she drew back to gauge my expression.

"Or we could..." I started. "We might..."

Her lips met mine again only firmer this time, more protracted. She drew back once more and said, "Or we could?"

"We could," I agreed.

We fell together as if we were both tumbling into a void, her body firm and responding to my embrace. Something otherworldly moved us into the bedroom and we fell onto the bed wrapped in each other's need. We made love in a way I had never experienced before. A meeting of bodies and a tangling of souls that reached deep and felt like home.

Despite the heat we lay close all night and in the gentle morning light our bodies met once again.

We dozed for a while until the full morning broke through the flimsy resistance offered by the draped cotton tablecloth and the room became bathed in brilliant sunshine. I slipped from the bed and made coffee.

Harley appeared just as I'd poured them. "Morning, Councillor," she said.

We took our coffees onto the veranda and watched the morning colour the valley one piece at a time.

After a while I said, "I don't make a habit of this, you know."

"Really?" she said. "That's a shame, you're rather good at it."

"I meant... Not while I was married... am married... I mean..."

She covered my hand with hers. "It's alright. Really."

"What time are your friends coming up?" Safer conversation.

"Niki and Tina? Not sure. After lunch I expect, they're not morning people."

"I need to go into town, I need to sort out a decent internet connection. This mobile dongle is useless here."

"Do you want me to wait here in case they turn up while you're out?"

"Would you? That would be great."

"No problem," said Harley. "You can leave Sancho here as well if you like. Make things easier."

"Oh, great, thanks."

"You'd better put some clothes on first." Harley smiled her best impish smile.

It was only then I realised I hadn't got round to getting dressed. Somehow it had felt unnecessary, especially in the heat. I threw on a shirt and shorts and headed down into Órgiva.

I figured Maria in the estate agents would be a good starting point. She was sat behind her desk when I entered.

"Hi, Terry," she greeted. "All good in Casa de las Estrellas?"

"Yes, fantastic. Looking for internet. Is it possible to get something up there? I know it's a bit remote."

"Have you tried Órgiva Telecom? Just down Calle Blanca?"

Her directions were easy and Órgiva Telecom seemed competent and efficient.

Pepe told me I could have up to sixty four megabytes, which was considerably faster than I'd been able to manage in Bahía Blanca and not much slower than England. I was staggered.

"It comes from microwave links," he said. "No wires. Telephone too, all in."

He arranged to send one of his engineers up the next day.

"For a survey?" I asked.

"No," he replied. "To fix it up for you."

I arrived back home to see two strange vehicles in the drive. An old Suzuki Vitara and another white Berlingo van, although not one I'd seen before.

I noticed Harley in a group of people near the well. She came over to me as I parked. She was wearing a white lacy sarong andnoticed me eyeing her attire.

"Oh, hope you don't mind," she said. "I just threw it on when I heard a car arrive."

"What? Oh no, it's..." It was only then I realised it was one of the tablecloths from the spare room. "It looks good," I said appreciatively. "What's happening?" I nodded to the group.

"Niki and Tina came up with Juan. He's a friend of theirs, a builder. He's putting the liner in the well."

"That's quick."

"Oh, and Fernando, one of the local Councilmen from yesterday, dropped by while you were out."

"Changed their mind about me?"

"No, you're out of luck on that one. He left this for you." She handed me a plastic carrier bag containing a large leather bound book. It looked to be about a hundred years old but I figured it couldn't really be that old. The gold embossed writing was too worn to make out what it said.

"What is it?"

"Not sure," Harley said. "I'm guessing it's their rule book or memorandums of whatsits. It's beyond my Spanish, that's for sure. You could ask Niki, she's much better than me."

I dropped the book in the kitchen then went into the

154

garden to see what was happening with the well. Juan was using a large wooden block to hammer a metal sleeve into the ground.

He looked up as I approached. "Buenos," he greeted and wiped a muddy arm across his sweat soaked brow. He indicated the hole and spoke rapidly at me. I understood some words, guessed at others and figured he was telling me it was an easy job and would soon be ready.

Niki and Tina were assembling parts of the wooden frame for the windmill. I offered to help and hold things but I just seemed to get in the way. I went into the kitchen to put the coffee on. Whilst the water was heating up I sat at the table with the book. It was a huge tome. The first part was all printed in a close typeset font. As the book progressed large sections were given over to handwritten text. Many variations on styles of writing and ink colour interspersed with more typeset sections. It was clearly intended to be a formal declaration of Council business along with important notes which were either notable events or amendments. The poor quality of the inks and the highly formal wording made it impossible for me to understand any more than a few words here and there. I closed the book and poured coffee.

As I took the tray outside another van pulled into the drive. It bore the logo of Órgiva Telecom. A man climbed out and waved greetings to everybody. He double kissed the girls and hugged Juan like an old friend. I greeted him with a good British handshake, he patted my shoulder.

I showed him where I wanted the internet router and he took a box of electronics up onto the roof. No ladders, he just sort of ran up the side of the house like squirrel. He wandered around on the roof taking a beam on the mountains behind us. At one point he used a pair of binoculars and a compass. He waved at a section of the roof and shouted down at me though his words were lost in a gentle breeze that was picking up. I guessed he was telling me he'd decided where the receiver should be positioned. I shouted approval.

Over the next couple of hours work continued at a furious pace on all fronts. More metal sleeves were hammered into the ground, bits of timber grew into a recognisable windmill and my roof sprouted a selection of electronic gizmos. The Órgiva Telecom engineer called me into the house and showed me a jumble of little black boxes and a tangle of wires. A telephone was plugged into one of the boxes. He switched it on and held it to my ear so I could witness the dial tone. I nodded in approval. I was actually quite speechless. I still had living memory of trying to organise British Telecom to supply me with a telephone in my first house. It had involved a six month waiting list and a mountain of paperwork.

He showed me how to plug my laptop into the router. A few quick experiments with websites proved the speed was far in excess of that promised. I logged into my emails and deleted all the offers of penis enlargements and Russian girls as he stuffed all his paraphernalia back into his toolboxes. He handed me a couple of sheets of paper which contained my account details, telephone number and router passwords. I tried shaking hands but we ended up hugging and he waved goodbyes to all then sped off backwards up the drive.

I resisted the temptation to go inside and play with my new toys and instead went back to the well. They seemed to be finishing up.

"Juan is just hooking up the electrics on the old pump," Tina said.

"The old pump?" I queried.

"Just as a backup. In case there is no wind one day. Although that doesn't happen here often."

The blades on the mill turned gently and gurgling sounds emanated from the hole in the ground.

Juan explained it would take a while to run clean. Harley invited everybody inside for a beer but Juan said he had another job to get to. I handed him the money he'd requested and added another twenty. He thanked me and headed off.

We cleared up then tested the water supply by showering the mud and sweat from ourselves. Tina and Niki stayed naked after their shower, Harley followed suit. I stayed in the house after my shower, pretending to do water and internet stuff while I struggled with how to dress. Going naked in front of other people seemed weird but staying clothed when the others were naked seemed even weirder. What if I had an erection? After last night with Harley the sight of her naked body was likely to have a profound effect.

"You alright, Terry?" I heard Harley call.

"Yes, I'm just... I'm checking for leaks."

"Well, don't be long. Can you bring some orange juice out with you?"

"Okay." I picked a carton from the fridge and stood in the middle of the kitchen, stressing. I took my shorts off and stood for a moment in just my shirt. I could say I had sunburn. On my arse? No, that wouldn't work. Cold then? No, it's thirty five degrees out there. I felt silly and put my shorts back on. This was crazy. I'd been to a mixed sauna in Finland when we were doing Snowstrike. I took my shorts off again. But then I'd had a towel of course.

"Terry?" Harley came into the kitchen. "You okay?" Her eyes surveyed me. I was stood in the centre of the kitchen wearing just a tightly buttoned shirt and holding a carton of orange juice in one hand and my shorts in the other. "Ah," she said. "I see."

"Sunburn," I offered.

"Take your shirt off."

"But then I'd be..."

"Take your shirt off, idiot." She snatched the shorts from my hand and threw them out of the door.

"But what if I have a... you know." I nodded downwards towards my groin.

She smiled and looked down at the source of my potential embarrassment. "Hmm, I think you're fairly safe on that front."

She was right. The adrenaline caused by my stress had created a retreat in the manhood department. Now that was even more embarrassing.

She took the carton of orange juice from my frozen hand and turned. "See you outside. And lose that shirt!"

I took the shirt off and stood for a moment. Sod it! I took some ice cubes from the bag in the freezer and went outside, Naked. Outside and naked. Outside, naked and in front of other people. It felt strange, liberating.

"Thought you'd got lost," Niki said.

"Just getting some ice." I placed the ice bowl on the table and sat strategically close to the table. Harley smiled at me and I relaxed.

"Terry's been invited to sit on the Concejo Abierto," said Harley.

"That's the Municipal Council, isn't?" Tina asked.

"The original local Councils," said Niki. "Mostly concerned with goat tracks and hunting rights these days I think. Certainly in the smaller municipalities. All the important stuff is dealt with by the City Councils or Provinces."

"But I've got my Spell Book," I said.

"Show Niki," said Harley. "She might be able to tell you what it's about."

I went to fetch the ancient leather bound tome. I had to stand up in my nakedness and walk naked past these naked women then into the house, all without clothes on and naked. I remembered this scenario from a dream although this wasn't quite the same. Unless Cherie Blair was in the kitchen. I walked nakedly into the kitchen and was relieved to find the absence of Cheri Blair. I grabbed the book and headed back outside, sliding smoothly back into my chair that partly concealed me behind the table. Harley gave me a knowing smile.

Niki opened the book with the reverence of a museum curator. "This predates Franco," she said as she scanned the opening pages. "They just gave you this?"

"Yes," I said. "In a plastic Dia bag. It must be worth a fortune."

"You planning on selling it?" asked Harley.

"Spain's full of this sort of stuff," said Niki. "The first bit seems to be a record of the formation of the municipality. Lots of names and honorifics." She carefully leafed through the delicate pages. "It's very old Spanish, very formal. Ah, here's the bit that lists the responsibilities." She peered closely at the yellowing paper. "Rights of access, acequia water, tithes, town boundaries. I should imagine you'll spend most of your time discussing the problems of straying goats or arguing over whose turn it is to borrow the town donkey."

"What's that bit about tithes?" I asked. "Is that a local tax or something?"

Ninki skimmed through the pages, holding a finger in one place then leafing through, clearly following references. "Okay, there's a bit here. Olive quota tithes. From what I can see a tithe was levied on the olive crops to pay for extracting the oil in a central mill." She read on silently for a moment. "The same for grain. Any grain or other produce milled locally was also subject to the tithe. Fascinating. This bit's cool, any babies born within the town boundaries are able to vote immediately whereas those born outside are not allowed to vote until twelve."

We chatted for a while longer as Niki extracted more interesting trivia from the book. It seemed that as a new resident I was not allowed to bear arms within the town boundaries or allow my fowl to enter any Council buildings. I wondered what scenario had arisen to provoke the inclusion of those particular rules. In general though Niki had been right, the Council seemed mostly concerned with trivia such as fundraising for the local fiestas and choosing who leads the procession on Saints' Days.

I took the book back into the kitchen and carefully wrapped it in its carrier bag. Niki and Tina headed off as the afternoon began to cool.

"We need to turn the water to the orange trees," Tina said.

I thanked them again for their help with the windmill and we watched them bounce their little car down the drive.

We sat for a while chatting, taking pleasure in the cooling air.

"Well, Councillor Terry," Harley said after a while. "I really should get back."

"Oh, okay." I felt slightly deflated. "I'll get dressed."

I dropped her outside her friend's yurt, a large construction topped in green canvas. We kissed and she said, "See you later." I drove away feeling slightly confused. I'd just passed through the centre of Órgiva when my phone rang. I glanced at the screen hoping it would be Harley then immediately realised I didn't even know if she had a phone, let alone have her number logged in mine. The screen announced it was Gerry.

I pulled over to answer the phone.

"Hi, Gerry," I greeted.

"Hey, Terry. You okay to talk for a minute?"

"Sure. What gives?"

"You remember a little while ago I mentioned the film I'd been contracted for? Number Three in the Who Dares series?"

"Vaguely," I said. "You're supplying the munitions?"

"Yeah, well they're stuck for a location for one scene. It's meant to be an Austrian mountain village in the mid-forties, only everywhere in Austria is far too modern and too expensive to dress for the period. It's only a short scene in a flashback so they don't have a huge budget for period sets. They were looking at Rumania, as everybody does these days, but the local mayor suddenly wanted a larger bung than agreed and it all fell out of bed at the last minute. Then when they mentioned that they also needed a car crash explosion into a bar I thought of you."

The thought intrigued me. "How can I help?"

"Remember how when we were doing Bond, I think it was Die Another Day?"

"Yes, but that was Cadiz? Supposed to be doubling for Havana if I remember wasn't it? Nothing like an Austrian village."

"I know, but remember how we went to Granada between shoots? Went to see the armoury museum there. There was this little village we stopped at for a beer. In the Sierra Nevadas or something."

"Vaguely, I suppose that would pass but I'm not sure I can remember where it was."

"But you're down that way, aren't you? Could you have a drive round the area, see if you could come up with somewhere quickly? They're desperate and there'd be a few bob in it for you. Especially if you could set the bang as well."

I thought for a moment. "I might just be able to help. Leave it with me."

"You're a star, Terry. By the way, how's things with Karen?"

"Don't know."

"Okay. Enough said. Talk soon."

I dropped the phone on the dashboard. Damnit. I hadn't really thought about Karen for a couple of days. It had felt as if I were on location somewhere, temporary separation and all perfectly normal. Just doing a job and normal life would be resumed soon. Only of course that wasn't really the case. Normal life was not going to be resumed. Nothing like it. I tried to probe the darker corners of my mind to see if I actually cared. I found nothing. Either I had buried that particular box very deep or there was nothing there to find.

I started the car and drove up the road for a hundred yards. I stopped suddenly, much to the annoyance of a following scooter who swung round me tooting loudly. I banged my fist on the steering wheel and shouted loudly, fleetingly thankful this car had been built before the advent of airbags. Sancho yapped furiously from the back seat. My hands gripped the steering wheel with a ferocity that would have crushed the life from any living person. Another shout filled the small interior and I swung the car round a hundred and eighty degrees and headed for Bahía Blanca.

Chapter Sixteen

The drive through the valley felt strange, subdued. I watched the mountains drift by, gradually calming as I neared the coast. The countless tunnels and bridges merged into a continuous blur until muscle memory drew me off the motorway at the correct junction. As I drove through the wide outer avenues an unaccountable feeling of claustrophobia descended like a blanket of fog. I pulled up outside the villa and sat in the car for a while. I didn't know why I was there or what I expected. I thought about driving away again but then the door opened and Dot appeared; she was just seeing Walter out. He walked down the path and waved at me as he passed. Dot obviously saw him acknowledging me and looked curiously in my direction. I couldn't hide. I left the car unlocked and headed up the path.

"She's not in," greeted Dot. "Karen. She's out. Shopping or something. I think."

"How are you keeping?" I asked.

"Oh, you know. Same as, really. Mustn't grumble. Too damned hot most of the time. How are you getting on up in the mountains?"

"Okay. House is mostly liveable now." This all felt very stilted and strange. "I've just come to collect a few things."

"Best come in then. I'll put the kettle on. Got some nice Bakewell tarts. Mr Kipling's they are."

"No thanks but a tea would be nice." I followed her into the house. It smelt strange, slightly sterile.

Dot filled the kettle and continued to try to make small talk as it boiled. She gave up after a minute and said, "I'll just ring Karen. See when she's coming back." She disappeared into the lounge leaving me to finish making the tea. I heard muffled speaking but couldn't make out what was being said. Although I could probably guess.

"She's on her way. Just finished at the hairdresser's."

"Thought she'd gone shopping?"

"What? Oh, yes. Buying shampoo. Always gets it at the hairdresser's."

"I'll just pop upstairs, there's some clothes I need. I can sort them out while I wait."

"She won't be long." Dot looked flustered.

I ignored her protestations and headed for the bedroom. It all seemed fairly normal. Clinically tidy and ordered. I hadn't come prepared so had nothing in which to put anything. I opened the wardrobe door where we usually kept the suitcases. There were three suitcases in the wardrobe. Two of them were ours, still with tags on marking previous trips. The other was pristine new, shiny black and expensive looking. I sat on the edge of the bed. What was I doing here? What had I expected to find? I heard a car pulling up to an urgent halt outside and headed downstairs.

Karen stalled as she stepped through the front door and saw me.

"Hello," I said. "How was the hairdresser's?"

She glanced towards her mother who had just appeared and was making funny expressions as she tried to explain psychically what she'd told me.

"Um, fine," Karen said. "How are you?"

"Disappointed," I said.

Karen paused for a moment then, "Terry, look... it's not what you think. It's just that... Well, you were never here and when you were here, you weren't here really. We came here for you and then... Well..." She realised I wasn't saying anything. She'd probably been rehearsing her speech all the way back from wherever she'd been and my part had been essential. I was probably supposed to be shouting at this point. "Look, I'm sorry," she finished quietly.

"I'm sure you are." I turned to leave.

"Terry, wait," she said.

"Why? What's to say? What's done is done and what's passed is best left passed."

I returned to the car and drove away with as much composure as I could manage. Once out of the estate I stopped to catch my breath. Well, that had been a spectacular waste of time. What was I thinking? All my life I'd been used to decisions, action. Taking charge and being in control, it's what I did. Now I sat here like a wet weekend in Basingstoke when I should be... should be what? What was one supposed to do in these situations? I could probably plant a neat little explosive device under Simon Mister Fucking Perfect Farrington wanker prat's car. Or I was sure Billy had some nice friends who I could pay to visit him one evening. In the end I opted for driving onto the Community Lawn that surrounded the nearly completed Olympic sized swimming pool, doing a series of doughnuts and then out through the ornamental hedge and onto the road. Let the leaf blowers sort *that* out. I realised it was just a mindless act of wanton vandalism but it felt good. So on the way out of the estate I drove straight over the newly constructed, and totally pointless, mini roundabout, neatly destroying the little wooden sign that announced this had been built with funds provided by the EU. So, not only another mindless act of wanton vandalism but this time with a nice touch of irony, I felt. I drove slowly back to my valley, vowing never to see any of them ever again.

For a change I drove back up the Old Road. It carved its way through a canyon that made Cheddar Gorge look like a ditch. I stopped at a bar that had for some unaccountable reason been constructed to resemble a castle. I sat with my beer, feeding tapas to Sancho and watched the few cars drift along the winding road. A lorry the size of a small village pulled onto the forecourt, neatly cutting off my view. I paid the bill and continued my journey. As I drove back through the valley my eyes scanned the riverbed area where the yurts gathered. Too far away to see anything other than a few of the larger constructions.

My little house felt very empty when I returned home. I needed noise. And gin. The speakers on my laptop were too small to play music at any sensible level so I opted for watching a movie on Netflix until I fell asleep with Sancho on my lap.

The morning found me in my bed with no recollection of how I'd got there. Sancho heard me stir and leapt onto the bed to give my face a good morning wash. I heard noise coming from outside and checked my watch. Seven thirty. I threw on a pair of shorts and blinked into the already brilliant sunshine outside.

"Buenas!" I heard a cheerful call. My eyes adjusted to the light and Paco came into focus.

"Hola," I greeted. "Que pasa?"

Despite my burgeoning hangover I caught enough of his reply to understand he wanted to lay the concrete bed for my forthcoming solar panels. I waved my agreement and felt my way back into the kitchen in search of coffee. I made coffee for myself, Paco, his mate and myself again. Eventually the day came into focus. They seemed to be managing perfectly well without my input so I gathered up Sancho and we headed off into town. Tien 21 is an electrical shop that seems to sell everything and they offered me a good selection of internet enabled televisions. I auditioned five but could see little difference between any of them so opted for the cheapest. I also bought a CD/MP3 player with a decent set of speakers. I felt slightly annoyed with myself that I'd left a perfectly good player and speakers in Bahía Blanca as that was one of the things I'd meant to collect yesterday. I dumped my purchases in the back of the car then braved Dia. A quick dash through the small supermarket yielded most of the things I needed and these were dumped into the boot with the television. I checked my watch, near enough lunch time. I headed for the Plaza and settled down with a beer and a bocadillo. The square bustled with unusual activity. A couple of marquees were being erected and a man on a cherry picker draped bunting from the street lamps.

"Hola, Terry," a female voice called from behind me.

My heart caught and I turned. It was Maria, the estate agent. She was seated at the table behind me. A clipboard on the table indicated she was probably waiting on a client.

"Oh, hola," I returned. "What's happening here?" I indicated the activity in the Plaza.

"Fiesta. Should be fun."

"What's this one about?"

"I'm not sure," she sipped her coffee. "I lose track. It's

only a small one. It's the patron Saints' Days which are usually the best. Most towns make those big ferias."

"Even places like San Tadeo?"

"They always used to. But I think the Council has no money. Same with many of the smaller towns now. Is very sad."

A couple, clearly English, threaded their way through the tables and as they approached Maria stood and greeted them with the traditional double kiss. I returned to breaking bits off my bocadillo and feeding them to Sancho.

I sat for a while enjoying the activity then headed for home. There was no sign of Paco when I arrived back although there was a new flat concreted area to the left of the overgrown garden. As I drew closer I noticed a new low shed had appeared, a simple breeze block construction with a wooden roof. I assumed it was to house the batteries. I was quite amazed at how quickly they'd completed all this.

I emptied the shopping and then took the television into the lounge. I felt sticky from the heat of the day so before setting to work I took a cool shower. As I dried off I searched for something loose and light to wear but then thought what the hell and didn't bother getting dressed.

Alpujarran traditional built houses have a natural resistance to having things attached to their walls. Firstly there's the problem of where to drill. In one place you encounter solid granite so hard that no amount of titanium tipped drilling has any effect whatsoever, yet two millimetres to the left and it's like drilling talcum powder. Eventually I managed to pepper the wall with a series of holes of varying sizes and angles. I just hoped I'd be able find enough reliable ones in the selection on which to secure the television. The next problem is always one of angles. Alpujarran houses are built with little consideration to the laws of straightness. Ceilings are never parallel to floors and walls generally have a slight undulation to them that makes one feel slightly seasick if observed for too long. The choice is whether to have the television level with the floor or the ceiling. I pondered this for a while then found my spirit level and decided to make it level with the planet. This, of course, meant that is was neither parallel to the floor or the ceiling. It did however give me a slight feeling of satisfaction that at least something in the house was straight with the universe. I switched it on and sat back to programme it. The set up was a lot faster than the attaching and soon I was watching Antiques Celebrity Bargain Swap. Lovely. Orange celebrities trying to enthuse over a nineteen seventies bubble lamp could only hold my attention for three minutes and two of those were a sort of bemused shock. I scanned through a small selection of the advertised three thousand channels and found 'Indiana Jones and The Last Crusade'. Great, that would do. All the more so as it had been filmed just down the road. I remembered it well. I settled back in my chair and Sancho snuggled onto my lap. I was fast asleep before my scene with the Nazi car chase crash came round.

I was awoken by the sounds of 'Yoo-hooing' and dragged myself into the sunshine before I realised I still didn't have any clothes on. I scurried back inside with a "Momento por favor" and found a pair of shorts.

When I ventured fully outside I saw Adam. He had a spade over his shoulder and a plastic carrier bag in his hand.

"Yo!" he greeted. "No need for the capitalist confines of exploitative child labour garb on my account."

"It's alright," I said. "I'd just got out of the shower. What's happening?"

"Come to talk to my babies. And I brought you this." He held the bag towards me.

"Tomatoes?" I asked with suspicion.

"No, you're in a different part of the cycle. Alejandro's special distillation. Hope you've got a sense of adventure."

"Oh, right." I took the bag and removed the bottle from inside. It looked like a litre of cheap lager. I assumed Alejandro was just reusing bottles. "Thank him for me, will you?"

"Aw, you still don't understand the cycle, do you? It's not him I should thank, not for you anyway. If you want me to thank anybody, which actually isn't necessary for the karma anyway but hey it's your version, if you need to send thanks out there then it should be to Eva for the honey."

"Honey? But I didn't have any honey?"

He sighed. "No, of course you didn't have honey. If you'd had the honey I wouldn't have been able to give it to Alberto in return for the eggs. Not cool, man!" He headed off down the path to talk to his plants.

I took the bottle inside and planted it carefully next to a bottle of Larious gin. I watched it for a moment, slightly fearful that it might explode at any instant. I made coffee to finish the waking process then took Sancho for a walk round the garden. He scampered after the butterflies and snuffled at something in the long grass. It would take forever to do anything with this lot. Maybe I should get goats. Or a horse. Chickens? Did horses and chickens get on? I'd have to ask somebody. The cooling air told me evening was on the way so I went inside to ready myself for fiesta night.

**

It was impossible to park anywhere close to town and I ended up near the Rio Chico and with Sancho wanting to sniff everything, a good twenty minutes walk to the centre of Órgiva. The street was blocked by barriers so we had to go round through a side road. As we came out I saw that the road had been cordoned off for a procession. I watched for a while trying to untangle the symbolism on show here. A large gold crucifix was held aloft on top of a flag-draped platform carried by a group of hooded men. I unconsciously scanned the surrounds. If there was any sign of a large wicker man I was running. A brass marching band started up and the whole spectacle moved slowly down the road. I continued up towards the Plaza, stopping off to buy a hotdog on the way. Sancho liked hotdogs apparently. In fact I lost it completely when he demonstrated that his jumping abilities had been kept a closely guarded secret all this time. I went to a nearby stand to replace my hotdog but came away with a beef burger instead. Sancho also liked beef burgers.

A large marquee in the centre of the Plaza gave host to a display of flamenco with lots of furious clapping from the packed audience along with strategic shouts of 'Ole' at appropriate moments. I watched for a while and although I appreciated the skill and the passion I found it as mysterious and impenetrable as jazz. We wandered down to the Almazara, a garden bar set back from the main road. A guitarist played folk in the corner and I settled at an empty table with a beer and tapas of some meat in a yellow sauce. Sancho liked meat in yellow sauce. I was on my second beer when Sancho suddenly leapt, pulling at the full extension of his lead. I turned to see what had caused his excitement. Harley was crouched at his level and allowing him to cover her in dog kisses.

"Oh, hi!" I said. "Somebody's pleased to see you."

"You mean you're not?" She tipped her head in an inquisitive manner.

"No. I mean yes. Of course I'm pleased to see you." I stood and hesitated. Polite double kiss thing or lover's kiss? Harley clearly sensed my confusion and pressed herself against me, her flimsy cotton dress offering no protection from the feel of her warmth. She held my face and stared into my soul then we kissed briefly but with a sense of belonging.

We sat and ordered more drinks.

"You disappeared," I said.

"Hmm. I didn't want to interfere." She nibbled meat from a wooden skewer, dropping a small piece for Sancho. "You had a crisis building. I thought I would just confuse what you had to do."

"How? How did you know?"

"I have this angel that lives in the crystal caves of the eighth incarnation of Aquarius. Tells me the secrets known only to the inner acolytes."

"The eighth incarnation of... huh?"

She laughed, "I'm a woman, you idiot. It's our job to know these things. We're biologically programmed to anticipate men's crises. To be fair, we usually cause most of them as well."

"Oh."

"How did it go? Your crisis?"

"I trashed an ornamental lawn and a mini roundabout."

"That's novel, most people choose the wedding album."

"I don't know where she's put it."

"Hmm. So, did it make you feel better? Your moment of anarchic gardening?"

"Yes." I thought for a moment. "Yes, I think it did."

"Good, then let's celebrate."

So we celebrated. We did the rounds of the bars, we laughed, we danced. We ate toffee apples and candy floss and held hands like teenagers.

By one o'clock the evening showed no signs of slowing down but I was dead on my feet. I held her and said, "So, you coming back to mine?"

She thought for a moment, then, "I've nowhere else to be." She smiled.

We threw our clothes off as soon as we entered the house, full of lust and intent. We made it as far as the bed then I assume we both passed out at the same time because it was Sancho who woke me by licking my face. I squinted my eyes at the window. Bright sunlight burned through the pink chintz tablecloth. I really should do something about real curtains. I turned towards Harley. She was spread eagled face down on the bed. I watched her carefully just to satisfy myself she was still breathing then slipped from the bed and headed to the kitchen. There might not be enough coffee.

I dropped the kettle twice and spilt water all over the tiny work surface. The escaped coffee granules added to the mess and dabbing at it with wet kitchen towel did little to alleviate the problem. I decided to come back to that after I'd drunk my first coffee. Or two.

I felt her warmth behind me fractionally before she spoke.

"Hey," she said. "Were we good last night?"

"Let's say yes," I said. "Coffee?"

She looked at the chaos. "Why don't I do that? You go... go do something else for a moment."

"If you're sure."

As I passed the front door I noticed a large brown envelope on the floor. It had clearly been pushed under the door at some point. The careful handwritten script addressed it to 'Snr Casa de las Estrellas'. I opened it with a degree of caution. Surely it was too soon for a bill for the roundabout?

The headed paper was clearly old although beautifully ornate. The heading I understood, Concejo Abierto del Municipio de San Tadeo. The rest of it was unintelligible, even had I been able to untangle the laboured handwriting.

"What you got there?" Harley sat next to me on the sofa and handed me my coffee.

"Thanks. Think it's something from the Council but I can't understand a word of it."

"Here, let me." She took the paper from my hand as I sipped at my coffee.

She studied it carefully for a moment. "I'm not sure," she said. "The writing's really bad but I'm guessing it's your official invitation to the next Council meeting."

"Can you make out when it is?"

"Looks like tomorrow. Not wasting any time are they?"

"Well if they've got fifteen years to catch up on, it could be a long meeting."

We took our coffees back to the bedroom and managed to catch up on the unfinished business of the night before.

Later, by some unspoken agreement, we headed to the yurt where she'd been staying to pick up her things. There wasn't much. A rucksack, some bedding and a guitar. "Didn't know you played?" I said.

"I don't," she said. "But somebody owed me some money. He didn't have any so I took this instead. Figured I could learn."

As I finished loading the car Harley said her goodbyes then we made our way home.

The following morning we set off early for the Council meeting. I wanted to be sure we knew where it was. Harley was coming as my interpreter but she kept trying to persuade me I didn't really need to understand anything anyway as I was only there to make up the numbers. "Just vote the same way the old fella does," she instructed.

"Which old fella?" I asked. "They're all old."

"The one with the hat."

"Not helping."

She laughed.

The Council room was in the old castle. It felt pleasantly

cool inside as we negotiated the maze of corridors until we found one with a sign outside it that announced Reunión de Concejo Abierto.

"Looks like the one," I said.

It took a bit of explaining to the trio that Harley was my interpreter. It was quite possible their lack of understanding was more likely due to their reluctance to have Harley sat at the main table and less to do with Harley's Spanish. But in the end they relented and great fuss was made in finding an extra chair and a cushion. The Council Room was laid out with the head table on a slight raised platform at one end of the room whilst around two hundred folding wooden chairs were neatly lined up across the rest of the room. The five of us sat at the table and waited. A man in uniform brought in a jug of water and four glasses. I let Harley share mine. We waited some more.

The door creaked open and we all perked up expectantly. An old man shuffled in and settled in the back row. He appeared to go to sleep immediately. I was just in danger of following suit when the leader of the Council, the old man not currently wearing his hat, struck his gavel three times calling the meeting to order.

One of the men, whose name I gathered was Eduardo, started reading from a large ledger. At first Harley started translating then gave up, saying, "They're just going over what happened at the last meeting."

"Shouldn't I know about that?" I whispered.

"Well, bearing in mind the last meeting was fifteen years ago I think the moment has probably passed."

Eventually the agenda moved to today's business. "Here we go," whispered Harley.

"Item one," Harley translated. "A request for a hunting licence for a parcel of land somewhere yada yada, blah blah."

"You sure that's what he said?"

Harley tried to suppress a giggle and attracted a disparaging look from Eduardo.

"Item two. A request for an increased allocation of acequia water due to the birth of... It sounded like old goats?

How can you have... no wait, *sheep* and goats. God, his Spanish is awful."

We voted that through.

"Item Three. The widow Gonzalez requests a new wheelchair ramp for her garden. They're discussing it. No funds. Voting it down."

We voted against the widow Gonzalez's request. We also voted against some new books for the library, a seat in the garden of remembrance and a Christmas party for the school. I felt slightly sick.

"Item Twenty One. Formal complaint over the leaking drains from the rainwater runoffs causing damage to... Yada yada yada. Ask for volunteers to fix it. Vote yes."

I was losing the will to live.

"Item Twenty Eight. Formal complaint over the disruption to the local birdlife caused by the wind turbine above the village. Jabber jabber. Big corporation yada yada. No chance in hell, vote no."

And so it went on. The business of the last fifteen years.

"Item Forty Nine. Fund raising for the Town Saint's Day Fiesta. Same old, same old. No funds. Vote no."

Eventually Eduardo struck his gavel another three times and the day's business was consigned to the ledger in great handwritten detail. I felt the whole affair had left me with a bad taste in my mouth and we headed for the Bar Mirador to get rid of the fug.

"Well, that was an eye-opener," I said after half of my beer went down in one.

"It's like it all over," said Harley. "The rural areas are really suffering while the Costas get the money."

"I'm sure it's not that simple, is it?"

"Money goes where money is. Spend eighty million on a new motorway that brings in more German tourist Euros to the beaches or bung a few thousand to a small forgotten village so they can celebrate their Saint's Day. No brainer really."

"But Órgiva seems to have money for their fiestas?"

"That's because they're big and spectacular. Brings in tourist numbers again. Makes it self-funding and then some.

173

But a small village like San Tadeo? Who's going to make the trip up here to watch somebody let off a box of garden fireworks?"

We continued chatting about the inequities of the EU funding machinery but my mind was only half on the conversation. My eyes had been drawn to the front of the Bar Mirador. I replayed my phone conversation with Gerry. I eyed the road leading into the small Plaza. The fountain and the positions of the lampposts. I found myself automatically calculating angles, velocities and camera positions.

"Terry? You listening?"

"What? Oh shit, sorry. Yes."

"I was saying we ought to go up in the mountains for a day. Blow the cobwebs out. I think we both need it?"

"I've got an idea." I grasped her hand. "It's a wild, crazy idea."

"Oh cool! They're the best sort. Does it involve lots of leather and chains?"

"What? No! I mean what? Maybe later. But I've a sort of idea that might help this village." My head swam with half formed and still incoherent thoughts.

"Well if it's not leather and chains what's it about?"

"Windmills," I said, feeling my adrenalin rising. "And car crashes. Come on, I need to do some research."

Chapter Seventeen

Next morning I awoke early, just before the usual explosion of light into the bedroom. I rolled towards Harley and held her for a while. She was still there and she was still real. I pottered into the kitchen and made coffee for both of us. Harley stirred as I took it in to her. She grunted thanks and pulled the sheet over her head.

I sat in the lounge and switched on the laptop. Windows wanted to perform some critical updates so I had to wait fifteen infuriating minutes while it cycled through its processes before it finally congratulated me with a little tune and announced it was now fully updated. I was just grateful Microsoft didn't make fire engines.

A short internet search informed me that the nearby group of wind turbines were installed and run by a huge international conglomerate called Iberviento. A bit more digging and I discovered that one of the giant windmills, the one above San Tadeo, was indeed within the municipal area of the town and had been installed some twelve years previously. I looked into Iberviento a bit more and discovered it was a Spanish company with subsidiaries which counted several well known power companies. The Council had been right, arguing with them would be pointless.

I felt Harley across my shoulder. I turned and we kissed.

"What you doing?" she asked.

"Windmills. You remember at the Council meeting the question about the wind turbine above the village?"

"Yes, they were complaining about the disruption to the birds, weren't they? Didn't have you down as a twitcher."

"I'm not. But I was curious about who owned it and when it was installed. It's a company called Iberviento. They're massive and seem to own half the windmills around Europe."

"I guess they're not worried about a handful of local wildlife then."

"I doubt it. But this was installed during the period the Council was in hiatus."

"Nice try, Terry, but even if they'd been meeting at the time, a company like that is not going to listen to the protests of a Council of octogenarian bird botherers."

"It's not about the birds. It's —"

The sound of a reversing vehicle outside snagged my attention. I grabbed a shirt and shorts and went to see what was happening.

A large white van was edging its way backwards along the drive. Every few metres it had to nudge forwards again to reposition for the narrow track. Eventually it stopped and a couple of men jumped out. It was Paco and his mate. He greeted us with a cheery wave and pulled down the tailgate to expose a pile of what I assumed were my solar panels. They began unloading and Harley made them coffee. I lent a hand. The panels were surprisingly light and we had those piled up alongside the house in a matter of minutes. The batteries on the other hand were very heavy and needed to be shifted down to the little hut. In all it took nearly an hour to unload everything by which time I was drenched in sweat. Paco's mate took the van away and I helped assemble the frames that would hold the panels. We drilled the bolts into the new concrete bed and the aluminium frames were securely fixed in place. The panels clipped easily to the frames and Paco strung the wires like a set of Christmas lights between them.

Paco's mate returned after about half an hour in their smaller van and they set to work digging a trench for the cables to the house. It was all beginning to get a bit too technical for my assistance so Harley and I went inside to make more coffee.

"They don't hang about," I commented.

"Darwin rules," said Harley.

"Huh?"

"There were so many building companies here during the boom that when it all went wrong half of them went pop, most of them Brits. The cheap beer finished off a lot of the rest so the only ones left were mostly the hard workers who are good at their jobs. Darwin."

"Interesting view."

We took the coffees outside. Paco explained he'd be disconnecting the electricity soon to do some work on the wiring and that it would be on and off for the next three hours.

"I need to ask Niki something anyway," I said.

We headed into Órgiva and down into the valley. We found Tina and Niki in their garden, busy spreading netting across rows of plants. I helped secure the netting to the cane stakes.

"Need a little more help with that ledger," I said to Niki when we'd finished.

We sat outside under a cane canopy. I slid the book across the table to her.

"He's suddenly got a thing about windmills," said Harley.

"You remember that bit about tithes and windmills?"

Niki leafed through the aged paper. "This bit?" she said after a few minutes. "Each mill owner is to tithe one libra, that's an old unit of weight, one libra in ten of the produce of the mill. That's a sort of local income tax I assume."

"What's that got to do with anything," asked Harley. "They were talking about windmills milling grain or olive oil. Not these sodding great turbines."

"Doesn't matter," I said. "It's the produce of the mill that's subject to the tithe, not the nature of it."

"And you're going to argue this with Iberviento?" asked Tina.

I sank back in my chair. She was right of course. The turbine may have been installed without the consent of the Council and it may well have a tithe obligation to the municipality but Mayor Eduardo was right. Big corporation, no point in arguing. Yada, yada. They certainly weren't going to listen to me. We drank orange juice and chatted for a while. Later, we headed back home feeling slightly dispirited.

"I'd thought for a moment that I could achieve something," I said as we drove up the hill. "It felt awful just listening to the requests for help. So impotent. Stupid really. I don't know why I thought I should be able to fix anything.

It's probably the same in every small village all over Europe."

"I remember a story about two men on a beach," Harley started. "The beach was littered with thousands of starfish which had been washed up in a storm. As the two men walked and talked, one of them kept picking up starfish and throwing them back into the sea. The other man asked him what he was doing and the man replied that he was saving the life of the starfish. The other man said, what's the point? There's thousands of them. You can't possibly make a difference. The first man picked up another starfish and threw it into the sea. As he did so, he said, 'It made a difference to that one.'"

We completed the rest of the journey in silence.

***

Paco was just clearing up when we arrived back. He told me the batteries had some charge in them but it would take several days for them to come up to full power so to be careful with evening usage. I helped them push the generator into the back of his van and we gathered up the last of his tools. I paid him in cash, no doubt assisting the black economy. Once inside I switched on the lights and music, taking pleasure in the thought it wasn't costing me anything. We took a couple of beers to the veranda.

"I do have another idea," I said.

"Go on," her voice was filled trepidation.

"You know I used to be in the film business? Special effects?"

"You did mention. Blowing things up mostly, I think you said?"

"Yes, well a company I used to do some work with need a location urgently. I think San Tadeo might fit the bill. It would need a bit of dressing... um, cosmetic changes to make it look like the period but I think it would work."

"How does that help? Do they pay lots of money or something?"

"Not a huge amount but it might go towards the fiesta or something. Do you know when it is?"

"Haven't the faintest idea. Haven't seen any posters around."

"Well, if anybody will know it'll be José at the Mirador. Come on, let's go."

The bar was quiet. It was too late for the shoppers yet still too early for the evening meal. We sat outside enjoying the cooling air. We ordered a couple of beers and a light meal of pork loins with patatas pobre. José brought out the drinks.

"You know when the fiesta is?" I asked.

"What fiesta?"

"The big fiesta. The town one." My Spanish was holding up and I felt pleased with myself.

"San Tadeo? Octobre twenty eight."

"Por que..." My Spanish collapsed and I turned to Harley. "Ask him why there's no posters around."

They spoke rapidly for a moment.

"He says everybody knows when it is and nobody comes from outside the town these days anyway."

The conversation continued in a sort of three way manner with Harley translating José when I struggled and finding those Spanish words for me that went beyond level Two of Rosetta Stone.

"How long does it go on for?" I asked.

"It's supposed to be three days but nothing much happens except on the actual day of Saint Jude. It's now just mostly a parade of the Relics."

"Saint Jude?" I queried. "I thought the saint was Saint Tadeo?"

"Saint Tadeo is Saint Jude. Or Judas. The church changed the name so as not to be confused with Judas the betrayer."

I pondered for a moment. "But isn't Saint Jude the patron saint of lost causes?"

José smiled. "We prefer to think of him as the bringer of hope." He disappeared back inside.

A few minutes later our meal arrived and we forked at pieces of garlic covered pork.

"Tell me about this film," Harley said.

"It's one of the 'Who Dares' series."

She paused, fork midway. "But they're huge! That's with Steven Hunter! Wow! Why didn't you say?"

I smiled. "This is just a minor shoot. It's a scene in flashback so Steven won't be here. In the film at that point his character, Charles Tremayne, hadn't even been born. Don't get too excited."

She thought for a while. "It would still be a big thing for the town. Do you think you can swing it?"

"Yes, providing I can convince José to let us trash his bar. And of course the Council."

José appeared with more drinks.

"I'll ask him," Harley said.

"No, wait, I need to –"

Too late, Harley and José were already talking way too fast for me to catch anything other than the gist. I did hear the words 'Who Dares' and 'Steven Hunter' though.

"He wants to know how much they will pay him?"

The three way translated conversation began again.

"Well, they usually make good any damage and pay for loss of business for any days you're closed," I said. "On top of that maybe a couple of thousand Euros. I'll see what I can do for you."

"Damage?" José queried.

I explained they wanted to crash a car through the front of the bar. It would then explode.

"But how?" He stared at his bar. "It will be ruined?"

"No," I said. "It's all special effects, don't worry. We'll take your window out first and change it for a fake one. The explosion is just flash and smoke, no real damage."

He seemed reassured. "I can play the handsome barman," he said with a smile.

"I'll ask if they need one!"

José hurried back inside, no doubt to spread the word that he was going to be a famous film star.

"So, how do you make these explosions without damaging anything?" Harley asked.

"It's to do with the type of explosive," I said. "A bit like fireworks which are designed to give lots of light and colour but low impact. We add a chemical which gives off lots of smoke..." I paused. Something had caught my memory. "Smoke..." I repeated.

"Smoke?" said Harley.

"Yes!" Something was clicking into place. "Smoke, that's it! Smoke and flash-bangs."

"Okay," she said hesitantly. "You said that. Smoke and flashes. I get it."

"No, you don't." My mind was racing. "It's all to do with windmills."

"Windmills?"

"Yes, windmills, flash-bangs. And the starfish."

"Starfish? Have you been at Adam's garden patch?"

"What? No. I might just have an idea. I need to go to Bahía Blanca."

Chapter Eighteen

The morning sun cast stark light over the neatly trimmed hedges and trees of Bahía Blanca.

As we drove through the estate Harley looked with amazement at the houses.

"What's with all the gates?" she asked.

"Paranoid Brits," I said. "They think the natives are going to rise up at any moment."

"They'll be in for a shock when the zombies come then."

I laughed as I visualised Frazer yelling at the zombies to get off his lawn.

As we drove past my villa I noticed a white Mercedes SLR Coupe parked outside on the street. I slowed to a stop alongside it.

"Don't," warned Harley.

"What?"

"I know what you're thinking and it won't do you any good."

I harrumphed and we drove on to the end of the estate.

"Should I wait in the car?" Harley asked.

"No, sod it." I rang the bell on the gate and waited. Clearly the cameras identified we were neither a native uprising nor marauding zombies and the double gates swung open. I edged the Stag up the deep gravel drive and parked it next to Billy's white Range Rover.

The smoked glass front door of the house swung open and Billy appeared.

"Tel!" he called as he approached. "And who's this?" He double kissed Harley, with just a little more familiarity than was normal.

"This is Harley," I said. "She's my... my friend."

"We're lovers," said Harley.

"Fantastic," said Billy, slapping me on the shoulder. "Absolutely fantastic. I heard there'd been a change in your domestic arrangements. Good for you." He ushered us through the hallway and into the rear garden. Harley surveyed the opulence with a sort of wide-eyed horror.

"Have a seat." He pointed to the wicker chairs round a table by the pool. "Ah, here's my precious."

Junie wandered into the garden, her eyes blinking at the sunlight as though she'd just woken.

"Hi, Terry," she said. She gave me an elongated hug. "How are you? I mean really? You know we're here for you." She ran her fingers across my face. "I'm loving the beard!"

I rubbed my chin. "Oh, just haven't got round to shaving for a couple of days."

She turned to Harley and repeated the hug with her. "Darling, lovely to meet you." She moved slightly away from Harley but holding both her hands. "My, though, Terry, she's a lovely little thing isn't she!"

Harley smiled. A carefully controlled smile that could almost be mistaken for a silent growl. She actually gave a little curtsy and I had to suppress a giggle.

"Get some drinks, love," said Billy. He turned to us and asked, "Buck's Fizz?" Then without waiting for an answer he turned to Junie. "There's a couple of bottles of Moet in the larder fridge I think. There's a dear."

We settled in the large cushioned chairs under the shade of a large parasol.

"So," said Billy. "What brings you down out of your mountain?"

"You remember some time ago you asked me about explosions?"

"Oh, yes."

"You said you wanted something showy but harmless? Do you still need it?"

"Sure." Billy leaned forwards, his interest clearly piqued.

"I'm not going to promise but what do you need exactly?"

Junie brought the drinks out along with a tray of canapés. "Isn't this lovely?" she said.

Billy chose a miniature biscuit with some green stuff on the top. He popped it into his mouth. He gestured to us to help ourselves.

"Lots of noise and smoke," he said after a moment. "Bit of a flash. Nobody hurt, nothing like that."

"Where?" I took a sip of my drink.

"On a boat. In Marbella bay."

"You want me to blow up a boat in Marbella Bay?" I was beginning to think this was a mistake. I had visions of some luxury cruiser, probably belonging to somebody he'd fallen out with.

"What? No. Don't want nothing blowing up. It's a..." He thought for a moment, clearly trying to present this in a way he thought I'd find acceptable. "It's a sort of a joke. Bit of a giggle really."

I picked up a tiny piece of toast with what appeared to be tomato ketchup on top and examined it before popping it into my mouth. It tasted salty.

"You've got to tell me a bit more than that, Billy. Who are you playing this...um... joke on?"

"The Coastguard."

"The Coastguard? I don't think the Coastguard are actually known for their sense of humour. Especially when it comes to explosions. And on boats."

"It'll be a laugh," Billy offered. "A bit Jeremy Beadle," he added.

"Why? Why would you want to play a joke on the Coastguard?"

He hesitated then leaned forward slightly as if mindful of being overheard. "I just need them to look the other way for ten minutes or so."

I was beginning to understand. "So you don't actually want a boat blowing up then?"

"No. Just to look like it. Isn't that what you guys do? Lots of noise and flash but no real damage?"

"You want a lot of noise and smoke, big flash, all on a boat in Marbella Bay?"

"That's the job." He emptied his glass in one. "What do you think?"

"Leave it with me."

"So what do you want from me?" he asked.

"What do you mean?"

"Well I'm fairly sure you didn't come all the way here just to do me a random favour now?"

I sipped at my drink while I pondered how to answer. "It's Simon Farrington," I said.

"You want me to send the boys round? He deserves it. Weasel worm. We were talking about it, me and Junie."

"No, I just wondered if you had any influence with him."

"Oh." Billy looked disappointed. "Sure, I have influence with him. Big time. My old dad used to say it's not what you know but who you know is what counts. Well, he was wrong." He popped a strange little sausage into his mouth. "It ain't what you know or who you know. It's who owes who a favour. That's what gets you on today. Who owes you a favour. Just so happens that little maggot owes me a favour. What do you need?"

"I've got a problem with a windmill."

***

We took the coast road back as I needed to stop off in Motril.

"Do you think he can do it?" Harley asked after twenty miles of silence.

"Billy? I have no doubts. Not so sure about Farrington."

"Okay." We fell silent again

We parked in the underground car park in the centre of Motril. A quick tour of a several pharmacies, three different hardware shops and a garden centre provided me with all the equipment I needed. Fortunately Spain was somewhat more lax over the sale of certain items than England. Oddly, it was the cell phone that caused most problems and it took several shops before I could buy one without having to give my real identity. We stopped off for a coffee at a busy bar and watched the world go about its normal business as I gathered my thoughts.

Simple job really. I had all the bits I needed, Billy had assured me a quiet place and plenty of time to set the charge and I didn't even have to worry about camera angles. No problem. Easy. Walk in the park.

"What's up?" asked Harley.

"Huh?"

"You look worried."

"Oh, just working it through. You know, going over the details."

"You don't have to do this," she said. "San Tadeo will survive. It's been there for eight hundred years so it's probably good for a few more yet."

"It's the right thing to do."

"The right thing? Blowing up a boat and blackmailing a politician? The right thing?"

"I know. But sometimes a man –"

"Don't start getting all John Wayne on me," she interrupted. "Or I'm going to..." she struggled for a suitable threat. "I'll set Sancho on you." She poked the dozing puppy under the table. "Kill, Sancho, kill."

"It'll be fine," I said. "Always did get a bit twitchy before a job."

***

"Podría estar en el coche con Steven."

"What did he say?" asked Ray.

The meeting room at the town hall was heaving, Word had got around that a big film was being shot in the area. We sat again at the table on the raised platform at the end of the hall. Ray Howard, Location Scout for Darkspace Films, sat at the far end of the table facing the rest of the Council.

"He said he wants to ride in the car with Steven Hunter," translated Harley.

Ray gave a controlled sigh then said, "Can you please explain again that Mister Hunter will not actually be here?"

Harley explained to Eduardo that this was just a minor scene set sixty years before the main action.

Eduardo looked puzzled for a moment then shrugged and jabbered rapidly with the man next to him.

"What's going on?" I whispered to Harley.

"I don't know, they're speaking way too quickly."

Somebody shouted from the audience.

"What's going on?"

"Somebody wants to know if everybody in the town gets a free cinema ticket."

Eduardo spoke again.

"He says his granddaughter is an actress," said Harley. "Apparently she could be Steven Hunter's fiancée."

"Oh, for heaven's sake," said Ray. He looked at Harley, "Don't translate that."

Harley smiled.

An elderly man in the audience stood and started singing; he actually had a very good voice. His wife pulled him back into his seat to a round of applause from the crowded room.

The Guardia Civil officer standing by the door raised his arms and spoke loudly and with exaggerated clarity above the noise. The room quietened and the officer turned to the platform and gave a beaming smile.

Ray looked at me. "Are we getting anywhere?" he asked, almost pleadingly.

"Bear with it," I said.

After another hour of arguing and spontaneous auditions we finally had an agreement from the Council that the town could be used for the filming. Ray had conceded to the conditions that Eduardo's name appeared in the credits and his granddaughter was seen in the background.

After all the hands had been shaken and the papers signed, Harley, Ray and I adjourned to Bar Mirador.

"Sorry about that," I said. "I don't know how it got out."

"No problem," Ray said. "Thanks for your help. We were in deep shit there when the Rumanians threw their toys out of the pram. I owe you one."

Billy's words came back to me. *"It's not what you know or who you know. It's who owes you. That's what counts."*

"Now you mention it," I said. "There is something you can do."

"Name it. You just saved my neck."

"What's the chances of getting Steven out here for a visit?"

Ray supped thoughtfully on his beer. "I'll have a word with him when I get back."

Chapter Nineteen

Marbella is not a place in which I would want to live. It reminded me too much of Los Angeles with its wide boulevards, expensive cars and even more expensive marinas. Billy had paid for a hotel for us for the night. It was set one level back from the sea front and a short walk from Puerto Banus.

We'd arrived early in the day and wandered the area to do the tourist bit. Although I'd been used to dripping opulence in some of the locations in which I'd worked this display of excess seemed all the more disturbing since my relocation to San Tadeo. Andalucía has forty percent unemployment yet there were shops here selling handbags for more than I'd paid for my house.

Harley stalled outside a tanning shop. "What the hell is that doing here?" she exclaimed. "It's thirty five degrees outside with a sun that could fry eggs and they put a tanning parlour here. The world's gone mad."

We stopped for a drink at a bar overlooking the marina. The sun glinted off the sea, forcing me to squint. The luxury yachts bobbed gently at their berths and a mixture of tourists and maintenance crew mingled on the piers. The nearby parking bays sported Ferraris, Lamborghinis and Maseratis. No humble Porches or Jaguars here. People strolled past as we sat. A peculiar mix of the super rich, the wannabes with their fake Rolexes and the locals going about their business.

I eyed the harbour. Billy had arranged for the boat I was to use to be moored in the small fishing harbour further down. Just a simple dinghy. The idea was that I set the charge, tow it out into the bay with another dinghy and let it loose. Billy had the phone number of the cell phone that would trigger the charge when he was ready. Big flash, lots of noise and smoke but only enough explosive power to blow a hole in the bottom of the boat, sinking the evidence. Simple. How could that possibly go wrong?

"Look there," Harley jerked me back. She was pointing at somebody just climbing out of a gullwing Mercedes. "He's just a child. How the hell can he afford something like that?"

"Probably chose his parents well."

We headed back to the hotel and I pulled my rucksack from under the bed. I laid out the components on the bed and assembled it all, with the exception of the phone. I'd connect that at the last minute.

"And that's it?" Harley asked. "That's all it is?"

"That's it," I said and carefully slid the bag back under the bed.

The hotel offered what seemed like every television channel in the world. We settled on a movie. It was some CGI heavy epic starring a fading WWE wrestler as a Greek warrior. It drifted into the background as I kept going over what I was about to do. Eventually the sky darkened and it was time to go to work.

The two dinghies were moored exactly where Billy had said they'd be. I waited until nobody was around then slipped the mooring, letting them drift out away before I started the motor. Harley watched me from the dock until she faded into the night. My seafaring skills were about on a par with those of Crocodile Dundee but all I needed to do was to head out into the middle of the bay. I was probably a good mile out when a huge black shape cut across me. The noise of my own little outboard had completely drowned out the low thrub of the floating gin palace as it ploughed through the water in front of me, leaving the glow of phosphorescence on the water and the sound of drunken laughter in my ears.

I cut the engine and made the tricky transition into the sacrificial boat. By the light of my small torch I completed the final connections and switched on the cell phone. All was well and I was just about to hop back across to the other boat when the cruiser circled round again. I froze and cut the torch. Had they seen me? The sound of laughter from on board told of teenagers and copious amounts of alcohol. A steady boom-boom from their music system drowned out the sound of the engines. Girlish squeals and splashing indicated probably pool games going on up top. I stayed still until they swept past. I had to cut loose now. The explosive device was live and I had no idea when Billy would trigger it, nor any way of contacting him. I certainly didn't want to be in the vicinity when it went off. I scrambled across to the other boat, mindful that the phone could ring at any moment. I slipped the rope holding the two boats together and they drifted apart. I was about to start the engine when the cruiser swung back towards me. What the hell were they doing? Whoops of champagne fuelled revelry broke the night as the cruiser cut between my boat and the little dinghy with the device. Shit! I waited until the cruiser had gone past then scanned the dark waters for the little dinghy. Nowhere. I risked the torched and threw the light all around where it had been before the boat had separated us. Nothing. The idiots must have sunk it. I cut the torch. I couldn't risk being caught out here. Okay this was a bollocks up. Billy was out there somewhere doing whatever the hell it was he was up to and I really didn't want to know about and any minute now he'd dial the phone and nothing would happen.

I wondered if I could quickly rig up some way of exploding the petrol in the outboard motor. I had petrol and I could adapt the spark plug to ignite it but there was no safe way of triggering it. I would have to be on top of it and that was not a good idea. I went through my pockets looking for something I could use. Anything. I had the torch, my own mobile phone. Could I ring Harley and get her to ring my phone back? It might work if I could just –

The explosion cut through the air like a thunder flash. The brilliant light cut at my eyes, leaving a retinal image of the cruiser against the light. What the hell? I stared at the boat. It was between me and the marina. The squeals of drunken exuberance had turned to shrieks of terror as clouds of luminous smoke billowed across the decks. Searchlights from the bridge raked the water as some of the partygoers jumped into the sea in panic.

It took me a few moments to realise what had happened. When the cruiser had cut between me and the dinghy it had either been swept along in the wash or it had caught on something. Either way the boat had taken my little floating bomb with it. When the signal had come the dinghy had exploded right up against the hull of the cruiser. It wouldn't have done any damage other than flashing the paintwork a bit but the chaos it had caused was epic. The cruiser started sounding its warning horns and every light blazed across its decks. The crew rapidly launched their own dinghy to search for the idiots who had panicked and jumped overboard. I used the still evolving chaos to start my own engine. I paused, wondering if I should go over to assist but figured the crew of the cruiser would have it all in hand and anyway the coastguard would probably be on their way. I headed back to the dock from where I had set out. At least from where I thought I'd set out but my navigational skills betrayed me and I ended up in a group of fishing boats. I tied up the boat and went n search of Harley. I found her about fifty metres further along the dock.

"What the hell happened?" she said. "Was that all your doing?"

"Yup, all me. Give me a hand. I need you to hold this torch at the place where this is supposed to be." I pointed at the dinghy. "Can't leave it here."

I took the boat back out again and guided it back to where we had started. I tied it up and swept the torch over it, checking I'd left nothing behind. All clear.

We made our way round to the marina to gain a clearer view of the unfolding drama. A huge coastguard cutter had come to assist. Massive searchlights swept the water looking for swimmers, its horns blaring and loudspeakers shouting instructions. Divers jumped into the water to assist someone who was having a screaming fit. We watched for a while longer then slid away from the gathering crowds.

"Well, that should do the job," said Harley.

"Hmm, not bad, Even if I do say so myself."

***

We raided the hotel mini bar, courtesy of Billy and rolled onto the bed in a fury of adrenaline fuelled passion. As we lay dozing in the tangled sheets the phone rang. I grunted into it.

"Hey, Terry," greeted the sound of Billy's voice. "Nice one. Love what you did with the yacht. Nice touch."

"Well, it was," I started then thought again. "It was quite complicated to pull off but I thought it would add to the fun."

"You're a diamond. Don't fancy another little job in Monte Carlo do you?"

"No! No thank you. I'm officially retiring. Just got one more bang to do then that's it."

"Shame, never mind. Stay there as long as you like. All on me. They owe me one."

"Thanks but we'll head back in the morning. Got some stuff to sort."

We ordered pizza from room service and settled down with a movie.

The morning brought a strong desire to escape Marbella. We cleared up any trace of ourselves and set off up the motorway and within two hours we were home in the peace and quiet of Casa de las Estrellas. We threw off our clothes and relaxed on the veranda, soaking in the view.

I fetched the bottle of Alejandro's homemade whisky. "I thought we might try this to celebrate."

I poured a drop in each of two glasses and sniffed. "Seems okay." I handed one to Harley.

She took her glass and sipped cautiously. "So, do you think that Farrington can pull it off?"

"I'm betting on it. I don't think upsetting Billy would be a good choice for him." I tasted the whiskey. It wasn't a Speyside but it had a certain charm. A hint of oranges?

"And you think Iberviento are going to listen to a scumbag MEP like him?"

"I guess we'll find out. It's the only hope, they're certainly not going to listen to local councillors. It depends on what leverage he has. The EU is responsible for funding a lot of these wind farms."

The whiskey left a distinct glow as it traced the route past my oesophagus. Not unpleasant.

Harley swirled her glass. "What do you think it's made of?"

I finished my glass. "Oranges, I think." I poured us both a refill. It tasted smoother with each sip.

"Very clever," said Harley.

"What is?"

"Orange whiskey. Orange whiskey is very clever. Not clever like Stephen Hawking of course. I mean he's *really* clever but for whiskey this is very clever."

I studied my glass for a moment. "I wonder what he was up to?"

"Usually sorting out black holes."

"Huh? No, not Stephen Hawking. I meant Billy. I wonder what Billy was up to. I know what Stephen Hawking does. I've got his book." This whiskey was really rather good.

Harley giggled. "I don't think Billy does black holes."

"I assume whatever he was up to involved a boat sneaking in from over the Med," I said.

"Hmm," Harley swirled the whiskey round her glass then finished it in one. "Boat coming in from North Africa? I wonder what that could possibly be?"

"Could be harmless." I topped up both glasses. "Could be... kaftans?"

"Or those nice dangly things, you know, they hang them from the ceiling," said Harley.

"Light bulbs?"

She burst into a fit of giggles. "No. You know, those feathery things. Dream catchers, that's the thing. Dream catchers."

"Dream catchers? They're Indian, not North African."

She pondered for a moment. "Oh, yes."

Laughter overtook us both. Possibly the release of the tension of the last twenty four hours, possibly the whiskey. We cuddled together and Sancho pushed himself up against my feet. It felt like home.

Chapter Twenty

I spent the next few days lining up the car crash effect. Darkspace Films had secured the licence for the explosives to be shipped to me directly so there was no need to scour Motril a second time. I used local craftsmen where possible and they built a replacement frontage for the bar, one which would disintegrate in a realistic manner but without structural damage to the building. I also commissioned them to be ready for a full repair job at the end of shooting. They built some dummy tables and chairs for the outside and a polystyrene bar that perfectly replicated the marble topped one in the Mirador. A couple of days later Katie, the Production Designer, arrived to begin transforming the Plaza area into an authentic 1940s Austrian village. As I'd thought, there wasn't a huge amount of background work to be done. Only one satellite dish to hide and some modern lighting to alter. Some of the windows needed false frontages and signage replaced but all in all she was pleasantly relieved to find the job fairly straightforward. With two days to spare before the film crew arrived the front of the Plaza was ready. I worked with Trevor, the stunt driver, for a day working out angles and timings. The script called for a series of bullets to go through the windscreen of a Citroen van and for it to career off the road, across the corner of the Plaza and into the bar. An explosion in the front of the van was supposed rip the bar apart.

All was set.

The next morning we were having coffee outside when I heard a car arrive. Sancho barked furiously. It was Eduardo from the Council. He talked excitedly at me and waved an envelope in my face. I called Harley over to translate.

"They've had a letter from Iberviento. They're sending a representative over to meet with the Council."

"When?" I asked.

A short interchange between Harley and Eduardo in which I thought I heard him say it was today.

"Today," said Harley.

"That's a bit short notice?"

"Apparently they sent the letter last week. It's only just got here." She noticed my expression and shrugged. "The Spanish postal service is like God, they both do things in their own time."

Eduardo ensured I understood that I was to be in the Council room at four then hurried off.

We stood and watched his little car tumble down the track in a cloud of dust.

"Well," she said. "That's a turn up. What do you think?"

"It looks like Farrington has stirred something up. The question is, what?"

"Maybe he's upset them and they've come to take their windmill back!"

***

The town Council meeting room was packed. These were fast becoming essential local events. Despite the brave efforts of the little notices everywhere the room drifted with smoke. A bottle of Lanjarón water and a carafe of red wine graced the head table. The representative from Iberviento sat at the far end of the table, in the interrogation position. He wore a white shirt and beige trousers. A pair of gold rimmed glasses perched on his hawk like nose. He played nervously with a gold pen.

We waited for people to stop packing into the room and then for everybody to stop swapping seats. After ten minutes the Guardia Civil officer pushed the big double doors closed against the stragglers and Eduardo banged his gavel. He called out the names of the Council members present and introduced Señor Ricardo Hidalgo, who suggested we referred to him simply as Ricardo.

"Señor Hidalgo has important communications from Iberviento," announced Eduardo.

Somebody in the audience shouted something about birds. I couldn't catch enough to understand but I didn't need Harley to translate for me.

Another man shouted something which I didn't understand and Harley told me he was convinced the mill's vibrations were driving rats into his goat sheds.

"Que es la cantidad crítica de los molinos que está causando una perturbación cósmica." I looked to see Adam standing at the back. He continued in what to me seemed fluent Spanish. When he'd finished I turned to Harley.

"He's complaining that the vibrations are causing a cosmic disturbance in the consciousness of the universe or something," she said.

Hidalgo looked unconcerned although slightly puzzled as the complaints against his windmills mounted. Eventually he turned to Eduardo and gave an almost imperceptible gesture to cut this short. Eduardo banged his gavel and shouted for order. The Guardia Civil officer from the back repeated the command. The room quietened.

Hidalgo started talking, I followed bits but a lot seemed complicated and technical. Harley translated the highlights. "He's explaining what a wonderful company Iberviento is. They've given a free windmill to a village in Kenya... They pay millions in tax for the benefit of Spain's citizens... They're saving the planet from oil dependence... Employ local people who would otherwise not be able feed their children and have to sell them into slavery... Help old ladies across the road –"

"You're making that up," I challenged.

"I lost interest halfway through," she said. "It's all bollocks anyway. How wonderful the big corporation, now let's all sing the company song."

Eduardo clapped as Hidalgo paused. One person in the audience followed suit. Eduardo clapped more loudly and nodded towards the room, his eyebrows threatening. Gradually the room rippled with subdued applause.

Hidalgo smiled graciously and held up his hand for silence. He continued speaking.

"Now he's on about how they support local communities. Why are we listening to this rubbish?"

"Stay with it. I think he's leading up to something."

"They recognise the strength of rural culture and feel that

as a responsible partner in this planet's welfare... Can I stab him yet?"

"Give him a moment. I think he's building up to something but this has to be their idea and they can't be seen to bow to external influence."

"In looking to see how we can better support the communities who have shown us their joint commitment and concern for the environment we have found some situations where some communities have demonstrated greater awareness for our mission goals and supported our targets in conservation and for this reason we are committed to return that support and as a responsible partner in the planet we offer our thanks to the people of San Tadeo." He paused to take a drink.

"Well that's what he said," said Harley as she took a welcome break from the translation while the crowd mumbled. "But what does he mean? It's all just nonsense words."

"It means somebody has leaned on them," I said.

Hidalgo started again, "We are aware of an agreement between our company and your proud community that started when you graciously allowed us to install one of our prototype turbines for evaluation. We can say now we have tested the machine and analysed the data which conforms with our expected results; therefore we can now ratify our agreement with this great and forward thinking community. From today we will be donating free of charge and as a gesture of the cooperation between us ten percent of the electricity generated by the turbine that is located within the boundaries of your great town."

"Huh?" queried Harley.

"He means it's been pointed out that they should have been paying out ten percent since the mill was installed," I said. "It also means they thought they could get away with it until somebody somewhere reminded them of it."

The room was silent for a moment then as if by some secret signal everybody began talking at once. Eduardo and his two fellow Councillors huddled into a bundle of rapid jabber that neither Harley nor I could even begin to comprehend. They seemed unconcerned that I'd been sidelined. Hidalgo kept his corporate smile firm as he gathered his papers then left the room without a word. The Guardia Civil officer held the door open for him then closed it as he left.

"What's all that mean?" Harley asked.

"These big turbines can kick out over two megawatts each. Enough to run around a thousand average houses." I thought for a moment then, "These houses round here? Maybe fifteen hundred. Ten percent of that... a hundred and fifty houses. If that's what they decide to do. What's the population here? Any idea?"

"Not a clue. Five hundred? A thousand?"

The meeting gradually broke up and we went home.

We sat on the veranda nursing beers and watching the valley fall into evening shade.

We chinked our beer cans together. "Result," Harley said.

"Result," I agreed.

Chapter Twenty One

By the morning of the shoot the townspeople had all gathered behind the barriers and they watched as Trevor, the stunt driver, took several dry runs, stopping just short of the bar. They gave a round of applause to each run. On one occasion Trevor climbed out of the car and gave an exaggerated bow to the people. They applauded more loudly.

I scanned the Plaza. Although I was really only responsible for the bullet strikes and the explosion I felt an obligation towards the rest of the proceedings as it was my location and I'd become the unofficial Fixer. I noticed a raised platform at the far end of the Plaza. I assumed it was in preparation for the fiesta in just over a week's time. The dolly tracks had been laid around the edge of the Plaza and the Grip had erected the platforms for the cameras.

By ten o'clock the crowds were becoming disturbingly large. Clearly word had spread around the nearby towns and villages. A group of about thirty cyclists arrived, many of whom were abusing the very concept of Lycra. We were scheduled to commence shooting at two as the light would be coming in at the right angles for our needs. I needed to set the charges on the car and the growing chaos in the Plaza didn't lend itself to dealing with delicate explosives, no matter how small they were. I suggested taking the car down to my house for a bit of peace and quiet. I led the way for Trevor in the stunt car. As we left the village I noticed an enterprising individual had opened up a nearby field as an impromptu car park. A big hand painted sign announced a five euro charge. There was already a long queue of cars snaking down the hill. We pulled into my track and parked outside the house.

"You been selling tickets, you old bugger?" Trevor pulled himself free of the stunt car. Not an easy task as the doors were welded shut and a roll cage took up much of the interior.

"Man's got to subsidise his lifestyle somehow," I answered. "Beer doesn't grow on trees."

Harley brought chilled orange juice and I set to work placing the charges. Tiny shaped explosive pellets were secured across the windscreen and side panels. When triggered they would give the effect of machine gun fire tracing the windscreen and side of the car. Small charges were placed on the clips holding the bonnet in place and the main charge was set just behind the radiator grill. That was the big, showy flash bang that would hopefully seem like a full explosion. I checked the time, midday just gone, time to move the car to the start of the run-up position. We'd chosen a small cut a half mile outside of town. Just time for Trevor to bring the speed up to exactly 25mph and ensure everything was true before driving into the Plaza. We drove to the end of my track and that's when we hit the traffic queue. Cars, vans and trucks were nose to tail going up the hill at the end of my track, Or rather, they weren't going. It was a jam that made the August Bank Holiday seaside run down the M5 seem like a drive in the country. Both sides of the road were gridlocked and some people had abandoned their cars on the verges.

I got out of my car and walked over to Trevor in the stunt car behind me. "I think we might have a bit of a problem," I said.

"You reckon?"

"We've got a bit of leeway, we'll try to wait it out. Not much else we can do."

"I'm not happy about taking a fully prepped car into that lot." He nodded towards the queue.

"Me neither but there's not much else we can do."

I got back into my car. "We could be here a while," I said to Harley.

"We could walk?" she suggested.

"We could, but Trevor can't. Without that car there's no shoot."

I eased forwards until the nose of the Stag was nudged between a white Fiat and an old Suzuki Vitara. I waved an acknowledgement at the Suzuki driver. We sat for fifteen minutes then all of a sudden we started to move. I watched in the mirror as Trevor eased into the line behind me. We inched painfully slowly up the hill, both sides of the road holding level, I pitied anybody wanting to go down the hill against this wave of vehicles. It was now nearly one o'clock and we were eating into our contingency time. The traffic moved forwards a bit faster and we approached the field being used as a car park. I tried to pull across to the other side of the road to avoid being swept into the field but was greeted by a cacophony of horns and shouts. I had nowhere to go but forwards into the field. I watched in the mirror as Trevor was forced to follow. A man in a dayglo vest waved me to stop then demanded five euros before he would let me pass. Harley tried explaining we were part of the film crew but that had no effect. We parted with five euros and drove to the far end of the field, hoping to find a way out up there. The top end of the field was as clogged as the rest and eventually we both parked up in the nearest gaps we could find.

"Well, this is a right bollocks up," Trevor said. "Exploding car trapped in crowded car park. What could possibly go wrong with that?"

"Give Eduardo a ring," I handed my phone to Harley. "See if he can do anything."

Within ten minutes we had two Guardia Civil cars with full sirens and lights escorting us out of the field and up the road once more. We reached the spot designated as the start point but of course it was now full of cars and the road around clogged. We managed to persuade the Guardia Civil officers to cordon of a different section of the road as a start point but we now had less distance to run up and time was getting short. I left Trevor in the stunt car and walked up to the Plaza. We had ten minutes before the scheduled shoot start and everything was set. We might just pull it off yet. The Guardia Civil pushed the crowds clear of the filming area and adjusted the barriers. I held the walkie talkie in one hand and the remote control for the explosives in the other. A familiar calm descended. I'd done everything I could, all was in the preparation and at this point it was too late to change anything. Explosions can't be unexploded nor cars uncrashed. This really would be the last time I'd do this. Time now to relax and enjoy the fun.

"Terry!" I heard somebody call. It was Clive, the Location Director. "What the hell am I supposed to do with her?" He pointed towards a young girl dressed in full flamenco finery and standing in front of the bar.

"Ask the Guardia to move her?" I suggested.

"She says you told her she could be in the film."

"What? She must be..." Oh hell, I remembered. Eduardo's granddaughter. I'd completely forgotten about her.

"Hang on," I yelled over to Clive. "I'll deal with it." I hurried over to the girl.

"Are you Steven Hunter?" she asked.

"No, he's not here today." She looked crestfallen. "Come on, we need to find you something better to wear."

"But my mother made this especially."

"It's lovely, but not really 1940s Austria." I looked around frantically.

My walkie talkie chirped. I stabbed the talk button. "Trevor? All okay?"

"You tell me. We're five minutes late and the engine's running."

We had a very small amount of fuel in the car as a precaution against fire. Just enough to do the job with a very small margin. "Turn it off," I said. "Slight delay."

"What now?"

"Mayor's granddaughter."

"Oh, that one. Okay, yell when ready. I'll stand down."

My eyes lighted on Harley. She was dressed as usual in a casual wrap and little else. I beckoned her over. "I need your dress."

"You'll look good in it," she said. "But couldn't it wait till later?"

"What? Oh, yes." My mind went to other places which weren't exactly helpful. "I mean I need to borrow it... Not for me... for..." My eyes scraped the crowd and I ran to retrieve the girl from a candyfloss stall. "Her," I said as I pushed her in front of Harley. "Mayor's granddaughter."

"Oh, yes, of course. I'd forgotten."

"Look at her. She can't be on film like that. It's supposed to be 1940s Austria not 1970s Benidorm."

The walkie talkie crackled. "What?" I yelled into it.

"How's it going? We got the go yet?"

"Two minutes. Promise." I clicked it off and looked at Harley. "Can you... I don't know. Can you do something with her?"

"And what am I supposed to wear?" Harley said.

I looked at the two of them. "You're about the same size," I said.

"You can't be serious." She looked the girl up and down. "Really?"

"Sorry," I said. "I don't have any choice. We promised Eduardo."

"You owe me," she said and took the girl off into the back of the bar.

Something was happening over on the platform at the opposite end of the Plaza. It looked like a brass band setting up.

Harley reappeared. She was wearing the garish red polka dot flamenco dress. "Most becoming," I said. "I'm putting that one in the fantasy bank for later."

She laughed. "Well, maybe later. But you owe me big time for this."

At least the girl looked less noticeable now. Not really in keeping with either place or period but she might disappear into the background. Until the IMDB trivia hunters spotted her of course, but I can't help that now. I sat her at one of the outside tables and told her to stay put. The tracking shot would pick her up. Momentarily.

I clicked the walkie talkie. "Stand by. Going in two." We were now twenty minutes behind schedule but the light was holding.

I scanned the scene. All looked okay. Everybody was in their place, the cameras were ready and the fire crew standing by. The director watched me intently, waiting for me to give the signal to Trevor. I put the walkie talkie to my mouth just as the band started to play. A raucous noise of amateur enthusiasm over musicianship. I stared at the platform. Eduardo was beaming with the pride of a father over a new born baby as the band abused their instruments with what was probably supposed to be an anthem. Maybe the town's anthem?

I spoke into the walkie talkie. "Stand down. Slight problem."

"What?" yelled Trevor. "I can't hear you. What's that racket?"

"Stand down," I repeated.

We waited what seemed an eternity for the band to finish. For a moment all was quiet and I spoke into the mouthpiece once more. "Hang on, Trev. I think we might be there."

"Better get a move on. I'll get a bloody parking ticket if I sit here much longer."

"Okay," I said. "Stand by." I heard the engine start from the little speaker. "Stand by," I repeated.

The sound of loudspeaker feedback squealed through the PA system on the stage. What the hell was going on now?

Eduardo shuffled to the centre of the stage. He tapped the microphone repeatedly causing more feedback. "Hola. Hola," he shouted into the microphone.

The director looked over at me with an exaggerated querulous expression. I shrugged and shook my head.

Eduardo continued shouting into the microphone but the howl-back and distortion along with his own particular brand of Spanish made it impossible for me to follow.

"What's he saying?" I asked Harley, trying hard not to look at her in the flamenco dress. It disturbed me.

"He says this is a great day for San Tadeo. A triumph for the office of the mayor that he brings such note to our community. Need me to carry on?"

"No, I get the idea. Let's hope he keeps it short." I scanned the sky.

Eduardo continued with his speech, drawing the occasional applause.

"Hang on," said Harley. "He's onto something else now. Meeting with the directors of Iberviento... What's he up to? Demanded they acknowledge his position as a leader of this great town yada yada. After long consultations with the Council –"

"What consultations were those I wonder?" I said.

"Shush, this is hard enough without your warbling. He forced Iberviento to donate electricity to the community. Oh this is good. Apparently this is all his doing as a great leader."

"Franco would be so proud."

Harley giggled then continued translating. "He's secured free electricity for all households with occupants aged over sixty or with small children... and the sick. Okay, that's actually quite cool. Starts next month after the fiesta. Also Iberviento are paying for all the electricity for the fiesta. Not bad."

"Got to give it to him," I said. "He knows how to play to an audience."

Eduardo sat down to a loud and for once, a very sincere applause. He beamed with pride. The noise subsided and everybody's attention returned to the film set. The director looked at me expectantly.

I scanned the scene. Nobody in the way, everything in position. I clicked the walkie talkie to speak.

"Go, go, go," I said with relief.

"Can't," Trevor said through the tinny speaker.

"Why?"

"I've run out of fucking petrol."

***

Half an hour later and the sun was moving, threatening to cast shadows over critical areas of the set. The Guardia Civil officer had secured petrol and rushed it to the stunt car. I'd had a quick word with Eduardo and in amongst some congratulations for his coup I managed to secure his assurance there would be no more disturbances.

Trevor's voice crackled at me. "We're fuelled up again and good to go here."

I looked once more around me. The director watched me carefully. I nodded to him and he ran up the cameras.

"Trev?"

"Yes?"

"Go, go, go."

A few seconds later the car drove into the Plaza at what seemed a breakneck speed but in reality was only 25mph. Just as it approached the edge of the pedestrian area I twisted the first control button, setting off the small charges across the windscreen. They exploded with small puffs of dust but very little sound. The Foley Artist would add that later. The car veered as if the driver had been shot and I heard a murmur from the crowd just as it smashed into the fake glass frontage, spilling chairs and tables in its wake. It crashed into the polystyrene bar which crumbled satisfyingly and parts of the ceiling collapsed onto it. The instant the car came to a halt I twisted the second control and a huge flash erupted from the front of the car, throwing the bonnet clear of the engine and flames leapt skyward amidst a cloud of smoke. We waited for what seemed an age then the director yelled, "Cut!" and the fire crew ran into the building, extinguishing the flames instantly. I waited with breath held as I always did until Trevor leapt out of the car and threw himself spread eagled on the ground. The fire crew covered him in foam. His suit hadn't caught but it was standard practise to act as if it had. Once Trevor had been given the all clear from the fire crew he walked from the wrecked bar and pulled his helmet off. The crowd erupted into spontaneous applause and the band struck up once more.

"Wow," I heard Harley say. "What a rush."

"It is a bit cool, isn't it?" I acknowledged and wrapped my arm around her shoulder.

Trevor came over and shook my hand. "Nice one, Terry. Up to your usual standard."

"Nice driving, Trev. We got there in the end."

Chapter Twenty Two

The repair crew had moved in as soon as the film crew started putting away their cameras and by the next day, the Bar Mirador was open for business once more. Harley and I sat at one of the tables and watched the rest of the clean up in action. False window fronts came down and disguises were lifted from in front of TV aerials and the satellite dish. The 1940s signage had been snatched long before by souvenir hunters along with any little bits of the fake bar front they could find. At the same time as the clean up was in progress, preparations were also underway for the three day fiesta to celebrate the town's patron saint, Saint Thaddaeus, or Saint Jude as he was also known. The Plaza sprouted lights of all descriptions from every available point. The town was clearly going to take full advantage of Iberviento's offer to pay for all the electricity for the fiesta.

"You know this fiesta is going to be huge, don't you?" Harley said.

"I hope so," I said. "They deserve it."

"And you're sure Steven Hunter will come?"

"Oh, he'll come alright. He's a genuinely nice guy. When Ray explained what was happening here he jumped at it. Of course, it won't do his profile any harm either." The beer tasted good and the sun warmed me through. Sancho nudged my leg in hopeful expectation of any escaping tapas. I think I felt more at peace than I had ever done before.

"You know nobody will ever talk to you again if he doesn't show, don't you?" Harley said.

"That is not a particular concern," I said. "Might be nice in fact, I think I'm talked out. It's the wicker man I'm worried about."

"Or the zombies?"

"Or the zombies," I conceded.

"I spoke to Marco the other day."

"Marco?"

"Marco, the guy I model for sometimes. Remember I mentioned him before? He said he'd help you start your painting if you fancied."

I pondered for a moment. "Mmm, might be an idea. When did you have in mind?"

"Thought we'd pop down tomorrow. Nothing else happening, is there?"

"No, sounds good. I'll get my painting kit together."

***

Marco's studio was a small, airy room perched on top of his house high on the Cerro Negro just outside Órgiva. Large open windows faced all sides and gave views over the Guadalfeo Valley. Marco was a tall slim man with a three day beard and dark hair. He wore a white cotton shirt and trousers. Four women and one man sat at easels facing a central cushioned raised platform. They were clearly English and chatted like old friends. They all greeted Harley and she introduced me as her partner. We exchanged names which I instantly forgot, apart from Titania as it was an unusual name and suited her fey appearance and Graham, as he was the only man.

"Ooh, lovely. We have a man!" said one of the women.

"Are you going to model for us? That would make a change."

"No, I'm here to learn to paint. Harley's going to model." I looked desperately to Harley. "Aren't you?"

"That was the idea," she said. "But if they'd rather paint a male for a change..."

"What? No, I don't think so. I couldn't do that. We'll stick to the plan."

Marco looked me up and down. "You would paint well though. Very interesting bone structure."

"No, it's not happening."

"You wouldn't have to be nude," said Marco. "Not if it makes you uncomfortable."

"Oh, that would be a shame," said the dark haired woman.

She eyed me up and down. "He looks like he's got an interesting body."

"And unfair. After all, Harley does it."

"Oh, come on," a middle aged blonde woman said. "It's been a long time since we've had a man."

"Speak for yourself," said Graham. Everybody laughed.

Two more women came in. They stopped when they saw me with Harley.

"Oh," said one of them. "Double models. How wonderful."

"No, it's just Terry today," Harley said. "I'm going to have a go at painting for a change."

I gaped at Harley. "Traitor!"

"Not shy, are you?" she goaded.

"No... Yes... What if... you know..."

"You were alright with Nicki and Tina?"

"That was different. We were all... you know."

"Don't be daft. You'll be fine. And it wouldn't matter anyway." She smiled mischievously. "They can always get more paint."

Marco took my upper arm and led me to the dais. "I was thinking Salviati's Reclining Male."

"We could do Michelangelo's David," said a dark haired woman. "I've always liked that."

And the suggestions continued.

"How about The Discus Thrower?"

"Don't be daft, we haven't got a discus."

"We could always use a plate."

"Rodin's Thinker would be good."

Marco looked at me. "What would you suggest, Terry?"

"Man Running Away?" I offered.

"I think we'll do Reclining Male." He tested my biceps. "I'm not sure you could hold a discus raised for very long."

I felt I should be insulted but I feared he might be right. "Reclining sounds good," I said.

He organised some cushions on the dais and asked me to lay back on them. He arranged me so I was resting on my left arm. I was supposed to be looking over my left shoulder but that was too uncomfortable so he allowed me to look forwards instead. When he'd decided on the position he suggested I disrobe and pointed to a side room I could use. It seemed odd to go somewhere private to take my clothes off only to come back naked but I complied. The side room was just a small storage cupboard but there was a hook on which to hang my clothes. I padded from the room naked, trying hard not to look at anybody. Harley whispered something as I passed her but I couldn't quite catch it. I settled on the dais and assumed the position on which Marco had decided.

I heard a bit of nervous giggling from a couple of the women.

"Never persuade my Alan to do that."

"I never even see my husband naked."

More giggles and Marco gave a little clap to bring order. He came over to me and rearranged my right arm and left leg. I tried very hard to ignore what was happening and focused on Harley. She winked at me and I forced a smile.

"Now then, ladies, and Graham," Marco said, "It takes courage to pose naked for an art class. Please be appreciative."

"Oh, we're appreciative alright!" More giggles.

Marco continued unfazed, "You'll see the male shape is different to the female form... Ladies, please!" He clapped his hands again. "Now remember this is Terry's first time so he may not be able to keep it up for as long as Harley did –"

The sound of laughter drowned his attempts to bring order. He tapped me on the shoulder. "They'll settle down in a minute. They're just nervous."

Gradually the giggles and raucous comments subsided and the room fell mostly quiet. Marco stepped behind each artist in turn offering little bits of advice or encouragement. When he looked at Harley's work he said, "That's an interesting interpretation."

I looked at her and raised a quizzical eyebrow. She gave me a mischievous grin.

I relaxed into my role. The position wasn't uncomfortable and the room pleasantly cool with the windows on all four sides open and offering a gentle breeze. I adapted to my nakedness surprisingly quickly and it seemed completely natural with quite a short time.

My mind drifted to the arrangements for the fiesta in a couple of days. Steven Hunter was due in tomorrow. He was staying in a small hotel in Órgiva under an assumed name. Hopefully that would stay quiet.

My eyes caught Harley's and she dipped her head so she was looking up at me slightly. A look that was strangely alluring.

Probably best to ignore her, she looked like she was up to something. Concentrate on the arrangements and try not to think about being here naked in front of these women. And Graham. Think about the coming fiesta, ignore Harley. The work in San Tadeo had been frenetic. The amount of lighting that had been strung up across the Plaza was extraordinary. They were certainly taking full advantage of their free electricity. My role in the proceedings was restricted to securing the film rushes from Darkspace so I planned on just enjoying the events.

Harley ran her hand through her hair, pushing it back. She arched her back in a stretch. I guessed it was uncomfortable hunched over the easel like that. I hadn't spent very long doing that, my attempts at painting so far had been fairly short lived. As she stretched her nipples strained against the thin white cotton of the shirt she wore.

The fiesta. It was scheduled to run for three days with various events staged throughout. It was likely to be huge. Posters had been distributed as far afield as Granada and Motril and Steven Hunter's attendance was going to be a big draw. Harley shifted in her seat and the silk wrap she used as a skirt slipped open, showing me the inside of her thigh. She obviously hadn't noticed as she just carried on painting.

Don't look. The fiesta was due to open with a meal and entertainment provided for all the elderly of the village. A big marquee had been erected to take the seating. Harley tugged absentmindedly at her shirt and it fell open a couple more buttons. She seemed not to notice and concentrated on her work. The smooth tanned flesh under the white cotton curved away gently.

The first night of the fiesta was going to be given over to a disco rave type event and I'd already decided to stay away from that one.

She turned to her right, appearing deep in thought. From this angle her shirt was sufficiently open to give a full view of her right breast. She tugged at her collar absentmindedly and the shirt fell open a bit more. Fortunately I was probably the only person to notice due the angle at which she sat. She'd be embarrassed if she realised. Or then again, knowing Harley, she probably wouldn't be overly concerned. She shifted position again and the skirt wrap fell open a bit more. Again, only visible from my position. It finally dawned on me that this was no accident. The movements and glimpses were all carefully calculated to be seen only by me. What was she up to? Best to blank this out.

The fiesta. Concentrate on the fiesta. A local rock band were due to play on... on... When were they due to play?

Another button fell open and I could now see clearly her right breast. Lightly tanned against the white of the shirt, her nipple... rock band, must make sure I see the rock band. I felt a stirring somewhere I really shouldn't be feeling a stirring. She was doing this on purpose. I caught her eyes and she smiled. The impish smile she knew I found irresistible. She held my gaze and moved her legs open slightly. The skirt fell free of one leg. My stirring stirred again. This was going to get embarrassing in a minute. I guessed that was her game.

The fiesta. Three days. Party. There was going to be a big paella on one day. Which day was that? Harley glanced around the room quickly to ensure nobody was looking in her direction and she opened her legs briefly. It was clear from the quick glimpse afforded that she was not wearing underwear.

Film rushes. Must make sure I pick those up in the... in the...

Another quick glance and she ran her fingers inside her semi open shirt. I heard badly suppressed giggles from one of the women. Apparently my stirring was becoming noticeable. Harley smiled at me and I did my best to glare without moving. She blew me a kiss and traced the shape of her nipple with her finger. I felt my little problem growing and heard more giggles from the ladies.

Marco clapped his hands. "Ladies, please. Decorum."

No amount of thinking about the fiesta was helping. Harley continued to tease and I tried to shift my position slightly to hide the problem.

One of the women said, "Marco, dear, the subject is moving."

"He can't help it," another voice said. More giggles.

"It must be very hard to stay still for so long."

"I think I need a bigger piece of paper," I heard Graham say and the room erupted into laughter.

Marco came over and touched me on the shoulder. "I think we might stop for today," he said. "You've done very well for your first time and don't be embarrassed. They're wicked little minxes." He guided me to the side room.

Once inside I closed the door with as much calm and nonchalance as I could muster. I leant back against the door and tried to regain control of my breathing. I waited a moment and then dressed and exited the room. The ladies stood in a semi circle and applauded as I appeared. I gave an exaggerated bow.

Harley took my arm and guided me to the door. "I'm going to kill you," I whispered. She laughed.

Chapter Twenty Three

We'd decided to walk up to the fiesta. It was about a mile but at least it would be downhill coming home. With the experience of the filming day still fresh in our minds the idea of trying to drive was a non-starter. The publicity that had been accorded was guaranteed to ensure this was going to be San Tadeo's biggest ever and probably one of the best attended in the region. The posters had proudly, and somewhat exaggeratedly, announced San Tadeo as the location for the next Who Dares movie starring Steven Hunter.

We left our house to walk into the village and had to weave our way through cars parked randomly in our track. There'd have been no taking the car out anyway, it seemed. The road up to the village teemed with cars and as we walked up the hill the trail of vehicles thickened until it came to a standstill. Fields on both sides of the road had been opened and were already filling up, despite the extortionate fees charged by the enterprising locals. We weaved our way round a group of abandoned vehicles and continued into the village. We were a bit early for the opening ceremony and headed for the Bar Mirador for a drink. José spotted us looking lost in the overcrowded outside area of his bar. He waved at us to wait then reappeared a few moments later with a folding table and a couple of chairs.

"For my special guests," he said. Either my Spanish was improving or he was speaking more clearly.

We sat with our beers and tapas of sardines and watched the commotion. The marquee bustled with activity as the elderly of the village were helped into their places by a multitude of volunteers. Some of them youngsters and others not much younger than the folks they were helping. Eventually the places were all filled and an air of expectation settled over the Plaza. The howl of microphone feedback announced something was about to happen. I stood up to see what was going on and over the sea of heads I watched as Eduardo went through his microphone tapping routine once more. Each time he banged it into his hand a howl of feedback echoed around the buildings.

Behind him a band started up with a vaguely tuneful march. A group of children then trooped up onto the platform. They were dressed in identical paramilitary uniforms and played a variety of instruments. They were greeted with enthusiastic applause, no doubt centred around proud parents. I sat back down and we listened to the music drift around the Plaza for another ten minutes. Eventually Eduardo took mastery of the microphone and began his opening address. Harley translated the highlights for me but it seemed that the success of the fiesta arrangements was due entirely to his unstinting hard work and personal sacrifice. He told of his victory over Iberviento and his negotiations with Darkspace which resulted in securing the use of San Tadeo in a world blockbuster movie. He talked for about twenty minutes, by which time the helpers in the marquee were fidgeting nervously as their charges became more impatient for their supper.

Finally Eduardo declared the fiesta open and the band burst into a painful but enthusiastic noise fest. The helpers in the marquee clattered the plates in front of their guests and all around me the crowds erupted into excited chatter.

The first night was likely to be the quietest of the three but already the crowds pressed shoulder to shoulder. The stall holders worked furiously dispensing hotdogs, candy floss, churros and all manner of tasty snacks. José had taken on extra staff but even they were unable to keep up with the orders.

By nine o'clock the stage was being set up for a DJ to rap his techno house or whatever it was he planned. It would probably involve very loud and metronomic bass tones so it was time for us to retreat. We headed back down the hill against a steady upward throng of people.

Sleep escaped us as the noise from the village drifted unabated around the valley. We sat outside for a long while enjoying the warm October evening. Eventually the noise subsided and we hit the bed just as the sun was tipping the mountains in the east.

***

We slept much of the morning then showered and headed up to the village to see what the afternoon's festivities would bring. The walk up the hill was once more a tortuous trail of people threading their way through abandoned vehicles. It reminded me very much of the early days of the Glastonbury festival in its chaotic prime.

A field on the outskirts of the village had been given over to a fair and already thronged with people. We went to watch some fire jugglers and I marvelled at their skill as they threw flaming swords between themselves. We headed up to the village. Somebody had taken a very wise decision to spread the fiesta wider and it now overflowed the village. The makeshift bars and food tents were spreading down the main road and every side street now boasted an array of stands and stalls. Street traders moved amongst the people offering selections of hooky DVDs, Rolex watches and designer perfumes. I noticed one of them selling the boxed set of the Who Dares movies. The case was labelled in Chinese but that didn't deter his customers who snapped them up.

I spotted Eduardo together with a small entourage in attendance as they wandered the fair. He was smiling beatifically at everybody as he passed.

As the afternoon wore on we headed into the Plaza and watched the group of ethnic drummers as they beat a furious but incredibly well rehearsed tattoo that seemed to go on for hours. José found us a table and looked after us with food and drink for which he refused all offers of payment. The scheduled procession of floats started at four o'clock and wound its way between the crowds and stands. Andy's mobile beer kegs once again took much of the attention of the crowds, to the point where the whole village centre became gridlocked. A pair of Guardia Civil officers headed over to try to open up the roads again but they became sidetracked by Andy's generosity and spent the next hour leaning against his stationary float and drinking beer. What should have taken an hour, took up most of the rest of the day as the floats gradually drifted through the village. Everything from simple trailer affairs with half a dozen children playing instruments, right through to professional mobile displays of incredible artistry. One which caught my eye was a complete scale model of Disney's Magic Castle complete with Snow White and... I could only count six dwarves, which was a bit of a worry.

The drummers cleared the stage and a group of children took their place. They wore blue and yellow uniforms and played a variety of instruments. They were surprisingly tuneful and played without a break for about half an hour, at which time they were replaced by another group of child musicians, this time wearing green and orange. This display went on for the rest of the afternoon with the only thing that seemed to change being the colour of the uniforms. I guessed this was some sort of competition involving local bands. By seven o'clock I'd worn out my tolerance for child protégés and we made our way to one of the food tents on the outskirts. We watched some flamenco as we ate burgers then headed back to the Plaza for an evening of dancing. Or at least to watch the dancing. The darkening skies and the dropping temperatures did little to curb the crowds but we gave up at midnight and headed home.

***

The final day of the fiesta began at midday although we didn't go up until six. José had kept us a table for the special evening. A huge canvas had been draped down the front of all the buildings at the far end of the Plaza. A hushed expectation permeated the village and although the stalls still thronged there was an air of anticipation.

"This is a bit different to the first fiesta I came to," I said.

"It's certainly taken off," Harley said. "I can't imagine how they're going to untangle all the cars at the end of it."

Sancho shuffled his feet and gave me his best 'good boy' face as he watched the plate of pork loin and chips on our table. I gave him a sliver of fat from the edge of the pork. I don't think he even swallowed, just opened his throat and it disappeared.

The lights in the Plaza dimmed and a hushed silence fell over the village.

"Here we go," I said.

A flurry of activity on the stage and suddenly the white canvas was flooded in a bright white light as the projector came to life. The crew on the stage fiddled with the angles to ensure the beam hit the canvas squarely and as the countdown numbers flashed on the massive screen they fine tuned the focus. The instantly recognisable main theme from the Who Dares series blared from the speakers fixed on gantries around the Plaza. A round of applause and some whoops echoed around the square as the film started. Steven Hunter's face appeared as he spoke directly to the camera. He gave thanks to the people of San Tadeo for their help with the latest film and offered free tickets to all residents when the film was finally released. That was met with a round of applause that completely drowned out the rest of his introduction. I'd had a preview of this so I knew what he was saying. He was introducing the rushes of the scenes filmed in San Tadeo and they'd also included a blooper reel.

The film started with wide shots of the village and an edited version of Eduardo's speech. Everybody cheered this. As the cameras panned around the village various individuals were clearly recognised to much cheering and shouting. Snippets of José serving at the bar were met with huge applause. The practise runs by Trevor in the stunt car met with much laughter and whoops of recognition each time somebody spotted themselves on screen. The film continued in this vein for around ten minutes. The director had done a great job in catching as much of the village and its inhabitants as possible. Then the main section of the film started. Once more the theme music struck up and now the camera panned what to all intents and purposes was a 1940s Austrian village. The few strategic set dressings coupled with clever camera angles had achieved a remarkable effect. The car then hurtled on to the screen appearing to travel much faster than the 25mph at which I knew it had been travelling. As it neared the corner of the Plaza the sounds of a machine gun ripped from the speakers and a trace of bullet holes shattered across the windscreen and raked down the side of the vehicle. A huge applause threatened to drown out the rest of the scene but the volume stepped up a level as the car veered seemingly out of control across the Plaza. It careened through a group of tables and chairs sending them flying in a cloud of splintered wood. The car hit the glass frontage and crashed through the marble bar inside. Instantly the bonnet of the car lifted in a huge explosion that filled the inside of the bar with fire and the Plaza with the sound of thunder. As the fire appeared to rage the titles rolled across the screen and the Who Dares theme started once more. A massive applause seemed to fill the whole valley.

"Wow," said Harley.

"I don't like the way the bonnet lifted," I said. "I think I should have put a slightly larger charge at the front end."

"Wow," said Harley once more.

The titles on the screen continued to roll and the audience hushed, then the director's voice came over the speakers, "And now, I would like you to welcome the star of the film, Mister Steven Hunter!"

More applause and shouts but they gradually subsided as nothing appeared to happen. The noise descended to murmuring with people looking all around wondering what had gone wrong.

"What's happening?" Harley asked. "Where is he?"

"Wait," I said.

Above the mumbling in the Plaza a steady rumble grew. Slowly at first and largely unnoticed but gradually becoming louder. As the noise grew it snagged the attention of more and more people. Everybody started looking around, wondering where the noise was coming from. The sound was rhythmic, a steady but rapid thrubbing.

The noise resolved itself into the sound of a helicopter. It grew louder as it approached. Searchlights, undoubtedly courtesy of Iberviento, exploded into life and raked the sky just as the music started up once more. The helicopter grew to a deafening level then suddenly appeared in the crossed beams of the searchlights. A smoke machine started from somewhere billowing white clouds that swirled under the rotor blades of the helicopter as it hovered low over the Plaza. The machine was now low enough to see that the side door was open. A dark shape stirred in the doorway then resolved into the shape of a man as he leapt from the door. A huge roar filled the Plaza as Steven Hunter abseiled down a rope straight into the centre of the crowd. Waiting Guardia Civil officers cleared an area for him as the crowd pressed forwards.

"Wow," said Harley. "Fucking wow!"

We were not going to get near Steven and it didn't matter. We'd catch up with him for a drink at some point before he returned to England. Tonight he belonged to the town.

***

For the rest of the evening we sat and watched the party. Sancho appeared to have grown as he was now able to steal tapas for himself. The laughter and the music. The smells of outdoor cooking mixed with the occasional drift of cannabis smoke. The bright lights which swung lazily in the breeze. The seemingly random loosing of fireworks momentarily taking centre stage. Children running between the feet of adults.

"Well, that all seemed to go alright," I said.

"But what happens next year when there's no big Hollywood star to boost the interest?

"One starfish at a time." I watched my town. "One starfish at a time."

I felt Harley squeeze my hand. "How do you feel?" she asked.

I looked around at the people. The people I'd come to know over the last few months. I felt Harley's warmth and Sancho settled on my feet.

"I feel like home," I said.

THE END

OTHER BOOKS FROM THE BEST SELLING AUTHOR...

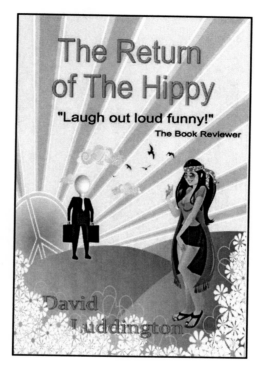

Tony Ryan is bemused. He thought he understood the way the world worked, but now, as a sacrificial lamb of the credit crunch he finds himself drifting... drifting into the clutches of the ever resourceful Pete who could find the angle in a Fairy Liquid bubble... and into the arms of the enigmatic hippy girl, Astrid, who's about to introduce Tony to rabbits, magic caves and the joys of mushrooms.

Charles Tremayne is a spy out of his time. After a long career spent rescuing prisoners from the KGB or helping defectors across the Berlin Wall the world has changed. The Wall has gone and no longer is there a need for a Russian speaking, ice-cold killer. The bad guys now all speak Arabic and state secrets are transmitted via satellite using blowfish algorithms impenetrable to anybody over the age of twelve. Counting down the days to his retirement by babysitting drunken visiting politicos he is seconded by MI6 for one last case. £250,000,000 of government money destined as a payoff for the dictator of a strategic African nation goes missing on its way to a remote Cornish airfield.

Tremayne is dispatched to retrieve the money and nothing is going to stand in his way. Armed with an IQ of 165 and a bewildering array of weaponry and gadgets he is not about to be outmanoeuvred by the inhabitants of a small Cornish fishing village. Or is he?

Tinker's Cottage nestles in a forgotten corner of deepest Somerset. It also happens to sit on a weak point in the space time continuum. Which is somewhat unfortunate for Ian Faulkener, a graphic novelist from London, who was hoping for some peace and quiet in which to recuperate following a very messy breakdown.

It was the cats that first alerted Ian to the fact that something was not quite right with Tinker's Cottage. Not only was he never sure just how many of them there actually were, but the mysterious way they seemed to disappear and reappear defied logic. The cats, and of course the Pope, disappearing literary agents, mislaid handymen and the insanity of Cherie Blair World.

As Ian tries to untangle the mystery of the doors of Tinker's cottage he risks becoming lost forever in the myriad alternate universes predicted by Schrodinger. Not to mention his cats.

Schrodinger's Cottage is a playful romp through a variety of alternate worlds peopled by an array of wonderful comic characters that are the trademark of David Luddington's novels.

For fans of the sadly missed Douglas Adams, Schrodinger's Cottage will be a welcome addition to their library. A heart-warming comedy with touches of inspired lunacy that pays homage to The Hitchhiker's Guide whilst firmly treading its own path.

To Follow On Facebook:

The Website: www.luddington.com

Twitter: @d_luddington

Lightning Source UK Ltd.
Milton Keynes UK
UKOW04f2019250915

9 781910 530085